VI KEELAND

We Shouldn't
Edited by: Jessica Royer Ocken
Proofreading by: Elaine York, Eda Price
Cover model: Lucas Bloms
Cover designer: Sommer Stein, Perfect Pear Creative, www.perfectpearcreative.com
Formatting by: Elaine York, Allusion Graphics, LLC, www.allusiongraphics.com

we shouldn't

There may be a fine line between love and hate...

...but straddling that line can be so much fun.

chapter 1

Bennett

"What the hell is she doing?"

When the light turned green, I kept jogging in place rather than crossing. The scene unfolding across the street was just too entertaining to interrupt. My car was parked in front of the office, and a curly-haired blonde with killer legs was leaning over the windshield—her hair apparently somehow stuck in my wiper blade.

Why? I had no fucking idea. But she seemed pretty pissed off, and the sight was comical to watch, so I kept my distance, curious to see how this would play out.

It was a typical breezy day in the Bay Area, and a gust of wind kicked up, causing her long hair to fly all over the place as she struggled with my car. That seemed to upset her even more. Frustrated, she yanked on her hair, but the clump wrapped around the wiper was too big, and it didn't come loose. Rather than trying to unwind it gently, she yanked harder, this time standing up as she tugged at her hair with both hands.

That did the trick. Her hair came loose. Unfortunately, my wiper blade was still attached to it, dangling. She grumbled what I suspected was a string of curses and then made a last, futile attempt to remove the tangled mess. The people who had crossed the street when I should've now began to approach where she stood, and blondie suddenly seemed to realize someone might take notice of her.

Instead of being angry that this crazy woman had damaged my one-week-old Audi, I couldn't help but laugh when she glanced around, then opened her raincoat and tucked the dangling wiper inside. She smoothed down her hair, cinched her belt, and turned to walk away as if nothing had happened.

I thought that was the end of the show, but apparently she thought better of what she'd done. *Or so it seemed.* Turning back, she returned to my car. She then proceeded to dig into her pocket for something and stick it under the remaining windshield wiper before scurrying off.

When the light turned green again, I crossed and jogged to my car, curious as to what her note would say. She must've been stuck there for a while and written it before I saw her, because she hadn't taken out a pen while I watched.

Lifting the remaining wiper, I slipped out the note and turned it over, only to find what she'd left behind wasn't an apology note at all. The blonde had left me a damn parking ticket.

What a morning. My car vandalized, no hot water at the gym next to the office, and now one of the elevators was out of service again. The morning rush crammed into the only functioning elevator car like sardines in a can. I looked down at my watch. *Shit.* My meeting with Jonas was supposed to start five minutes ago.

And we were stopping at every damn floor.

The doors slid open on the seventh floor, one floor below mine.

"Excuse me," a woman behind me said.

I stepped to the side to let people out, and the woman caught my attention as she passed. She smelled good, like suntan lotion and the beach. I watched her step off. Just as the elevator doors began to close, she turned back, and our gazes locked for a brief second.

Gorgeous blue eyes smiled at me.

I started to smile back...then stopped, blinking and taking in her whole face—and her *hair*—just as the doors slid shut.

Holy shit. The woman from this morning.

I tried to get the person standing in front of the elevator panel on the other side of the car to press the open button, but we'd started moving before she even figured out I was talking to her.

Perfect. Just perfect. Goes with the rest of the damn day.

I arrived in Jonas's office almost ten minutes behind schedule.

"Sorry I'm late. Crappy morning."

"No problem. Things are a little hectic here today with the move."

I sat down in one of the visitor's chairs across from the boss and let out a deep breath.

"How's your team doing with everything going on today?" he asked.

"As well as can be expected. Would go over much better if I could tell everyone their jobs were safe."

"No one is losing any job at the moment."

"If you could stop that sentence after the word *job*, that would be great."

Jonas sat back in his chair and sighed. "I know it's not easy. But this merger will be good for the company in the end. Wren may be the smaller player, but they have a nice portfolio of clients."

Two weeks ago, the company I'd been working for since straight out of college had merged with another large ad agency. Everyone had been on edge ever since, nervous about what the acquisition of Wren Media meant for their position at Foster Burnett. For the last two weeks, I'd spent half my mornings reassuring my team, even though I had no fucking idea what the future of two major ad houses consolidating might look like.

We were the bigger company, so that's what I'd been reminding people. Today was the physical consolidation into the San Francisco office where I worked. People carrying boxes had infiltrated our space, and we were supposed to smile and greet them. It wasn't fucking easy—especially when my own job could be at stake. This company didn't need two creative directors, and Wren had its own marketing team, which was moving into our space right at this very moment.

While Jonas had assured me my job with the company was safe, he hadn't yet said that any of us wouldn't be transferred. The Dallas office was larger, and a recent rumor had floated around that more transfers were in the cards.

I had no plans on moving anywhere.

"So, tell me about the woman I'm going to crush. I asked around. Jim Falcon worked at Wren for a few years and said she was pretty close to retirement anyway. Hope I'm not going to make some blue-haired woman cry."

Jonas's brows drew down. "Retirement? Annalise?"

"Jim told me she uses a walker sometimes—trouble with her knees or some shit. I had to get maintenance to widen the aisle between the cubicles where the staff sits so she can get through. But I refuse to feel guilty for whipping the ass of this woman just because she's older and has some health problems. I'm sending her packing to Texas, if it comes down to it."

"Bennett...I think maybe Jim is confused. Annalise doesn't have a walker."

I shook my head. "Are you kidding? Don't even tell me that. It cost me a bottle of Johnny Walker Blue Label to get my work order moved up to the top of the list with the maintenance department."

Jonas shook his head. "Annalise isn't—" He stopped mid-sentence and looked up over my head toward the door. "Good timing. Here she is now. Come on in, Annalise. I want you to meet Bennett Fox."

I turned in my chair to see my new competition—the old biddy I was about to annihilate—and nearly fell over. My head swung back to Jonas.

"Who is this?"

"This is Annalise O'Neil, your counterpart over at Wren. I guess Jim Falcon confused her with someone else."

I turned back to the woman walking toward me. Annalise O'Neil certainly wasn't the old woman I had pictured in my head. *Not in the fucking slightest.* She was late twenties, at best. And gorgeous—drop-dead gorgeous. Killer long, tanned legs, curves that could cause a man to drive off a cliff, and a wild mane of wavy blonde hair that framed a seriously model-worthy face. Without warning, my body reacted—my dick, which had been floundering around disinterested for the last month since news of the merger broke, suddenly perked up. Testosterone squared my shoulders and lifted my chin. If I were a peacock, my colorful feathers would've fanned wide.

My competition was a fucking knockout.

I shook my head and laughed. Jim Falcon hadn't made any mistake. The fucker did it to screw with me. The guy was a wiseass. I should've known. He must've been laughing his ass off when I had the guys from maintenance disassembling and reassembling the cubicles to make room for her walker.

What a dick. Although it was pretty funny. He got me, that's for sure.

But that wasn't what had me smiling from ear to ear.

Nope. Not at all.

Shit was about to get interesting, and it had nothing to do with my kicking the ass of a woman who walked just fine.

My competition—Annalise O'Neil, the beautiful woman standing right in front of me inside my boss's office, the woman I was about to go head to head with...

...was also the woman from this morning, the one who had ripped my wiper blade off and left me a damn parking ticket in its place, the smiling woman from the elevator.

"Annalise, is it?" I stood, straightening my tie with a nod. "Bennett Fox."

"Nice to meet you, Bennett."

"Oh, trust me, the pleasure is all mine."

Annalise

Figures.

It was the gorgeous guy I'd seen in the elevator. And here I thought we'd had a little spark.

Bennett Fox grinned like he'd already been named my boss and extended his hand. "Welcome to Foster Burnett."

Ugh. He wasn't just good looking; he knew it, too.

"That would be Foster, Burnett and *Wren,* as of a few weeks ago, right?" I iced my subtle reminder that this was now *our* place of employment with a smile, suddenly thankful my parents had made me wear braces until I was nearly sixteen.

"Of course." My new nemesis smiled just as brightly. Apparently his parents had sprung for orthodontic care, too.

Bennett Fox was also tall. I once read an article that said the average height of a man in the US was five-foot-nine-and-a-half inches; less than fifteen percent of men stood taller than six feet. Yet the average height of more than sixty-eight percent of Fortune 500 CEOs was over six feet. Subconsciously, we related size to power in more ways than just brawn.

Andrew was six foot two. I'd guess this guy was about the same.

Bennett pulled out the guest chair next to him. "Please, have a seat."

Tall and with gentlemanly manners. I disliked him already.

During the ensuing twenty-minute pep talk given by Jonas Stern—in which he attempted to convince us we weren't vying for the same position, but instead forging the way as leaders of the now-largest ad agency in the United States—I stole glances at Bennett Fox.

Shoes: definitely expensive. Conservative, oxford in style, but with a modern edge of topstitching. Ferragamo would be my guess. *Big feet, too.*

Suit: dark navy, tailored to fit his tall, broad frame. The kind of understated luxury that said he had money, but didn't need to flaunt it to impress you.

He had one long leg casually crossed over the other knee, as if we were discussing the weather rather than being told everything we'd worked twelve hours a day, six days a week for was suddenly at risk of being in vain.

At one point, Jonas had said something we both agreed with, and we looked at each other, nodding. Given the opportunity for a closer inspection, my eyes roamed his handsome face. Strong jaw, daringly straight, perfect nose—the type of bone structure passed down from generation to generation that was better and more useful than any monetary inheritance. But his eyes were the showstopper: a deep, penetrating green that popped from his smooth, tanned skin. Those were currently staring right at me.

I looked away, returning my attention to Jonas. "So what happens at the end of the ninety-day integration period? Will there be *two* Creative Directors of West Coast Marketing?"

Jonas looked back and forth between us and sighed. "No. But no one is going to lose his or her job. I was just about to tell Bennett the news. Rob Gatts announced he'll be retiring in a few months. So there will be a position opening up for a creative director to replace him."

I had no idea what that meant. But apparently Bennett did.

"So one of us gets shipped off to Dallas to replace Rob in the southwest region?" he asked.

Jonas's face told me Bennett wouldn't be happy about the prospect of heading to Texas. "Yes."

All three of us let that sink in for a moment. The possibility of having to relocate to Texas shifted my mind back into gear, though.

"Who will make the decision?" I asked. "Because obviously you've been working with Bennett..."

Jonas shook his head and waved off what I was beginning to question. "Decisions like this—where two senior management positions are being merged into one office—the board will oversee and make the final determination of who gets first pick."

Bennett was just as confused as me. "The board members don't work with us on a daily basis."

"No, they don't. So they've come up with a method of making their decision."

"Which is?"

"It'll be based on three major client pitches. You'll both come up with campaigns on your own and present them. The clients will pick which they like best."

Bennett looked rattled for the first time. His perfect composure and self-assuredness took a hit as he leaned forward and raked long fingers through his hair.

"You've got to be kidding me. More than ten years, and my job here comes down to a few pitches? I've landed half-a-billion dollars of ad accounts for this company."

"I'm sorry, Bennett. I really am. But one of the conditions of the Wren merger was that due consideration be given to the Wren employees in positions that might be eliminated because of duplicity. The deal almost didn't go through because Mrs. Wren was so insistent that she not sell her husband's company, only to have the new organization strip away all of Wren's hard-working employees."

That made me smile. Mr. Wren was taking care of his employees even after he was gone.

"I'm up for the challenge." I looked at Bennett, who was clearly pissed off. "May the best woman win."

He scowled. "You mean *man*."

We sat for another hour, going through all of our current accounts and discussing which would be reassigned so we could focus on integrating our teams and the pitches that would decide our fate.

When we got to the Bianchi Winery account, Bennett said, "That's in two days. I'm ready for that pitch."

I had known there were two competitors other than me presenting to the account. Hell, I'd been the one to suggest the work go out for pitches to make sure they were getting the best advertising out there. But I hadn't been aware that Foster Burnett was one of the other firms involved. And, of course, the merger changed everything. I couldn't afford to let the new management think I could possibly lose an existing account.

"I don't think it's necessary for us both to pitch. Bianchi has been my account for years. In fact, because of my relationship with them, I was the one who suggested—"

The jerk interrupted me. "Mrs. Bianchi was very interested in my early ideas. I have no doubt she'll go with one of my concepts."

God, this guy is arrogant. "I'm sure your ideas are great. But what I was going to say is that I have a relationship with the winery, and I'm certain they'll work with me exclusively if I suggest that because—"

He interrupted me again. "If you're so certain, why not let the client decide? Sounds to me like you're more afraid of a little competition than certain of your relationship." Bennett looked at Jonas. "The client should see both."

"Alright. Alright," Jonas said. "We're one company now. I'd rather say one pitch for an existing client, but since you're both done already, I don't see any harm in showing both. As long as you two are capable of putting on a united front for Foster, Burnett and Wren, we should let the client be the judge on this one."

An obnoxious smile slid across Bennett's face. "Fine with me. I'm not afraid of a little competition...unlike some people."

"We're not competition anymore. Perhaps that hasn't sunk into your head yet." I sighed and mumbled under my breath, "It does look like the information would have to penetrate a lot of hair gel to get there."

Bennett ran his fingers through his lush mane. "You noticed my great hair, huh?"

I rolled my eyes.

Jonas shook his head. "Okay, you two. I can see this isn't going to be easy. And I'm sorry to do this to you both." He turned to Bennett. "We've worked together a long time. I know this must sting. But you're a professional, and I know you'll do your best to get through this." Then he turned to me. "And we may have just met, Annalise, but I've heard nothing but wonderful things about you, too."

After that, Jonas asked Bennett to see if he could find a spare office for me to set up in for now. Apparently, people were still being moved around, and my permanent office wasn't ready yet—well, as permanent as it might be under the circumstances. I stayed behind to discuss some of my accounts with Jonas until early afternoon.

When we were done, he walked me to Bennett's office. Foster Burnett's space was definitely nicer than what I was used to at Wren. Bennett's office was sleek and modern, not to mention twice the size of my old one. He was on the phone but motioned for us to come in.

"Yes, I can do that. How about Friday at around three?" Bennett looked at me, but spoke into the phone.

While we waited for him to finish his call, Jonas's phone rang. He excused himself and stepped out of the office to speak. Jonas returned just as Bennett hung up.

"I need to run upstairs for a meeting," Jonas said. "Were you able to find a place for Annalise?"

"I found the perfect spot for her."

Something about the way Bennett responded seemed sarcastic, but I didn't know the man well, and it didn't seem to bother Jonas at all.

"Great. It's been a long day with a lot for you both to take in. Don't stay too late tonight."

"Thanks, Jonas," I said.

"Have a good night."

I watched him depart and then turned my attention back to Bennett. Both of us must've been waiting for the other to speak first.

I finally broke the silence. "So...this whole situation is awkward."

Bennett came out from behind his desk. "Jonas is right. It's been a long day. Why don't I show you where I set you up? I think I'm gonna call it an early night for a change."

"That would be great. Thank you."

I followed him down the long hall until we came to a closed door. There was one of those nameplate holders on the door, but the name had been slipped out.

Bennett nodded his head toward it. "I'll call down to purchasing and get them to order you a new sign for your office before I go tonight."

Well, that was nice of him. Maybe it wouldn't be so awkward between us after all.

"Thank you."

He smiled and opened the door, stepping aside for me to enter first. "No problem. Here you go. Home sweet home."

I took a step in, just as Bennett flicked on the lights.

What the hell?

The room had a folding table and a chair set up, but it was definitely not an office. It was a small supply closet at best—and not even the nice kind with organized chrome shelves where office supplies were stored. *This* was a janitor's closet, one that smelled like bathroom cleaner and day-old, musty water, most likely because of the yellow bucket and wet mop sitting beside my new makeshift desk.

I turned to Bennett. "You expect me to work in here? Like this?"

A flicker of amusement danced in his eyes. "Well, you'll also be needing paper, of course."

My brow furrowed. *Is he joking?*

Reaching into his pocket, he walked to the folding table and slapped a lone piece of paper down at the center of it. Turning to exit, he stopped directly in front of me and winked.

"You have a good night. I'm going to go get my car fixed now."

Stunned, I was still standing just inside the closet when the door slammed behind him. The whoosh of air from its closing caused the paper he'd left to fly into the air. It floated for a few seconds, then settled at my feet.

I stared at it blankly at first.

Squinting as it came into focus, I realized something was written on it.

He left me a note? I bent and picked it up for a closer look.

What the hell?

The paper Bennett had left wasn't a note at all—it was a parking ticket.

And not any parking ticket.

My parking ticket.

The same damn one I'd left on someone's windshield this morning.

chapter 3

Annalise

"I need a drink like you wouldn't believe." I pulled out a chair and looked around for a waiter before I'd even sat down.

"And here I thought you wanted to hang out with me because of my winning personality, not the free meal you get every week."

My best friend, Madison, had the best job in the world—a food critic for the *San Francisco Observer*. Four nights a week, she went to a different restaurant for a meal that would eventually turn into a review. On Thursdays, I joined her. Basically she was my free meal ticket. More often than not, it was the only day I left the office before nine and the only decent meal I ate all week because of the sixty-hour workweeks I tended to put in.

A lot of good that's done me.

The waiter walked over and extended the wine menu. Madison waved him off. "We'll have two merlots... whatever you recommend is fine."

The order was her standard answer, and I knew it was the first step in reviewing the restaurant's service. She liked to evaluate what the waiter brought. Would he ask her questions about her taste so he could make a good choice? Or go for the most expensive glass on the menu for the sole purpose of maximizing his tip?

"No problem. I'll pick something out."

"Actually." I held up a finger. "Can I change that order, please? Make that one merlot and one Tito's and seltzer with lime."

"Of course."

Madison barely waited until the waiter was out of earshot. "*Uh-oh*. Vodka seltzer. What happened? Is Andrew seeing someone?"

I shook my head. "No. Worse."

Her eyes widened. "Worse than Andrew seeing someone? You had a car accident again?"

Well, maybe I exaggerated a little. Finding out my boyfriend of eight years was dating another woman would definitely devastate me. Three months ago, he'd told me he *needed a break*. Not exactly the three little words I had expected him to say at the end of our night out for Valentine's Day dinner. But I'd tried to be understanding. He'd had a lot of change over the last year—his second novel had tanked, his sixty-year-old father was diagnosed with liver cancer and died three weeks to the day after the diagnosis, and his mother decided to remarry only nine months after becoming a widow.

So I agreed to the temporary separation, even though his idea of a break was more Ross than Rachel—we were both free to see other people, if we wanted to. He'd sworn there was no one else, and it wasn't his intention to go out and sleep around. But he also felt an agreement *not* to see

24

other people would keep us tethered and not allow him the freedom he felt he needed.

And when it came to driving... I'd hated it ever since the first month I got my license because of a pretty bad accident that had turned me into a nervous driver. I'd never gotten over it. Just last year I'd had a small fender bender in a parking lot, and any of my fear that had been quelled reared its ugly head. Another accident so soon might push me over the edge.

"Maybe not as bad as that," I said. "But it's up there."

"What happened? Bad first day at the new office? And here I was thinking I'd get to hear about all the hot guys at the new place of employment."

Madison didn't understand Andrew's need for a break, and she'd been encouraging me to get back out in the dating world and move on.

The waiter arrived with our drinks, and Madison told him we weren't ready to order. She asked him to give us ten minutes to decide.

I sipped my vodka. It burned going down. "Actually, there was one hot guy."

She put her elbows on the table and rested her head atop her hands. "Details. Give me details about him. The story about your bad day can wait."

"Well...he's tall, has bone structure a sculptor would envy, and reeks of confidence."

"How does he smell?"

"I don't know. I didn't get close enough to sniff him." I plucked the lime from the rim of my glass and squeezed the juice into my drink. "Well, that's not true. I did. But when he was that close, we were in a supply closet, and all I could smell was cleaning supplies and musty water." I sipped.

Madison's eyes lit up. "You didn't! The two of you... in the supply closet on your first day at the new office?"

"I did. But it's not what you think."

"Start from the beginning."

I smirked. "Alright."

She definitely thought this story was going to have a different ending.

"I had a trunk full of last-minute boxes with files and junk from my old office that had to be moved into the new space. I tried to find a parking spot, but there was nothing for blocks...so I parked illegally and made a few trips up to the office with my stuff. On my next-to-last trip down, there was a ticket on my windshield."

"That sucks."

"Tell me about it. Almost two-hundred bucks for those these days."

"Crappy start to the day," she said. "But it could have been worse, I suppose, with you and cars."

I had to laugh. "Oh, it got worse. That was the *best* part of my day."

"What else happened?"

"The meter maid was a few cars away from mine, still giving out tickets. I figured I'd already gotten the ticket, so I might as well finish my unloading. I carried the last of my boxes up to my new office, and when I came back downstairs, every car had a ticket to match mine. Except one. The car parked right in front of me."

"So the car arrived after the cop left, evading the ticket?"

"Nope. I'm positive it was there before me. She just skipped that one. The reason I'm certain is that it was the same make and model Audi I have, only a newer year. The first time I passed it, I peeked inside to see if they had changed anything in the interior on the newer edition. I noticed there was a pair of driving gloves with the Porsche logo on the front seat. So I know it was the same car that had been parked there for more than an hour because the gloves were still there."

Madison sipped her wine and scrunched up her face.

"The wine's not good?"

"No, it's fine. But driving gloves? Only race car drivers and pompous jerks wear driving gloves."

I tipped my drink to her before bringing it to my lips. "Exactly! That's exactly what I thought when I saw them. So I re-gifted my parking ticket to the pompous jerk. My car was the same make, model, and color. Why should I have been out two-hundred bucks when Mr. Porsche gloves hadn't gotten a fine? The ticket didn't have a name, only the make, model, and VIN number of the car, and the license plate on my carbon copy was barely legible. I figured he wouldn't know his VIN and would probably pay it—he *was* parked illegally, after all."

My best friend smiled from ear to ear. "You're my hero."

"You might want to let me finish the story before you declare that."

Her smile wilted. "You got caught?"

"I didn't think so. But I had a little mishap. When I leaned over and lifted the wiper to tuck the ticket underneath, somehow a piece of my hair got caught and tangled."

Madison's brow furrowed. "In the wiper blade?"

"I know. Strange. But it was so windy today, and when I went to unwind it, I made it worse. You know my crazy thick hair. I could lose a hairbrush in it for a few days and no one would notice. These waves have a mind of their own."

"How did you get it out?"

"I yanked until it came free. Only when it finally detached from the car, the windshield wiper was attached to my hair instead of the brand-new Audi it belonged to."

Madison's hand flew to her mouth as she cracked up. "Oh my God."

"Yeah."

"Did you leave the owner a note?"

I took a healthy gulp of my drink, which tasted a little better the more I drank. "Does the ticket count as a note?"

"Well...at least there's an upside?"

"There is? Tell me, because right about now, after the day I had, I'm not seeing any upside at all."

"There's a Greek god in the office. That's good. How long has it been since you've been on a date—eight years?"

"Trust me. The Greek god won't be asking me out on a date."

"Married?"

"Worse."

"Gay?"

I laughed. "Nope. He's the owner of the Audi I vandalized and then re-gifted my parking ticket to, and apparently he saw me do it."

"Crap."

"Yeah. *Crap*. Oh, and I have to work with him on a daily basis."

"Oh shit. What does he do?"

"He's the regional creative director for the company we merged with."

"Wait a minute. Isn't that your title?"

"Yep. And there's only room for one of us."

A waiter who wasn't even ours walked by. Madison put out her hand and grabbed him. "We need another vodka seltzer and glass of merlot. *Immediately.*"

⁓

The next morning, I made a stop on the way to the office. As much as I hated what was happening with my job, apparently, I was going to have to work with Bennett for the next few months. And...let's face it, I'd been wrong. I'd damaged his car and left a parking ticket instead of a note. If someone had done that to me... Well, I doubted I would be even as polite as he'd been throughout the day. He'd waited until we were alone to call me out on my shit, when he could've made me look bad in front of my new boss.

His car was illegally parked in the same spot as yesterday when I arrived. Last night, when I'd replayed the day in my head, I thought perhaps his car had been skipped over by accident because the meter maid lost track and thought she'd ticketed it already since it looked identical to mine from the outside. But if that were the case, and he'd already gotten away with it once, why would he park there again today and risk getting another ticket?

There were only a few logical answers. One, he was rich and arrogant. Two, he was an idiot. Or three, he *knew* he wouldn't be getting a parking ticket.

Bennett's office door was closed, but I noticed from the bottom that his light was on. I lifted my hand to knock, but hesitated. It would've been easier if he weren't so damn good looking.

Grow a pair, Annalise.

I straightened my spine and stood tall before knocking loudly on the door. After a minute, relief started to wash over me as I decided Bennett wasn't in there. He must have left his light on. I was just about to turn away when, without warning, the door whipped open.

I jumped in surprise and clutched my chest. "You scared the shit out of me."

Bennett removed one earbud from his ear. "Did you just say I scared you?"

"Yes. I wasn't expecting you to open the door."

He pulled the other earbud out and let them dangle around his neck. His brow furrowed. "You knocked on my office door but weren't expecting me to open it?"

"Your door was shut, and it was quiet. I didn't think you were in there."

Bennett held up his iPhone "I just got back from my run. Had my earbuds in."

Music blared from them, and I recognized the song.

"'Enter Sandman?' Really?" My voice hinted at my amusement.

"What's wrong with Metallica?"

"Nothing. Nothing at all. You just don't *look* like someone who listens to Metallica."

He squinted. "And exactly what *do I* look like I listen to?"

I gave him the onceover. He wasn't dressed in the expensive suit and wingtips he'd had on yesterday. Yet even wearing casual clothes—a body-hugging black Under Armour T-shirt and low-hanging sweats—there was something about him that reeked of refinement.

Although the way that vein bulged from his bicep was more *fine* than re*fine*ment at the moment. Bennett was older than me, I'd guess—early thirties, perhaps—but his body was firm and muscular, and I imagined he looked even more incredible without that shirt on.

Blinking myself back from a semi-daze, I remembered he'd asked me a question. "Classical. I would have taken you for more of a classical music person than Metallica."

"That's kind of stereotyping, isn't it? In that case, what should I assume about you? You're blond and beautiful."

"I'm not stupid."

He folded his arms over his chest and cocked one brow. "You did get your head stuck to the windshield of my car."

He had a point. And I was most definitely not starting off on the right foot by arguing with him again this morning. Getting myself back on track, I held up the long, slim package I'd picked up on my way to the office.

"That reminds me, I wanted to apologize for yesterday."

Bennett seemed to assess me for a minute. Then he took the wiper blade from my hand. "How the hell did you get your hair stuck to my car, anyway?"

I felt my face heat. "Let me start off by saying cars aren't my thing. I don't like to drive them, and have crap luck with them working properly. At the old office, I could walk to work. Now I have to drive every day. Anyway, I got a parking ticket yesterday morning while I was unpacking

31

boxes from my car. We happen to have the same make, model, and color Audi. Yours was parked illegally, too, but you hadn't gotten a ticket. So I tried to put mine under your windshield wiper, hoping you would pay it. Only a gust of wind came, and my hair somehow got tangled when I lifted the wiper. When I tried to unravel it, I made it worse. I really didn't mean to vandalize your car."

His face wasn't giving anything away. "You only meant to make me pay your parking ticket, not break my wiper."

"That's right."

He smirked. "Now it all makes sense."

Bennett had a water bottle in his hand. He brought it to his lips and took a long gulp, his eyes never leaving me. When he was done, he nodded.

"Apology accepted."

"Really?"

"We have to work together. Might as well keep it professional."

I was relieved. "Thank you."

"I shower at the gym downstairs after my morning run. Give me about twenty minutes, and we can get started going over our accounts."

"Okay. Great. See you in a bit."

Maybe I'd underestimated Bennett. Just because he was good looking, I had assumed he would be an egomaniac, and I'd never live down my moment of insanity. When I reached my supply closet office, I jiggled the key in the lock. It was stuck, but eventually it clanked and the door opened. The smell of cleaning supplies immediately permeated my nose. At least I understood why he'd stuck me in here now. Sighing, I flicked on the light and was surprised to find someone had left a bag on my desk.

Assuming it was probably the janitor, I picked it up to move it to where the other chemicals were piled and spotted a handwritten note on top.

You'll be needing this. —Bennett

A gift for me?

Setting my laptop and purse down, I dug inside the bag. It was light—definitely not cleaning chemicals—and the contents were wrapped in tissue paper.

Curious, I unwrapped it.

A cowboy hat?

What?

You'll be needing this.

Hmm...

You'll be needing this.

As in, for my job.

In Texas.

Maybe Bennett wasn't that mature after all.

chapter 4

Bennett

Tomorrow maybe I should leave some lingerie.

Right on time, Annalise strutted into my office carrying a large cardboard box. She had on the cowboy hat I'd left her to be a dick. Only now that she was wearing it, I was *thinking* with my dick.

She looked sexy as hell with her wild blonde hair sticking out all over. *I bet she'd look hot as shit in a black lace corset and some spiky heels to go with that cowboy hat.* I shook my head to knock that visual from my imagination. But my mind wasn't having it. It was busy thinking of a million ways I'd like to see her wear it.

Riding me.

Reverse cowgirl.

Yeah, not smart, Fox.

I looked away for a minute before clearing my throat and walking over to take the box from her hands. "Looks good on you. You're going to fit right in at the new office in a few months."

"At least maybe I'll have a place to work down there that won't get me high from sniffing chemicals all day."

"I was just screwing with you. Your real office is being set up for you as we speak."

"Oh. Wow. Thanks."

"No problem. I'm sure the cake in the urinals makes the new office smell a lot better."

"I'm not—"

I raised a hand and cut her off. "Joking. The office is the same layout as mine, two doors over. I know you'd like to be closer to me, but that's the best I could drum up."

"Are you always this obnoxious so early in the morning?" She held up a tall coffee mug with a pink sparkly A on it. "Because I'm just starting my second cup, and if that's the case, I'm going to need to caffeinate more before I get here."

I chuckled. "Yep, get used to it. I've been told mornings are my least obnoxious time, so you might want to fill that big mug with something stronger after lunch."

She rolled her eyes.

Marina, my assistant—*our* assistant—walked in and dropped an envelope on my desk. She offered Annalise a smile and said good morning, while pretending I wasn't in the room.

I shook my head when she walked out. "By the way, I feel compelled to warn you: don't accidentally eat your new assistant's lunch."

Annalise seemed to think I was kidding. "Okay."

"Don't say I didn't warn you."

I walked over to the round table in the corner where I normally held small meetings and set her box down. Noticing the label, I said, "Bianchi Winery? I thought we were going over all of our accounts to even out the workload and reassign clients between our teams?"

"We are. But I figured it couldn't hurt to show each other our presentations for tomorrow. Maybe we can agree on which is the best one, and we won't have to go up against each other?"

I smirked. "Afraid you're gonna lose, huh?"

She sighed. "Forget it. Let's just go over the accounts like Jonas asked."

God, she's touchy. "Alright. Why don't we work here? There's more room to spread out."

She nodded and pulled out an accordion file folder from her box. As she unfastened the elastic band that kept it neatly compressed, the file expanded, displaying a few dozen compartmentalized, individual slots. Each slot had a color-coded label with something typed on it.

"What's that?"

"It's my Quick Kit."

"Your what?"

"Quick Kit." She pulled out a bunch of papers from one of the slots and fanned them across the table. "There's a client contact sheet with the name and numbers of all the key players, a fact sheet that gives a summary of the product lines we market, a list of my team members who work on the account, some summary budget information, graphics of the client's logos, a listing of preferred fonts and PMS color codes, and a summary of the current project."

I stared at her.

"What?"

"What's all that for?"

"Well, I keep the Quick Kit in the file cabinet in the marketing bullpen area so that whenever a client calls, anyone can grab the information and be able to discuss the account after just a few minutes of looking over these documents. I also use it when I'm called to meetings to give account updates to the executive team. But I figured we could use it today when we talk about each account."

Shit. She's one of those—all super organized and neurotic.

I pointed my eyes to her folder. "And what's with all the different colors?"

"Each account has its own color, and all of the collateral and files are color coded so it's easy to file and pull together information."

I scratched my chin. "You know, I have a theory about people who use color-coding systems."

"Oh yeah? What's that?"

"They die early from stress."

She laughed, but then saw my face.

"Oh, you're not kidding, are you?"

I shook my head slowly.

She straightened her folder in front of her. "Alright. I'll bite. Tell me, why is it that people who prefer color coding die earlier?"

"I told you. Stress."

"That's ridiculous. If anything, my stress level is reduced because of my color-coding system. I'm able to find things more easily and don't have to waste time opening every drawer and going through piles of old collateral laying around. I can just scan for a color."

"That may be true. In fact, I'm pretty sure you'll hear me yelling *fuck* a few times a week when I can't find something I'm looking for."

"See?"

I held up a finger. "But it's not the color coding in itself that causes stress; it's the incessant need for organization that leads to stress. Someone who color codes thinks everything has its place, and the world doesn't work that way. Not everyone wants to be that organized, and when they don't follow your systems, it inherently makes you stressed."

"I think you're exaggerating. Just because I like color coding doesn't mean I'm a neurotic organization freak and get upset when things are out of place."

"Oh yeah? Give me your phone."

"What?"

"Give me your phone. Don't worry. I won't go through and check out all the duck-lip selfies you have stored in there. I just want to check something out."

Reluctantly, Annalise held out her phone to me. Things were just as I suspected. Every app was filed and organized. There were six different folders, and those were labeled: Social Media, Entertainment, Shopping, Travel, Work Apps, and Utilities. Not one single app was outside of the little organized bubbles. I clicked into social media bubble, dragged the Facebook app out, and let it loose. Then I went into the Shopping folder, took the Amazon icon, and dragged it into the social media bubble. I pulled the e-Art app from the Work bubble and let it dangle loose on her background.

Once I handed it back to her, she scrunched up her face. "What is that supposed to prove?"

"Your apps are messy now. It's gonna start to drive you nuts. Each time you open up your phone to do something, you'll have a strong urge to file the icons back where they belong. By the end of the week, it will cause you so much stress, you'll give in and fix it all to keep your blood pressure down."

"That's ridiculous."

I shrugged. "Okay. We'll see."

Annalise straightened in her seat. "And what exactly is your system for managing accounts? What are you going to use to review the accounts together today? A list written on the back of an envelope in crayon?"

"Nope. Don't need a list." I sat back in my chair and tapped my finger to my temple. "Photographic memory. It's all up here."

"God help us if that's where all the information is," she mumbled.

Annalise spent the next two hours going over all of her accounts. I'd never admit it out loud, but her hyper-organized file gave her access to a hell of a lot of data right at her fingertips. She was clearly on top of her game.

We set aside a few of her summary sheets to note which accounts she thought she could reassign.

When it came time to talk about my accounts, not surprisingly, Annalise planned to take notes instead of just listening like I did.

"I forgot to bring a notepad," she said. "Can I borrow one?"

"Sure." For the sake of teamwork, I grabbed two pads and a pen from my desk drawer. Not thinking anything of it, I tossed one on the table in front of her and the other in front of where I'd been sitting. Annalise noticed the ink on the front before I did. She turned the pad to face her.

Shit.

I attempted to grab it from her hand, but she pulled it back and out of my reach. "What do we have here? Did you draw all of this?"

I held out my hand. "Give me that."

She ignored me in favor of studying my doodles some more. "No."

I arched a brow. "No? You're not going to give me my notepad back? How old are you?"

"Umm...apparently..." She waved the notebook in the air, displaying my art. "...the same age as the twelve-year-old boy who drew these things. If this is what you do all day at work, I'm not sure what I was worried about. I was thinking I had to compete for the job against a seasoned professional."

I had a bad habit of doodling while I listened to music. I did it whenever I was stuck creatively or needed a palate cleanser in between projects. I had no fucking idea why, but the mindless sketching helped clear my busy head, which in turn allowed the creativity to get its turn inside. The habit wouldn't be so bad—maybe a little embarrassing that a thirty-one-year-old man still draws *cartoon superheroes* at his desk—but nothing to get me in trouble...that is, if the superheroes I doodled daily were *male*. But they weren't. My superheroes were all women...with pronounced body parts, sort of like the caricatures you can get done by a street artist where your head is five times the size of your body and you're roller-skating or surfing. You know the ones, right?

Probably have one of yourself riding a unicycle tucked away in the back of your closet somewhere. It's ripped and wrinkled, yet you still haven't thrown the damn thing away. Well, mine are similar. Only it isn't the heads of my creations that are exaggerated. *It's the tits. Or the ass.* Occasionally the lips, if the mood hit me. You get the idea.

Jonas had recently warned me again about not leaving that shit around the office after a little incident with a woman from human resources who had stopped in unexpectedly and gotten a glimpse.

I snatched the pad from Annalise's hand, ripped out the page, and crumpled it into a ball. "I doodle to relax. I didn't realize I'd grabbed that pad. I usually rip the page off and toss it out when I'm done. I apologize."

She tilted her head, like she was examining me. "You apologize, huh? What exactly are you sorry for? Me seeing them or you sketching characters that objectify women on company time?"

I'm guessing this is a trick question. Of course, I was only sorry she'd seen them. "Both."

She squinted and stared at me. "You're full of shit."

I walked back to my desk, opened the drawer, and deposited the wadded-up doodle page. Closing it, I said, "I don't think you're qualified to know when I'm full of shit yet. We've spent, what, an hour with each other in total?"

"Let me ask you something. If I was a guy—say one of your buddies here that you probably go out with for happy hour once in a while—would you have apologized to him?"

Of course not. Another trick question. I had to think about the right way to answer this one. Luckily, I'd been through HR sensitivity and sexual harassment training, so I was armed with the right answer.

"If I thought it would offend him, yes." I left out that it wouldn't offend any of the guys I socialized with outside of the office...mostly because I don't hang out with *pussies*. Figured Jonas would be happy with my restraint if he knew.

"So you apologized to me because you thought it might offend me?"

Easy one. "Yes."

I hoped that was the end of the discussion, so I took a seat. Annalise followed suit. But she wasn't letting it go that quickly. "So objectifying women is okay, just not when you think you might offend someone with it?"

"I didn't say that. You're assuming I objectify women. I don't think I do."

She tossed me a look that called bullshit.

"I think *you're* the one who objectifies women."

"Me?" Her eyebrows jumped. "*I* objectify women? How so?"

"Well, that drawing was a superhero—the woman had the power to fly. Every day, she leaps from tall buildings and fights crime like a badass. And here you are assuming that because she's a little on the buxom side she's some sort of demented fantasy. You didn't even take into consideration that Savannah Storm has an IQ of 160 and just yesterday saved an old lady from getting creamed by a bus."

Annalise lifted one brow. "Savannah Storm?"

I shrugged. "Even her name is badass, isn't it?"

She shook her head, and I saw the splinter of a smile threatening. "And how exactly was I to know what a badass Savannah was simply from your doodle?"

Somehow I managed to maintain a serious face. "She was wearing a cape, wasn't she?"

Annalise cracked and laughed. "I'm sorry. I must've missed that big clue due to the fact that each one of her breasts was larger than my head. I mean, her IQ should have been obvious from the cape."

I shrugged. "It happens. But you should really watch jumping to those rash judgments. Some people might be offended and think you're objectifying women."

"I'll keep that in mind."

"Good. Then maybe we can get to the important accounts now—*mine*."

chapter 5

Annalise

I tried to warn him.

Even last night, when we'd finished going over our accounts together, I again attempted to bring up today's pitch to Bianchi Winery. But the smug jerk stopped me before I could explain *why* I knew he didn't have a shot in hell at landing the account.

So screw it, I hope he wasted his entire morning on a dog-and-pony show that was totally unnecessary.

I mumbled to myself as I pulled down the half-mile-long dirt road and parked by the giant weeping willow. Coming here always brought a wave of calm over me. Being greeted by rows and rows of neatly planted grapevines, swaying willow trees, and stacked barrels let the serenity seep in through my pores. Getting out of my car, I closed my eyes, took a deep, cleansing breath in, and exhaled some of the stress from the week. *Peace.*

Or so I thought.

Until I opened my eyes and noticed a car parked off to the right, next to the big, old green tractor. And that car was almost identical to mine.

He's still here.

Bennett's appointment had been at ten o'clock this morning. I glanced at the time on my watch, double-checking that I wasn't hours early. But I wasn't. It was almost three o'clock in the afternoon. I'd figured he'd be long gone by the time I arrived. What the hell could they have been talking about for five hours?

Knox, the vineyard manager, walked out of the small retail shop carrying a crate of wine just as I finished getting my files out of the car. He'd worked at the winery since before the first grape seeds were sowed.

"Hey, Annie." He waved.

I slammed the trunk shut and swung my leather art attaché over my shoulder. "Hey, Knox. You need me to open my trunk again so you can stash my weekend bottles?" I teased.

"Pretty sure I could stash every last bottle in your trunk and Mr. Bianchi wouldn't mind."

I smiled. He was sort of right about that. "Is Matteo in the office or up at the house? I have a business meeting with him."

"Last I saw, he was walking the fields with a visitor. But they might be in the cellar by now. I think he was giving him the full tour."

"Thanks, Knox. Don't let them work you too hard!"

The door to the office wasn't locked, but no one was inside. So I set my presentation stuff down on the reception desk and went looking for where everyone was hiding. The retail shop door was open, but no one answered when I called. I was just about to turn and head up to the main house when I heard the echoing of voices

45

as I passed by the door leading from the shop to the wine cellar and tasting room.

"Hello?" I carefully navigated the stone stairwell in my high heels.

Matteo's voice, speaking in Italian, boomed in the distance. But when I reached the bottom, the only person I found was Bennett. He was sitting at one of the alcove tasting tables, his shirtsleeves rolled up, his tie loosened, and a wine glass taster flight on the table in front of him. Three of the four glasses were empty.

"Drinking on the job?" I arched a brow.

He linked his fingers behind his head and leaned back to revel in his smugness. "What can I say? The owners love me."

I held back my laughter. "Oh, do they? So you haven't let them see the real you, then?"

Bennett flashed a smile. A gorgeous one. *Jerk*.

"You wasted a trip out here, Texas. Tried to tell you, but you wouldn't listen."

I sighed. "Where's Matteo?"

"He just got a call and stepped into the fermentation room."

"Have you seen Margo?"

"She ran out to the grocery store."

"What are you still doing here, anyway? Were you late for your presentation?"

"Of course not. Matteo offered to give me a tour so I could see the new vines they planted this year, and then Margo insisted I do a full tasting. I'm like one of the family now." He leaned toward me and lowered his voice. "Although I'm pretty sure Mrs. Bianchi's into me. Like I said, you got no shot at winning this one."

I somehow managed to keep a straight face. "Margo... Mrs. Bianchi... is *into you*? You do know Matteo's her husband, right?"

"Didn't say I was gonna try anything. Just calling it like I see it."

I shook my head. "You're unbelievable."

The sound of a door opening and shutting turned both our heads toward the back of the tasting room. Every sound reverberated twice as loud down here, including Matteo's steps as he walked toward us. He opened his arms and spoke with his thick Italian accent when he looked up and saw me. "My Annie. You're here. I didn't hear you come in."

Matteo embraced me in a warm hug, then held my face and kissed both of my cheeks. "I was on the phone with my brother. The man, he's still an idiot, even after all these years. He bought goats." He pinched together all five fingers in the universal Italian gesture for *capeesh!* "Goats! The moron, he bought goats to live on his land in the hills. And he's surprised when they eat half his crops. Such an idiot." Matteo shook his head. "But never mind that. I introduce you." He turned to Bennett. "This gentleman is Mr. Fox. He's from one of the big advertising companies you made us to call."

"Umm...yeah. We've met. I didn't get a chance to talk to you guys because things have been crazy at the office. But, Bennett and I...we work for the same company now. Foster Burnett, the company he worked for when you made the appointment to meet with him a few months ago, it merged with the company I work for, Wren Media. It's now one big advertising agency—Foster, Burnett and Wren. So, yes, Bennett and I have met. We work... together."

"Oh good." He clapped. "Because your friend, he's joining us for dinner tonight."

My eyes jumped to meet Bennett's gloating ones. "You're staying for dinner?"

He grinned like a Cheshire cat and winked. "*Mrs. Bianchi invited me.*"

Matteo had no clue that Bennett's big, dumb smile was him trying to get a rise out of me since the full-of-himself bastard thought he was invited because the Mrs. was *into him*.

The notion was hilarious, really. Because I knew Margo Bianchi, and *trust me*, she hadn't invited Bennett Fox to stay for dinner because she was into him.

And I knew that not because she adored her husband—which happened to be true—but because Margo Bianchi was a perpetual matchmaker. There was only one reason she would invite a young man to dinner. Because she wanted to set him up with her *daughter*.

"Oh? Mrs. Bianchi invited you, did she?" I couldn't wait to wipe that smirk off his face.

Bennett picked up his wine and swirled it around a few times before bringing it to his grinning lips. "She did."

I exaggerated a smile. "That's great. I think you'll really enjoy *my mother's* cooking."

Bennett was mid-sip. I watched his brows draw down in confusion and then rise up in shock—right before he started to choke on his wine.

"I can't believe you invited the enemy to dinner."

My mother lifted the top off a pot and stirred her sauce. "He's a very handsome man. And he has a good job."

"Yes. I know. He has *my job*, Mom."

"He's thirty-one, a good age for a man to start settling down. If you start to make babies in your forties like a lot of young people today, you have a teenager in your fifties when you're running out of energy to keep up."

I refilled my wine glass. When it came to mothers, I'd always thought of myself as lucky. After she and my father split up, she'd practically raised me on her own. She worked full time and yet never missed a soccer game or school function. While most of my friends were bitching about their meddling, married mother or absent, divorced mom who was out on the prowl for a new husband, I never complained—until I hit the ripe old age of twenty-five. Apparently, that was when the shadow of an old maid started to follow women around, according to the way my mother acted.

"Bennett is not your future son-in-law, Mom. Trust me on that one. He's an arrogant, condescending, cartoon-drawing, job-stealing pain in the ass."

My mom set the ladle down on the greasy spoon and pursed her lips at me. "I think you're exaggerating, honey."

I leveled her with a stare. "He thought you invited him to stay for dinner because you were into him."

Her forehead creased. "Into him?"

"Yes. As in...you were interested in him for yourself. And he knows you're married."

She laughed. "Oh, honey. He's a handsome man. I'm guessing *most* women *are* into him, so he's gotten used to mistaking a woman being friendly with a woman being friendly for a reason."

It started to feel like I could say *anything* about Bennett, and Mom would have an excuse for it.

"He's trying to steal my job."

"Your companies merged. That's an unfortunate situation, but it's not something that he had anything to do with."

"He abuses kittens," I deadpanned.

My mother shook her head. "You're trying to find any excuse you can not to like the man."

"I don't have to find any excuse; he hands me the reasons on a silver platter whenever I'm in his presence."

Mom lowered the flame to simmer and took another bottle out of the wine refrigerator. "Do you think Bennett will like the '02 Cab?"

I gave up. "Sure. I think he'll love it."

⟜

"So did you grow up here? Living at a winery?"

I'd avoided Bennett before dinner by going outside on the porch to play with Sherlock—my mom and Matteo's chocolate lab. Unfortunately, he found me.

"No. I wish." I tossed a tennis ball over the porch railing and into the rows of vines. Sherlock took off running. "My mom and I lived in the Palisades area for most of my life. She didn't meet Matteo until I was in college. I bought him for her for her fiftieth birthday."

Bennett leaned against the post, one hand casually tucked into his pants pocket. "Don't let my mother know that. All I got her was a Keurig that she stashed away in the back of a closet to collect dust."

I smiled. "Growing up, she always said she wanted to go to Italy. I'd just gotten my first job when she was about to turn fifty, so I saved up for a ten-day tour of Rome and Tuscany. Matteo owned one of the vineyards our tour stopped at. They hit it off, and two months after she came back, he had his vineyard up for sale and decided to move to the US to be closer to her." I pointed to the grape farm. "He bought this place, and they got married right over there on the one-year anniversary of the day they met."

"Wow. That's pretty cool."

"Yeah. He's a great guy. My mom deserved to meet him."

Sherlock came running back with the ball in his mouth, but instead of dropping it at my feet, the traitor took it to Bennett. He reached down and scratched his head.

"What's your name, boy?"

"His name's Sherlock."

Bennett whipped the ball back out to the farm, and off went man's best friend. "So you could've mentioned that Bianchi Winery was your family."

My jaw dropped. "Are you joking? I tried to. Multiple times. But every time I attempted to tell you, you interrupted me to drone on about how you were going to win the account and how much the owners love you.

You were pretty cocky about it. Especially this afternoon, telling me *my mother* was into you."

"Yeah. Sorry about saying that. I just wanted to screw with you. Rattle your confidence before your presentation."

"Nice. Very nice."

He unleashed his charming smile. "What can I say? All's fair in love and war."

"So we're at war, are we? And here I was thinking the better candidate would get the job based on merit, not because the other one sabotaged them."

Bennett stood and winked. "I wasn't talking about war. You love me already."

I laughed. "God, you're such a pompous ass."

I stayed on the porch to finish playing catch with Sherlock while Bennett wandered inside the house. I was surprised when he came back out with his suit jacket on, a glass of wine in one hand, and his leather portfolio case in the other.

"Where are you off to?"

He extended the glass of wine to me, but when I reached out to take it, he pulled it back and sipped. "Your mom asked me to bring you this on the way out."

"Where are you going?"

"Figured I'd head home."

"Should you be driving? My parents tend to pour wine like it's water."

"Nah, I'm good. I only did one set of tastings, and I drank them over a few hours."

"Oh. Okay. But we haven't had dinner, yet."

"I know. And I apologized to your parents. I told them something came up, and I had to run."

"*Did* something come up?"

"I don't want to interject myself into your family time. Your mom mentioned you hadn't seen each other in a few months."

"Work's been crazy ever since Mr. Wren died."

Bennett held his hands up. "I get it. Trust me, my mother would tell you I don't call or see her nearly enough."

"You don't have to leave."

"It's okay. I can admit defeat on the rare occasion that it happens. You won this battle, but you won't win the war, Texas. I'll let you present your ideas to them undistracted by me."

I stood. "My mother is going to be so disappointed. She was probably planning on discussing what kind of underwear you wear over dinner to make sure you're not killing off sperm with tighty whities for the protection of her future grandchildren."

Bennett took another sip of wine and offered me the now-half-empty glass. But when I went to take it, he didn't let go. Instead, he leaned in close while our fingertips touched. "Tell Mom not to worry. My boys are healthy." He winked at me and let go of the wine. "I prefer commando."

I chuckled and watched him walk to his car. He loaded his presentation supplies into the trunk and slammed it shut.

"Hey!" I yelled.

He looked up.

"Do you ever sketch yourself? Commando could be a good superhero name."

Bennett circled to his car door. He opened it and held onto the top as he yelled back. "You'll be dreaming about it tonight, Texas. And I don't have to guess what part you'll exaggerate."

chapter 6

Bennett

"You're late."

I looked at my watch. "It's three minutes after twelve. The 405 had a backup."

Fanny wagged her crooked, arthritis-stricken finger at me. "Don't be bringing him back late just because you couldn't get here on time."

I bit my tongue, holding back what I really wanted to say in favor of, "Yes, ma'am."

She squinted at me, seeming unsure whether my response was patronizing or if I was really being respectful. The latter was impossible since you need to *have* respect for a person in order to show them some.

We stood on the porch of her little house, staring at each other. I looked around her into the window, but the blinds were drawn.

"Is he ready?"

She held out her hand, palm up. I should've realized that was the hold up. Digging into my jeans pocket, I pulled out the check, the same payoff I'd given her every first Saturday of the month for eight years so she'd let me spend time with my godson.

She scrutinized it as if I was going to try to rip her off, then tucked it into her bra. My eyes burned from accidentally seeing some wrinkled cleavage as I watched.

She stepped aside. "He's in his room, punished all morning for having a foul mouth. Better not be getting that language from you."

Yeah. That's probably where he gets it. It's the five hours every other week I get to spend with him that screws him up. Not your drunk-ass fourth or fifth—I've lost count—redneck husband who yells shut your fuckin piehole *at least twice during my five-minute pick up and drop off.*

Lucas's eyes lit up when I opened the door to his room. He jumped from his bed. "Bennett! You came!"

"Of course I came. I wouldn't miss our visit. You know that."

"Grandma said you might not want to spend time with me because I'm rotten."

That made my blood boil. She had no right to use my visits as a scare tactic.

I sat down on his bed so we were eye to eye. "First, you're not rotten. Second, I will never stop visiting you. Not for any reason."

He looked down.

"Lucas?"

I waited until his eyes made their way back to mine. "Not ever. Okay, buddy?"

He nodded his mop-top head, but I wasn't so sure he believed me.

"Come on. Why don't we get out of here? We have a big day planned."

That brightened Lucas's eyes. "Hang on. I need to do something."

He reached under his pillow, grabbed a few books, and walked over to his backpack. I figured he was putting away his school stuff until I got a good look at the cover of the top book in his hands.

My brows drew together. "What is that book?"

Lucas held it up. "They're my mom's journals. Grandma found them in the attic and gave them to me after she read them."

A memory of Sophie sitting on the curb writing in that thing flashed in my head. I'd forgotten all about those journals.

"Let me see that."

The first book was a leather-bound journal with an embossed gold flower on the front, which had mostly faded away. I smiled as I flipped through the pages and shook my head. "Your mother wrote in this thing on the first of every month—never on the second, and always in red pen."

"She starts the page with *Dear Me*, like she doesn't know she's writing the letters to herself. And she ends them with these weird poems."

"They're called haiku."

"They don't even rhyme."

I laughed, thinking back to the first time Soph showed me one. I'd told her I was better with limericks. What was the one I'd recited? Oh wait... *There once was a man named Lass. He had two giant balls made of brass.*

And in stormy weather, they clung right together, and lightning shot out of his ass. Yeah, that was it.

She'd told me to stick to drawing.

Once, in high school, she'd fallen asleep when we were hanging out, and I got my hands on this one and read it. She was pissed when she woke up and caught me almost done with it.

I looked over at Lucas. "Your grandmother knows you're reading this?"

He frowned. "She said to learn everything about my mom and then do the opposite. Said it would help me get to know who you are better, too."

Fucking Fanny. What was she up to? "I'm not sure it's such a good idea for you to be reading these right now. Maybe when you're a little older."

He shrugged. "I just started. She talks about you a lot. You taught her how to stop throwing like a girl."

I smiled. "Yeah. We were close."

I couldn't remember the specifics of the parts I'd read a long time ago, but I was reasonably certain it wasn't something an eleven-year-old should be reading about his dead mother.

"What do you say I hang on to these for you for a while and maybe pick out some parts for you to read? I don't think you'll want to read your mom talking about boys and stuff, and that's what girls usually write in journals."

Lucas scrunched up his face. "Keep 'em. It was kinda boring anyway."

"Thanks, buddy."

"Are we going fishing today?" he asked.

"Did you make us new lures?"

He ran to his bed and crawled under until only his feet were sticking out. His smile was ear-to-ear when he came back out with the wooden box I'd given him and opened it.

"I made a woolly bugger, a bunny leech, and a gold-ribbed hare's ear."

I had no clue what the hell any of them looked like, but I knew if I Googled them, his lures would be made to perfection. Lucas was obsessed with everything fly fishing. About a year ago, he'd started watching some reality TV show about it, and his enthusiasm hadn't dimmed. Which meant I'd had to figure out how to fly fish.

Once I'd been watching a YouTube video about lakes in Northern California to fly fish in, and when I'd mentioned I was thinking of taking him up for the day, he started to recite all the best spots to fish for different things around the lake. Apparently, he'd watched the same video I'd stumbled upon—only about a hundred times.

I took the lures from the box and checked out his handiwork. They looked no different than the ones you'd buy in the store.

"Wow. Good job." I held up one. "I call dibs on using the woolly bugger first."

Lucas chuckled. "Okay. But that one's the bunny leech."

"I knew that."

"Sure you did."

"So how's school going, buddy? We're getting close to summer break."

"School's okay," he frowned. "But I don't want to go to Minnetonka."

My body turned rigid. I knew Lucas's dad lived there. But I didn't think anyone else knew that. "Why would you go to Minnetonka?"

"Grandma's making me go to her sister's. She lives in the middle of nowhere. I've seen pictures. And when she comes to see us, all she does is sit on the couch and watch dumb soap operas and ask me to rub her feet." He paused. "She's got onions."

"Onions?"

"Yeah. On her feet. They're like weird bumps that are all bony and stuff, and she wants me to rub them. It's gross."

I chuckled. "Oh. Bunions. Yeah, they can be pretty gnarly. How long are you guys staying?"

"Grandma said a whole month. Her sister's having..." Lucas held his fingers up to make air quotes "...lady-parts surgery."

His delivery would have made me laugh if we'd been discussing anything other than him leaving for a month and going to a place his mother never had any intention of taking him. "She said I'm gonna meet a whole bunch of family. But I'd rather stay home and go to soccer camp."

What the hell was Fanny up to now? The two of us definitely needed to have a talk when I dropped Lucas off this afternoon. She hadn't mentioned anything to me about missing any visits, and I'd already paid for the summer-long soccer camp it seemed he would miss. But I'd learned better than to promise Lucas I could make his grandmother see what was best for him, so I attempted to put the topic on the backburner for later and not let it ruin our Saturday.

"How're things going with Lulu?" Girls were a new topic of discussion lately.

Lucas cast his line out into the lake, and we watched it plunk down into the water at least sixty feet away. I'd be lucky to reach half that. He locked the drag and looked my way. "She likes Billy Anderson. He's on the football team."

Ah. Now it makes sense. Two weeks ago when I came to pick him up, he'd asked me if I could talk to his grandmother about him trying out for the football team. She'd told him it was too dangerous of a sport. He'd never expressed an interest in anything but soccer before, and God knows I tried to get him to throw a baseball and football around. But he was almost twelve now—about the age I was when I discovered twelve-year-old Cheri Patton would jump up and down and cheer for me if I scored a touchdown. *Damn, that girl had great pom-poms.*

"Oh yeah? Well, don't worry. There're plenty of fish in the sea."

"Yeah." He moped. "I think I'm gonna like an ugly one next time."

I held back my laughter. "An ugly one?"

"All the pretty ones are so bossy and mean. But the ugly ones are usually pretty cool."

Maybe he should be advising me on girls, instead of the other way around.

"That sounds like a good plan. But let me give you one piece of advice."

"What?"

"Don't tell the girl you decided to like her because she wasn't one of the pretty ones."

"Yeah. I won't." He reeled in his line with a smirk on his face. "I bet the girl wearing your shirt when you changed her tire a few weeks ago was really, really mean."

I laughed. The kid didn't miss a thing. Normally, I didn't bring women around Lucas. Not that I didn't think he wouldn't be cool with it, but because the relationships I had didn't generally last too long. Except a few weeks ago when he'd met Elena—the hot little meter maid who took care of more than one fantasy I'd had about a girl in uniform. We'd spent the night before my regular every-other-Saturday visit with Lucas at my place. Ten minutes after I'd picked him up, she called my cell to say her car needed a jump outside of my building—where I'd left her still in my bed. I couldn't very well not go back and take care of her car when she'd taken such good care of me. So Lucas met Elena. I'd said she was a friend, but apparently he'd put two and two together. *The little shit.*

"Elena was very nice." *Until I didn't call the entire next week.* Then she told me to fuck off. And suddenly yesterday I started getting parking tickets when I parked in my usual spot outside the office.

"My friend Jack says you should ask a girl three questions, and if she answers no to any of them, you shouldn't like her."

"Oh yeah? What questions are those?"

Lucas counted off on his fingers, holding up his thumb for one. "First, you ask if she's ever let anyone copy

62

her homework." He raised his pointer finger. "Second, you ask if she can eat more than one slice of pizza. And third..." He added his middle finger. "You need to know if she's ever gone out in her pajamas."

"Interesting." I scratched at my chin. I might have to test this theory myself. "Does Lulu eat more than one slice of pizza?"

"She eats *salad*."

He said it like the word was a curse. But there was something to that. When I take a woman to a nice Italian restaurant or steakhouse and she orders a salad—half the time not finishing it because she's *too full*—that's never a good sign.

"Let me ask you something. How did your friend Jack come up with this test?"

"He's got an older brother who's eighteen. He also told him that if you tell a girl you have three testicles, she'll always let you show her your wiener."

That one I'd most definitely be trying out. I wondered if it would work on Little Miss Daddy Owns a Winery.

"Uh, I don't think you should try out that last piece of advice. Could get you arrested for indecent exposure."

Lucas and I spent our entire day fly-fishing. He caught a bucket full of trout. I caught a tan. When I drove him back to Fanny's house, she was her usual friendly self. I had to stick my foot in the door to keep her from slamming it shut in my face after Lucas and I said goodbye.

"I need to speak to you a minute."

Both hands flew to her hips. "Is your check not gonna clear?"

God forbid that happen.

"My check is fine. As was the one that I gave to Kick Start, the day camp I paid for Lucas to go to this summer."

Fanny was a pain in the ass, but she was sharp. She didn't need anything explained to her.

"Have to help out my sister. He'll get to go for half of it."

"And what about my Saturday visits?"

She ignored my question. "You know, he's been asking a lot of questions about his mother this week. I found some old journals of Sophia's. They make for some *pretty interesting* reading."

"He's too young to read his mother's journals."

"That's the problem with young people today. Parents protect them too much. Reality isn't always perfect. The sooner they learn that the better."

"There's a difference between giving a kid a dose of reality and scarring him for life."

"I guess we're lucky it's up to me to determine what will scar him and what won't, then."

Yeah, right. "What about my weekends?"

"You can keep him until six instead of five when we get back. It'll make up the lost hours."

Unbelievable. "I promised him I'd see him every other Saturday. I don't want to let him down."

She flashed a vicious smile. "Think that ship's already sailed."

My jaw flexed. "We had an agreement."

"Maybe it's time we renegotiate that agreement. My electricity's gone up because of the new phone and computer you bought him."

"You get your check right on time every month, and I pay for plenty of extras like camp, school supplies, and whatever else he needs."

"You want him to go to that camp so badly. *You* keep him for the month I'll be taking care of my sister."

"I work late and travel all the time." Not to mention my job was at stake, and I'd be working even more the upcoming months.

Fanny stepped back from the doorway, into the house. "Looks like you'll be breaking your promise come next month then, won't you? Just like you did to his mother. Some things never change."

She slammed the door in my face.

chapter 7

August 1st

Dear Me,

Today we made a friend! It didn't start out like we were going to be friends, though. I was practicing throwing a softball at the pitch back the old owners left in front of our new house, and a boy stopped on his bicycle to watch me. He said I threw like a girl. I said thank you, even though I knew he didn't say it to be nice. Bennett got off his bike and let it fall to the ground, not bothering to use his kickstand. It looked like he did that a lot because the bike is pretty scuffed up.

Anyway, he walked over and took the ball out of my hand and showed me how to hold it so I wouldn't throw like a girl anymore. We spent the rest of the afternoon playing together. And guess what? Bennett and me have the same teacher when school starts next week. Oh, and he doesn't like to be called Ben.

After we were done playing ball, I was going to show him around the new house. But mom's new boyfriend Arnie was home. He works at night, so I'm not supposed to make noise during the day because he sleeps. So we went to Bennett's house, and his mom made us cookies. Bennett showed me a notebook of stuff he made. He draws really good pictures of superheroes! Guess what else? I told him about the poetry I write, and he didn't laugh. So today my poem is dedicated to him.

> *The summer is rain.*
> *A little girl sings outside.*
> *She drowns in music.*

This letter will self-destruct in ten minutes.

Anonymously,
Sophie

chapter 8

Annalise

Something was off.

Not one insult or smart-ass comment since I walked into his office twenty minutes ago. I'd typed up our list of the accounts we'd each agreed to keep and which we were pushing off to staff. But I realized a few we were reassigning had upcoming meetings already scheduled, and we should probably attend those to smooth out the transition. I rattled off the clients and dates while Bennett sat behind his desk, continuously tossing a tennis ball in the air and catching it.

"Yeah. That's fine," he said.

"What about the Morgan Food campaign? We didn't talk about that one because the request for proposal hadn't come in yet. It arrived this morning."

"You can take it."

My brows drew down. *Hmmm.* Not going to question that one aloud.

I crossed that off my list and kept going. "I think we should have a staff meeting—a joint one. Show both our teams that we can act as one, even if it's just an act for their benefit. It'll boost morale."

"Okay."

I crossed another item off, then set my pad and pen down and watched him more closely. "And the Arlo Dairy campaign. I thought maybe you could do some of those exaggerated-body-part superhero sketches to include with our presentation."

Bennett tossed that damn ball up into the air then caught it. Again. "That's fine."

I *knew* he hadn't been paying attention. "Maybe you could sketch the VP of Operations. I bet she'd look great with a bigger rack."

Bennett tossed the ball up and his head swung in my direction. His glazed-over eyes seemed to come back into focus, like he just woke up from a nap and for the first time saw me sitting there.

The ball fell to the ground. "What did you just say?"

"Where are you? I've been sitting here for twenty minutes, and you've been so agreeable I thought you might have the flu or something."

He shook his head and blinked a few times. "Sorry. I just have a lot on my mind." Turning his chair to face me, he picked up a tall coffee from his desk. "What were you saying?"

"Just now or the whole time?"

He stared at me blankly.

I huffed, but started over. The second time around, when he actually paid attention, my adversary wasn't as agreeable. Yet he still seemed off. When we were done going through my list, I thought he might need some cheering up.

"My parents really liked you…"

"Especially your mom." He winked.

Now *that* comment seemed more like the Bennett I'd come to know over the last week.

"Must be early-onset senility. Anyway, they showed me your proposal for their ad campaign. It was really good."

"Of course it was."

For a second, I reconsidered what I'd spent days mulling over. His blazing ego didn't need any more fanning. But my parents deserved the best advertising campaign possible. And that wasn't mine, unfortunately.

"As much as it pains me to say it, your ideas were better. We'd like to go forward on the radio copy and magazine sketches you proposed. I have a few tweaks, and I'd obviously like to stay on the campaign as the point person, but we can manage this campaign together. And I'll let Jonas know it's my family and give you credit for bringing in the better pitch."

Bennett stared at me for a long moment, saying nothing. Then he leaned back into his chair, steepled his fingers, and squinted at me like I was a suspect. "Why would you do that? What's the catch?"

"Do what? Tell Jonas?"

He shook his head. "All of it. We're in the middle of fighting for our jobs, and you're going to hand me a W that's an easy point for you."

"Because it's the right thing to do. Your advertising is better for the client."

"Because it's your family?"

I wasn't quite sure about the answer to that. The fact that it was my parents' winery was a no-brainer.

But what would I do if this were a regular client we had both pitched? I honestly didn't know if I'd be handing him anything. I'd like to think my morals would have me putting the client first, no matter what. Yet this was my job on the line...

"Well, yes. The fact that it's my parents made it an easy decision to put the client first."

Bennett scratched his chin. "Alright. Thank you."

"You're welcome." I opened my to-do-list notebook again. "Now, next order of business. Jonas sent us an email this morning on the Venus Vodka campaign. He wants ideas by this Friday, and he doesn't want us to tell him who came up with which pitch. I think he wants to make sure we have direction early because he doesn't trust we'll be able to work together well enough."

"Would you do that for any client?"

"Be ready early when the boss asks? Of course."

He shook his head. "No. Use my campaign if you thought it was better than yours."

Apparently I was the only one who'd changed subjects. I closed my book and leaned back in my seat. "I'm honestly not sure. I like to think I would put any client first, that I'd act ethically in their best interest, but I love my job, and I've invested seven years working my way up with Wren. So, I'm ashamed to say, I can't really answer that with certainty."

Bennett's face had been stoic, but a slow grin spread across it now. "We might get along after all."

"What would you do in that situation? Do what's best for the client or for yourself?"

"Easy. I'd bury your ass, and the client would get second best. Although, on the off chance my work was actually second best, it would be by a hair, so the client wouldn't be suffering much."

I laughed. Such a damn cocky bastard, but at least he was honest. "Good to know what I'm up against."

We spent the next half hour going through open issues and then decided we would get started on the Venus campaign later in the day because we both had afternoons jam-packed with meetings.

"I have an appointment with a client at two. I can probably be back at the office by about five," I said.

"I'll order us in some dinner. What are you? A vegetarian, vegan, pescatarian, beegan?

I stood. "Why do I have to be any of those?"

Bennett shrugged. "You just seem like the type."

Too bad eye rolls weren't a form of exercise. God knows, I'd be in tip-top shape after being around this man. "I eat anything. I'm not picky."

I'd made it to the door when Bennett stopped me. "Hey, Texas?"

"What?" I needed to stop answering to that name.

"Have you ever let anyone copy your homework?"

My nose wrinkled. "Homework?"

"Yeah. At school. Back in the day. Could have been in grammar school, high school, or even college."

Madison might not have done a single math assignment on her own for most of algebra. "Of course I did. Why do you ask?"

"No reason."

My appointment went longer than I'd anticipated, and the office was almost emptied out by the time I got back. Marina, Bennett's assistant—or rather *our* assistant—was just packing up her desk.

"Hey, sorry I'm late. Did you let Bennett know I got delayed?"

She nodded as she pulled her purse from the drawer. "Are you ordering dinner? Because my Lean Cuisines are clearly marked with my name in the freezer in the employee kitchen."

"Umm. Yeah. Bennett said he was going to order dinner for us."

She frowned. "I also have two cans of ginger ale, four Sargento cheddar cheese sticks, and a half-used squeezable Smucker's grape jelly in there."

"Okay. Well, I wasn't planning on helping myself to someone's food in the refrigerator. But that's good to know."

"There're menus in the top, right-hand drawer."

"Okay. Thank you. Is Bennett in his office?"

"He went for a run. Normally he runs in the morning, but he went out about forty-five minutes ago since I told him you were going to be late." Marina glanced around the room, then leaned in closer and lowered her voice. "Between us girls, you might want to watch your supplies around him."

"Supplies?"

"Paper clips, notepads, staplers—some people around here have sticky fingers, if you know what I mean."

"I'll...remember that. Thanks for the heads up, Marina."

Twenty minutes later, Bennett popped his head into my office. His hair was wet and slicked back, and he'd changed into a T-shirt and jeans. He held a pizza box in one hand. "You ready?"

"Did you pay for that pizza or swipe it from Marina?"

He dropped his head. "She got to you already."

I grinned. "She did. But I'm curious to hear the backstory from you."

"Well, unless you like cold pizza, that'll have to wait. Because explaining how *nuts* that woman is might take a while."

I laughed. "Okay. Where do you want to work?" I nodded to the box sitting on the guest chair on the other side of my desk. "I packed some stuff to prepare just in case you wanted to go elsewhere."

He walked toward my desk. "Of course you did. Wanna know what I did to prepare?"

"What?"

"I picked up two shot glasses at the little touristy shop down the block, just in case we feel the need to test drive the product." Bennett plopped the pizza box on top of my box and lifted from the bottom. He tilted his head toward the door. "Come on. Let's spread out in the bullpen. I think everyone else is gone for the day."

The Foster Burnett marketing bullpen was very different than the one we'd had at Wren. Aside from it being twice

74

the size—which made sense since Foster Burnett had twice the employees of Wren—it was set up like a dream college dorm lounge. Both bullpens had two couches and a coffee table, but that's where the similarities ended. Wren had framed inspirational quotes, easels holding white boards, a large drafting table for sketching ideas, and a small fridge with soft drinks. Foster Burnett had one long wall painted black that doubled as an enormous chalkboard, a foosball table, a full-sized Ms. Pac-Man arcade game, colorful beanbag chairs, dozens of origami animals hanging from the ceiling, and two well-stocked 1950's vending machines for soda and snacks in which everything cost only twenty-five cents.

"This room is nothing like the one we had at the old office."

Bennett leaned forward and tore a second slice of pizza from the pie, sliding it onto his paper plate. He held the box open. "You ready for another one?"

"No, thanks. Not yet."

He nodded and folded his pizza in half. "What was Wren's bullpen like?"

"Less dorm room décor and more corporate team building."

"Framed picture of a pack of wolves with some bullshit teamwork slogan?"

We didn't have that particular one, but I knew the print he was referring to.

"Exactly."

"I set up this room when we moved up to this floor. Tried to get them to put a few showers in, but HR wouldn't go for it."

"Showers?"

"I do my best thinking in the shower."

"Huh. I feel like my best epiphanies come in the shower, too. I've always wondered why that is."

"It takes away all outside stimuli and allows our mind to switch into daydreaming mode by relaxing the prefrontal cortex of the brain. It's known as DMN, default mode network. When the brain is in DMN, we use different regions of it—literally opening up our minds."

He shoved a quarter of his slice into his mouth, seeming not to notice the surprise on my face.

"Wow. I didn't know that. I mean, I knew why we sometimes need to get out of the office or play a video game to free up our headspace. But I'd never heard the scientific explanation behind it."

I flipped open the pizza box and took out another slice. Lifting it into my mouth, I looked up and found Bennett watching me intently.

"What?" I wiped at my cheek with the napkin in my other hand. "Do I have sauce on my face or something?"

"Just surprised you eat more than one slice of pizza."

I narrowed my eyes. "Are you saying I *shouldn't* eat more than one?"

He held up his hands. "Not at all. That wasn't a weight comment."

"Then what did it mean?"

Bennett shook his head. "Nothing. Just something a friend of mine said about girls who actually eat."

"I grew up eating a bowl of pasta as a side dish. I can eat."

I caught Bennett's eyes doing a quick sweep over my body, as if a comment was about to come, but then he shoved more pizza into his mouth.

"So what's the deal with Marina?" I asked. "She rattled off a detailed inventory of the food she has in the fridge to let me know she'll be very aware if anything goes missing."

Bennett slumped into the couch. "I *accidentally* ate her lunch two years ago."

"You thought her lunch was yours and ate it by mistake?"

"No. I knew it wasn't mine. I don't bring lunch. But I was working really late one night and thought it was Fred's in accounting, so I ate it. It was one goddamned peanut butter and jelly sandwich, and now I'm accused of stealing her stapler or something every other week."

"Well, I hear the rate of recidivism for first-time lunch thieves is pretty high."

"I made the mistake of telling Jim Falcon. Now every once in a while, he swipes something off her desk and plants it on mine. He thinks it's funny, but I'm pretty sure she's about three paperclips away from poisoning my coffee."

"Something tells me she isn't the only woman to feel that way about you."

⌒‿

Once we put the pizza away, the two of us couldn't agree on anything.

First we took turns sharing our loose ideas for the Venus Vodka campaign. The company had solicited a full branding pitch for their latest flavored-vodka product. We needed to come up with a cohesive package: proposed product names, logo ideas, taglines, and an overall marketing strategy. Not surprisingly, my ideas and Bennett's were a mile apart. All of my suggestions had a feminine ring. All of Bennett's were masculine.

"Men ages eighteen to forty drink the most alcohol," he said.

"Yes. But this is *flavored* vodka. Honey flavored. The primary drinkers of flavored alcohol are women."

"That doesn't mean we have to paint the bottle pink and sell it with a straw inside."

"I wasn't suggesting that. But Buzz isn't a girly name."

"It is when you add a bumble bee on the label. If the branding is too feminine, men aren't going to pick the bottle up to carry to the register."

"Are you serious? You're really suggesting that if something is too feminine, men aren't going to pick it up?"

"I'm not suggesting it. It's a fact."

We'd been arguing for the last half hour. If we were going to get anywhere working together, we needed to spend less time trying to sell the other one and more time coming up with ideas. I sighed. *What a shame.* I really loved Buzz vodka with a bee on the label. "I think we need a system."

"Of course you do," Bennett mumbled.

I scowled. "We each get three vetoes. If one of us invokes veto power, that means we think the concept is wholly unworkable, and there is no point in trying to shape it into a campaign. If one of us vetoes, we have to immediately move on and not try to debate why it's a good idea." I looked at my watch. "It's a quarter to eight already. We could spend all night arguing."

"Fine. If it gets you to give up on your bee campaign, let's do it." Bennett looked down at his watch. "And it's seven fifty-one, not quarter to eight."

Yep. Another eye roll.

Bennett decided to play some Ms. Pac-Man to try to clear his head. I needed to relax a little to get into brainstorming mode, too. So I slipped off my heels and stood. Pacing helped me think. I shook out my hands as I walked.

"Honey vodka...honey flavor. Sweet. Sugar. Candy." I began to run through word associations aloud. "Syrup. Hive. *Bzz. Bzz.* Fuzzy. Yellow."

"What the hell are you doing?" The sound of his Pac-Man being gobbled punctuated his sentence.

I stopped. "Trying to clear my mind and start thinking fresh."

Bennett shook his head. "Your yapping is doing the opposite of clearing mine. I've got a better idea for you."

"What? Run home and shower?"

He reached into the box he'd carried in for me and took out the sealed, unlabeled bottle that Venus had sent over with the RFP. Then he dug two little shot glasses out of his pocket.

I'd thought he was kidding earlier when he said he bought them in preparation for our brainstorming session.

"We need to sample the product. Nothing like a little alcohol to clear your mind."

chapter 9

Bennett

Annalise O'Neil was a lightweight.

We'd only done two shots—for research purposes, of course—and already her demeanor had changed. She waved her pointer finger in the air. The only thing missing was a light bulb in a bubble above her head. "I got it. Me so *honey.*"

She pronounced the *honey* so it sounded like *horny.* Then proceeded to crack herself up.

I liked drunk Annalise. "That's actually a damn good idea."

"Isn't it?"

"Except it's already taken."

"Nooooo."

"Yep. There's a pale ale named Me So Honey. It's actually pretty good."

"You've tasted it?"

"Of course. How could I pass a beer with that name and not bring it to my buddy's? Who hasn't brought a bottle of Ménage à Trois wine to a party for the same reason?"

Annalise kicked her bare feet up on the coffee table. "Me! I've never bought it."

"Well, that's because you're uptight."

Her eyes went wide. "I am not uptight."

"So you've had a ménage à trois, then?" It was fun screwing with her.

"No. But that doesn't make me uptight."

I leaned forward and poured two more shots of vodka. Annalise hesitated, but I nudged. "One more. It'll help clear your mind."

She'd made a face after the first two shots. But this one went down smooth. *Yep.* Annalise was definitely a damn lightweight.

She slammed the empty shot glass down on the table a little too hard. "Ménage à blah. I was dumped once for not wanting to swing."

My brows jumped. Totally not what I expected to come out of her mouth. "Your boyfriend wanted you to sleep with another guy?"

"Yep. In my first year of college. And of course, he'd get to sleep with another woman."

I sucked back my shot. "That never appealed to me. I'm not big on sharing a woman."

Annalise snort-laughed. "Maybe you should date me. That'll make you want to sleep with other women."

I let that comment sink in a minute before responding. *Did she just tell me she sucks in bed?* "Ummm...come again?"

She cackled so hard she tipped over on the couch. I had no idea what the fuck she was laughing about, but I started to laugh, too. Watching her loosen up and be amused at her own comments was pretty damn funny.

81

When her tipsy giggle fit subsided, she let out a wistful sigh. "Men suck. No offense."

I shrugged. Men do suck, especially me. "None taken."

"Sorry. I think the shots went to my head." She sat up straight and smoothed out her hair. "Let's get back to brainstorming. My brain took a detour, apparently."

"Oh no you don't. You can't just drop that dating you makes men sleep with other women and move on. I'm a man, remember? I suck. I can't move on from that without an explanation. Are you bad in bed or something?"

Annalise forced a smile, but it was a pretty damn sad one. "No. At least I don't think so. I've been told I'm good at..." She looked down and then back up under those thick lashes. "...certain things. I just meant because I got dumped for declining swapping once and now... my boyfriend...*ex*-boyfriend...Andrew and I...we're on a break."

That answer had a lot of information in it, but I couldn't get past *certain things*.

Was she flexible?

Give great head?

I once knew a woman who did this amazing thing with my balls...

I swallowed. *Fuck.*

"Ummm... You're right. We should get back to work. Excuse me for a minute." I abruptly got up and went to the bathroom to splash water on my face. A few minutes later I'd managed to wrangle my thoughts away from what talents Annalise might have.

Returning to the bullpen, I took a seat across from her. "How about Wild Honey? Men and women both

82

respond well to the word *wild*. We can market by some association with the name—wild parties, wild adventures, wild animals."

Annalise seemed to ponder my suggestion for a while. At least that's what I'd assumed she was doing until she spoke.

"You're a guy. What does *on a break* really mean to you?"

Shit. Do I answer that honestly or tell her what she wants to hear?

"Veto."

Her forehead wrinkled. "What?"

"You said we each have three vetoes, and when one of us hates something the other comes up with, all we have to do is say veto and we move on—no debating the idea. I'm invoking my first veto power. I'm not touching that question."

"Come on. I really want to know. I've only gotten a woman's perspective. And you don't strike me as the type of guy to bullshit me."

I studied her carefully. She'd been giggling a few minutes ago, but she also seemed to be sincere in wanting an answer. So I took a deep breath.

"Okay. To me, being on a break means I want to have my cake and eat it, too. I don't want to commit to just one woman, but I also don't want her to commit to anyone else—in case the day comes when I decide I'm ready to settle down. So I keep her on the hook, while I go fishing somewhere else for a while."

She frowned. "Andrew said he needed to discover who he is. *On Valentine's Day*. I got dumped on *Valentine's Day*."

83

What a dick.

"How long were you together?"

"Eight years. Since junior year in college."

She'd probably hate me for it, but someone had to tell her the truth.

"So he's what...twenty-eight...thirty?"

"Twenty-nine. He was a year ahead of me."

"He's jerking you around."

Her jaw dropped. "You don't even know him."

"Don't need to. No stand-up, twenty-nine-year-old man who loves a woman is going to set her free because he needs to *find himself*. Especially on fucking Valentine's Day."

She straightened her spine. "And you know this because you're such a stand-up guy?"

"Didn't say that. In fact, I'm the opposite of a stand-up guy. Never even had a girlfriend on Valentine's Day. I make sure I get rid of them beforehand so there's no expectation of candlelight and romance. That's why I can say with certainty that your ex doesn't really need a break to find himself. Because it takes an asshole to know an asshole."

Annalise's blue eyes blazed. Her lips pursed, and her cheeks flushed with anger. If I'd been uncertain I was the asshole I'd just admitted to being before, the fact that seeing her getting pissed off made my dick twitch would've proved it.

She stared at me for a solid two minutes and then got up to stand at the foosball table. "Let's go," she said. "I feel the need to kick your ass."

It was hours later before we made any real progress. But once we started, we got on a roll, and the two of us really started gelling. I'd say one thing, she'd take it and run for a while, that would spark an idea in me, and in the last half hour, we'd come up with a name, sketched out a rough idea for a logo, and jotted down a dozen complementing ad concepts.

Annalise yawned.

I took a look at my watch. "It's almost midnight. What do you say we call it a night? We have a good start. I can work on the logo tomorrow morning and get something drawn up on the Mac. Maybe we can toss around some more ideas Wednesday so we can nail down which ones we want to present to Jonas."

She leaned down and slipped on her heels. "That sounds good. I'm wiped out. And I think I may be starting to get a hangover from those shots earlier, if that's even possible."

Bent over like that, her blouse gaped, and I had a clear view right down her shirt. The gentlemanly thing to do would have been to turn away. But you already know I'm an asshole. Plus...she had a black lacy bra on. Black lace against pale skin is my kryptonite—something about the contrast let my imagination run wild with a *cook in the kitchen, whore in the bedroom* fantasy.

Which had me thinking...

I bet she'd look great in a chef's hat and stilettos.

I definitely needed to get laid. Not a good idea to be fantasizing about someone at work, no less a woman

I planned to annihilate. The news of the merger might have deflated my perpetual hard-on, but apparently Miss O'Neil had pulled me through that dry spell. It wasn't the first time my dick had perked up around her.

I diverted my eyes in the nick of time, a half second before she looked up at me.

Her smile was genuine. "We did good tonight. I'll admit, I wasn't so sure we could work together."

"I'm easy to work with."

She rolled her eyes—a common response to my shtick, I'd noticed. But this time, it was more playful than real.

We packed up what we'd brought into the bullpen, and Annalise wrapped the leftover pizza in some tinfoil she found in a drawer.

"Can I borrow the Sharpie you were using to sketch before? I want to label these."

I reached into my pocket and handed it to her. In big, bold letters, she wrote across the front of the silver foil: NOT MARINA'S.

"She's going to think I did that."

She smirked. "I know. I agreed you were easy to work with. I didn't say you weren't an asshole. I saw you looking down my shirt before."

I stilled, unsure how to react to her comment, and closed my eyes. The sound of her heels clicking on the floor told me when it was safe to open them. A few steps from the door, she spoke without stopping or turning around. But I could tell from her voice she was amused.

"Good night, Bennett. And stop watching my ass."

chapter 10

Annalise

I hadn't been to the gym in more than three months.

Andrew was a creature of habit and went daily at six a.m. sharp. I'd tried to join him at least three days a week when we were together, even though I preferred to exercise in the evening. But after our break started, it became awkward to see him there. We'd wave and say hello. Once or twice we even chatted. But the goodbye at the end of our conversation made my heart ache all over again. I'd stopped going for my sanity.

Until today.

I had no idea what possessed me to pick today of all days to go back to the gym, especially since it had been nearly one in the morning by the time I got home from work last night. But I arrived at five fifty, wanting to be already on the treadmill by the time Andrew walked in... *if* he walked in. We hadn't seen each other in more than two months, since the wedding of a mutual friend from college, and it had been almost three weeks since we'd even exchanged texts.

Picking a treadmill in the corner—one with a straight view to the locker room exit as well as the front door—I popped in my earbuds and hit shuffle on Pandora on my iPhone. The first five minutes were rough. Maybe avoiding exercise all together hadn't been that good of an idea after all. I huffed and puffed like a two-pack-a-day smoker until eventually my adrenaline kicked in, and I found my groove with the pace I'd set.

Although finding my groove didn't stop me from staring at the doors like I was waiting for Ryan Reynolds to walk through at any second.

At ten after six, I felt my shoulders start to relax. Andrew was never late. Unlike me, he was a stickler for time. He must not be coming today. For all I knew, he could be away, or had even changed gyms. Although the latter wasn't too likely. Andrew didn't do change—he ate the same whole wheat toast with two spoonfuls of organic peanut butter at five fifteen every morning and walked into the door at the gym at six. By seven, he sat in front of the computer at his desk to start his daily writing.

With the anxiety of anticipating his arrival dissipating, I upped my speed to six miles an hour and made the mental decision to not stop until I'd run a full three miles. It was probably better that he didn't show up and find me since I was feeling so out of sorts lately, anyway.

After I hit the three-mile marker, I did a ten-minute cool down walk and then wiped off the machine. I hadn't brought clothes to shower, but I needed to pick up my purse from the locker and stop in the ladies' room before heading home to get ready for work. I'd made it halfway to the locker room when the front door opened and two people walked in, Andrew being the second person. My heart raced faster than it had on the treadmill. And that was *before* the woman who'd walked in right before him turned to laugh at whatever he'd just said.

They'd come together.

I stopped in place about two seconds before Andrew looked up and saw me. I must've looked like a deer in the headlights about to get creamed by a Mack truck. He said something I couldn't hear to the woman he'd walked in with, and she looked up at me, frowned, and headed toward the elliptical machines.

Andrew took a few hesitant steps toward me.

"Hey. How are you? I didn't expect to see you here."

Obviously.

I nodded and swallowed back the taste of salt in my throat. "You're late."

"I changed up my routine. Writing later in the day. Even at night sometimes."

I forced a fake smile. "That's great."

"I heard about Wren. How are things going with the merger?"

"It's tough."

Small talk was killing me. I looked over my shoulder and found the woman he'd walked in with watching us. She turned her head away immediately. My pride wanted me to not mention her and escape with my head held high.

But I couldn't help myself. "New workout partner?"

"We didn't arrive together, if that's what you're thinking."

I couldn't hold back my emotions any longer. My lip started to tremble, so I bit down. The taste of metal flooded my mouth as I sucked in blood.

"I need to get to work. It was nice seeing you." I walked away before he could say anything. But he never even made an attempt to stop me.

To say I'd been distracted this morning was an understatement. I'd spent three hours answering half-a-dozen emails and staring at copy that needed approval by noon, but I still couldn't get past the first two sentences. I also mustn't have heard Bennett walk into my office or even begin to speak.

"Earth to Texas."

I looked up.

He waved his hands in my line of vision. "Are you in there?"

I blinked a few times and shook my head. "Sorry. I was daydreaming on a campaign."

Bennett squinted like he knew I was full of shit, but surprisingly, he let it go. "Come with me." He nodded his head back toward my office door.

"Where?"

"Just come. I want to show you something."

The fight had been sucked out of me today. So I sighed and got up. I followed him over to an alcove down the hall that held a file cabinet with closed accounts. He opened it and took out a random file. "Check out Marina."

I looked down at the file. Whatever page was on the top was upside down. "Huh?"

He discreetly pointed his eyes in the direction of our assistant, whose desk was in our line of sight down the hall.

Following, my eyes widened "Is that..."

He turned a page in the upside-down file and grinned from ear to ear. "Yup. I think so. I did a drive-by and checked her garbage: two wadded up balls of tinfoil. And our leftovers are missing. I went looking for them to have for lunch, and when she saw me pass by, she smiled like she was on the crazy town bus with Jack Nicholson driving to go fishing."

I laughed—something I didn't think I'd do for a while after this morning. "You know what I think?"

"What?"

I shut the folder he was pretending to look at and dropped it into the file cabinet. "I think you're both nuts." I slammed the drawer.

He followed me back to my office. "At least when I ate hers, it was a legit accident."

"Right. You meant to steal from someone else."

"Exactly."

I sat down behind my desk. Bennett helped himself to a visitor's chair. Apparently, he wasn't leaving.

"Did you bring lunch?"

"No. I forgot it in the fridge at home, actually."

He picked up a small picture frame on my desk and examined it. It held a picture of mom and me on her wedding day to Matteo. *Andrew* had taken it. Bennett grinned and set it back down. "My girl looked beautiful."

I shook my head. *Wiseass.*

"I had a lunch meeting that canceled. Want to order in and I can show you the new logo concepts I did this morning? I'm in the mood for Greek."

God, he'd already drawn new logos. I couldn't afford to be distracted.

"Sure. I'll take a gyro with the sauce on the side."

"Great." He stood. "And I'll take a falafel with a side order of patates tiganites—those fried potato things."

"What are you telling me for?"

He jammed his hands into his pockets. "So you can order. The name of the place is Santorini Palace. It's on Main Street."

"Me? Why am *I* ordering? You asked me to order with you."

He pulled a billfold from his pocket and slipped out two twenties. "I'll pay. But you have to order."

"Is ordering *beneath* you or something?"

He walked to my door. "I went out with the woman who takes the orders a few months ago. Her family owns the place."

"So?"

"I don't want her to spit in my food."

I shook my head. "You're unbelievable."

"The yellow and black look really good."

We'd just finished lunch, and Bennett now showed me four different versions of the logo he'd developed this morning based on the sketches we came up with last night. He really was a talented artist. I pointed to the last one. "I like this one the best. The font is crisper."

"Sold. We'll move forward with that for our meeting with Jonas on Friday. Did you make any progress on the tagline and ad ideas."

"I...sort of had a bad morning."

"Get your head stuck in some other handsome guy's windshield wiper?"

I smiled half-heartedly. "I wish. I just...I had a rough start to the day." As if on cue, my phone began to buzz. *Andrew* flashed on the screen. I stared at it.

After the second ring, Bennett looked at me. "Aren't you gonna answer that? *Andy's* calling."

"No."

I'd thought I'd hidden my sadness, but after the phone stopped ringing, Bennett said. "You want to talk about it?"

My eyes jumped to his. His concern seemed genuine. "No. But thank you."

He nodded and gave me a minute by cleaning up our empty food containers. When he sat back down, he turned over the paper he'd brought in with the logos and started to draw something. "I have an idea for an ad."

I stared down at the paper the entire time he sketched, lost in thought.

"What do you think?"

I sighed. "I ran into Andrew at the gym this morning with another woman."

Bennett wrinkled up the paper he'd just sketched on and wadded it into a ball. He leaned back in his chair, stretched his long legs out in front of him, and folded his arms across his chest.

"You just happened to run into him?"

I thought about saying yes, but decided to admit I was a loser. I hung my head and shook it.

"Who was the woman?"

"I don't know. He didn't say."

"What did he say?"

"Not much. He was definitely surprised to see me. I hadn't gone to the gym in a while since it became awkward seeing him there."

"And you're sure they're a couple?"

I shrugged. "He said they hadn't come together. I think he saw in my face what it looked like to me—the same way the two of us used to walk into the gym together after spending the night at my place."

"You said yourself that you could both see other people."

"Saying it and *seeing* it are two different things."

My phone began to buzz again. Both of us stared at Andrew's name flashing on the phone. Before I could stop him, Bennett grabbed my phone and swiped to answer.

"Hello?"

My eyes bulged from my head as I glared a death warning at him.

"She's..." He paused for a few heartbeats. At least I think that's how long it was; my heart had stopped beating. "...busy right now."

He listened and then shook his head. "This is Bennett, a good friend of Annalise's. And who is this?"

Quiet.

"*Arthur*. Got it. I'll let her know you called."

Pause.

"Oh. *Andrew*. Alright, Andy. You take care now."

Bennett swiped to end the call and tossed the phone back onto the table.

"What the hell did you just do?"

"Gave the undeserving prick something to think about."

"You have a lot of nerve picking up my phone and answering it."

He bent his head so we were eyelevel and stared. "Someone has to have balls with that jerk."

Then he got up and walked out of my office.

chapter 11

Bennett

Women are way too fucking sensitive.

I reread an email from Human Resources for the third time.

Bennett,

As you are aware, the recent merger has left many employees feeling anxious about the long-term status of their positions here at Foster, Burnett and Wren. Because of that, statements from management may be scrutinized by employees in a manner that they had not been before. As such, we ask that you, as well as all senior managers, please be cognizant of the sensitivity of your responses to employees. Please refrain from criticisms such as telling an employee that they make "too big of a deal out of things" and to "suck it up." Although no formal complaint has been filed, these types of comments can be considered harassment and lend to a difficult work environment.

Thank you,
Mary Harmon

I knew exactly who had complained. *Finley Harper.* Doesn't the name just scream *I have a stick up my ass*? This was all Annalise's fault. Finley was a transplant from Wren, of course. None of my crew had ever gone to HR. Hell, just last week I'd told Jim Falcon I didn't care if he had to blow the client, I was firing his ass if the CEO of Monroe Paint didn't come out of the conference room smiling like the fucking idiot he was after our meeting was over.

I shook my head. Annalise and her goddamn color-coding and team spirit. She probably cries along with the people she has to fire. And, come to think of it, where the hell had she been? I hadn't seen her since yesterday at lunch when I answered the call from her sorry-ass excuse of an ex.

Maybe I should start to say and do the opposite of everything I thought from now on around these people from Wren. Next time Finley spends a half hour complaining that a client doesn't like designs done to their exact specifications, instead of telling her to suck it up and get back to work, I'll sit down and ask her how it makes her *feel* to have a client unhappy with her work. Maybe over some tea.

And Annalise—when she asks me what I think about her so-called *break*, instead of being honest and telling her that her dick of an ex wants his dick sucked by someone other than her, I'll explain that it's normal for men to want a period of separation every so often, and that I'd bet dollars to donuts he comes back a happier and more well-adjusted man because of her understanding.

Wake the fuck up, people.

I hit reply and started to type a response to Mary in HR, then thought better of it. Instead, I went looking for Miss Sunshine who had never delivered the copy for our meeting with Jonas tomorrow.

Annalise's door was open, but her head was buried in her computer screen. I knocked twice to get her attention and then walked in.

"Before I say anything, are you recording this conversation to bring to Human Resources? If so, let me go back to my office and change into my pink pussy pants."

She looked up, and it felt like I'd been hit with a sledgehammer to the chest.

Crying.

Annalise was crying. At least she had been recently. Unconsciously, I rubbed at a dull ache on the left side of my ribcage.

Her face was red and puffy, and a streak of mascara ran down her cheek.

I took a few steps back toward the door, and for a split second I debated not stopping. I mean, what could she be crying over? Chances are, it was either work or her ex. I was the least-competent person to give relationship advice to anyone. And work? This woman was my adversary, for God's sake. Helping her was helping myself right out of a fucking job.

Yet instead of walking back over the threshold, I found myself pulling the door closed—with me still inside.

"You okay?" My voice was hesitant.

Women were always unpredictable, but a crying woman needed to be treated like a wounded puma lying in the plain you're trying to cross. She could continue to lie in pain, licking wounds inflicted by someone else in silence, or she could decide at any moment to tear into an innocent bystander and feast on him for lunch.

Basically, I was scared shitless of a woman in tears.

Annalise sat up straighter in her seat and started to shuffle papers around her desk.

"Fine. I'm just finishing up the copy for the Venus meeting with Jonas tomorrow. Sorry I didn't get it to you sooner. I've just been...busy."

She'd opened the door, giving me the chance to bail on discussing anything personal, and again I failed to back up. What the fuck was wrong with me? She was waving the *Advance to Go (Collect $200)* card in my face; yet I reached out and plucked the *Go Directly to Jail* card from the pile instead.

I took a seat in a guest chair in front of me. "You wanna talk about it?"

What the fuck?

Did that just come out of my mouth?

Again?

I knew I shouldn't have watched *The Notebook* a few weeks ago, but I'd been too hungover to get up and find the remote to change the channel.

Annalise looked up once more. This time our eyes met. I watched as she tried to pretend nothing was wrong and then...her bottom lip began to tremble.

"I...I spoke to Andrew a little while ago."

The douchebag. Great. Figures he'd hurt her over the phone while she's at work. Any guy who utters the words *"We should take a break"* has no balls to begin with.

I had no idea what to say, so I went with as little as possible—less likely I'd stick my foot in my mouth. "Sorry."

She sniffled. "I tried not to call him. I really did. He sent me a few texts after you answered my phone yesterday, saying we needed to talk. But it was making me crazy to see his texts and not respond." She laughed through her tears. "More crazy than having my icons in all the wrong folders has made me over the last week."

I grinned. "You're welcome. I probably just added three years back to your life by helping you overcome the demons of organizational control."

Annalise opened her drawer and fished out a tissue. Wiping her eyes, she said, "How many years do I get added back if I fixed them after four days?"

I nodded. "We'll work on it. Next week you'll give me your full-page to-do list, and we'll try to make it five days without you checking shit off."

"How do you know I have a full-page to-do list?"

I gave her a look that said *Are you joking, Captain Obvious?*

She sighed. "I bet Andrew knew I'd call him back, too."

I had no doubt about that either. The guy was a douchebag *because* he knew what he could get away with and kept her dangling at the end of that point.

"I might be the last person who should give relationship advice, but I do know men. And any guy who ends things over the phone is a jerkoff and not worth your tears."

"Oh. Andrew didn't end things."

"He didn't? Then why are you crying?"

"Because he asked me to meet him tomorrow after work for dinner."

I furrowed my brows. "I'm lost. Why is that a bad thing?"

"Because Andrew is a good man. He wouldn't tell me it was fully over on the phone." Her eyes started to fill with water again. "He asked me to meet him after work at the Royal Excelsior. I'm sure it's because he's going to buy me an expensive dinner before he ends things in person."

"The Royal Excelsior? Isn't that the place in the Royal Hotel downtown? I have a client a few blocks away."

She nodded and wiped her nose.

Okay. So I'm a big enough man to admit when I'm wrong. And obviously I was wrong thinking her ex was asshole enough to end shit on the phone. I hadn't realized the guy was a *giant* asshole and was going to fuck her first before ending it.

"You shouldn't go meet him."

Annalise offered a sad smile. "Thank you. But I need to."

I struggled with my thoughts. Did I lay it out for her—explain that the guy didn't want to break things off, he wanted to get laid? Hell, if he was smart—which I was reasonably certain he was, looking at the gorgeous woman sitting in front of me that he'd managed to keep on ice for months—he'd probably manage to let her think the roll in the hay was her damn idea.

Or did I keep my nose out of it? After all, she was a grown woman, capable of making her own decisions. And she was also my nemesis.

But she looks so damn vulnerable.

"Listen. I already put my thoughts out there about this guy saying he needed a break. So I'm pretty sure you don't want to hear what I have to say...but be careful."

"Be careful about what?"

"Men. In general. We can come off as nice guys when we're really dicks."

She looked confused. "Why don't you just spit out what you're trying to say, Bennett?"

"You won't fault me for being honest?"

She squinted at me. *Yep. She's going to fault me for being honest.* But now I'd opened my damn mouth and was stuck, so screw it.

"I'm just saying...don't let him take advantage of you. He asked you to meet him for dinner at a hotel for a reason. Unless he's telling you he made a huge mistake and wants you back, don't hop into bed with him. Listen carefully to the words he chooses. Saying he misses you isn't committing to jack shit and might just be to lower your defenses and raise your skirt."

Annalise stared at me. Her face had been blotchy from crying, but red started to fill in the white spots. *She's pissed.*

"You don't know what the hell you're talking about."

I raised my hands in surrender. "Just looking out for you."

"Do me a favor and don't." She stood. "I'll have the copy to you in an hour or two. Is there anything else you need?"

I could take a hint. Standing, I buttoned my jacket. "Actually, yeah. Maybe you can talk to Finley about removing the stick up her ass and coming to me if she has a problem, rather than marching over to Human Resources. We're a team now—all on the same side."

She pursed her lips. "Fine."

I walked to the door and put my hand on the knob before turning back. I never could leave well enough alone. "Also, I'd prefer that copy in an hour, rather than two."

chapter 12

Bennett

I needed to see the client.

That's what I kept telling myself anyway. It had been six months since I'd met with Green Homes, and they were solid. So a quick pop-in visit on my way home tonight wasn't out of the ordinary. The fact that they were located downtown, two blocks from the Royal Hotel, just happened to be a coincidence.

And the parking garages were always full in this area. So it wasn't unusual that I'd parked in one three blocks away and had to walk right past the Royal after my meeting ended.

At six o'clock in the evening.

My schedule had been full during the earlier part of the day, mostly.

I wasn't much of a believer in coincidence. I was more of an actions-make-things-happen kind of guy. But the fact that I was standing in front of the Royal Hotel—pure chance.

A fluke.

Happenstance.

Whatever.

Opening the door leading to the lobby? Now that, that wasn't coincidence. That shit was morbid curiosity.

I looked around the atrium, intentionally positioned behind a wide marble column so I could look things over without too many people seeing me. It was pretty quiet for early evening. To the left was the check-in area. One customer stood being helped while a few employees milled around behind the long counter. To the right was an empty bank of elevators. Straight across, on the other side of a large, circular fountain, was the lobby bar. A dozen or so people sat around. I scanned for her face.

Nothing.

She'd left the office at four thirty, so she must be here by now. Hopefully she was inside the restaurant ordering expensive shit from the menu, compliments of the douchebag, and not suckered up to a room upstairs.

Annalise's screwed-up relationship was none of my business. I should have turned around and left. I didn't really care if she got screwed over.

Coincidence.

Morbid curiosity.

Those were the reasons I'd stepped foot into the lobby. And the reason I walked toward the bar, rather than hauling ass out the front door?

I'm thirsty. Why can't I have a drink?

The bar was L-shaped. I sat in the far corner against the wall so that liquor bottles and the fancy old antique cash register blocked me from most people who happened to walk into the lobby. I had a clear shot at the restaurant doors, though. The bartender set a napkin down in front of me. "What can I get you?"

"I'll take a beer. Whatever you have on tap is fine."

"You got it."

When he returned, he asked if I wanted to see a menu. I didn't, so he nodded and started to walk away until I stopped him.

"Any chance you saw a blonde?" I motioned with both hands to my head. "A lot of wavy blonde hair. Ivory skin. Big blue eyes. If she was with a man, I'm guessing he looked like she was out of his league."

The bartender nodded. "He had a Mister Rogers sweater on. She was taller in those heels."

"Did you happen to see where they went?"

He hesitated. "Are you her husband or something?"

"No. Just a friend."

"You're not gonna cause any trouble, are you?"

I shook my head. "None whatsoever."

He lifted his chin. "They went to the restaurant. Closed out their tab about twenty minutes ago."

I blew out a deep breath. Sure, I felt relief. But it wasn't because I gave a shit whether Annalise slept with the douchebag or not. It was because I didn't need crying at the office. I had to work with her now—in close proximity.

I sat at the bar and nursed my beer for the better part of half an hour. The door to the restaurant opened and closed, and the initial stakeout excitement I'd felt started to lose its luster. I considered bolting.

Until the door opened, and I caught a glimpse of the woman coming out.

"Shit." I looked down into the empty peanut dish I'd polished off, attempting to avoid eye contact. After thirty seconds, I chanced a sneak peek up. She wasn't standing in front of the restaurant door anymore. I breathed a sigh of anxious relief. But it only lasted one breath. Because on my next inhale, I diverted my eyes from the door and found Annalise in my peripheral vision, walking right toward me.

And she didn't look too happy.

Her hands gripped her hips. "What do you think you're doing?"

I tried to play it off casually by picking up my empty beer and bringing it to my lips. "Hey, Texas. What are you doing here?"

She scowled. "Don't even try it, Fox."

"What?"

"Why are you following me?"

I feigned being offended, raising my hand to my chest. "Following you? I'm meeting a friend. I had a client meeting a few blocks over."

"Yeah? Where's your friend?"

I looked down at my watch. "He's...late."

"What time were you supposed to meet him?"

"Umm. Six o'clock."

"Who are you meeting?"

"What?"

"You heard me. What's your friend's name?"

Damn. This was an inquisition. Her rapid-fire questions threw me off. I said the first name that came to my head. "Jim. Jim Falcon. Yeah. Ummm...I just met with a client, and we were going to have drinks after to go over my meeting."

She added some badass squinting to her scowl. "You're so full of shit. You're following me."

"I left the office at three today to go see a client," I lied, knowing my door had been closed so she wouldn't have known if I was still in when she left. "What time did you leave?"

"Four thirty."

"So how exactly could I have followed you? I think *you're* following *me*."

"Are you nuts? Seriously, I think you need a shrink, Bennett. I've been watching you through the door to the restaurant for a half hour. You're staring at the door every time it opens."

I threw up my hands like I was exasperated. "The door is in my line of view."

"Go home, Bennett."

"I'm waiting for my friend."

"I don't know what you think you're doing, but I'm a big girl and can take care of myself. I don't need your protection. If I want to *fuck* Andrew, whether he wants to get back together with me or not, that's *my* decision. Not yours. Maybe you should spend some time thinking about why you don't have a relationship of your own, rather than being so concerned with mine."

Before I could get another word in, Annalise turned and stomped back to the restaurant. I sat there for a few minutes collecting my thoughts.

What the hell am *I doing here?* I'd lost my damn mind.

The bartender walked over and leaned one elbow on the bar. "She'll come around. They only get that pissed off when there's something there."

He saw the confused look on my face and chuckled. "Can I get you anything else?"

"You got any ass back there? Because mine just got chewed out."

He smiled. "Beer's on me. Hope your night gets better."

"Yeah. Me, too. Thanks."

I took my time walking the three blocks to the parking garage and then sat in the car and shot off a text to Jim Falcon before I forgot.

Bennett: If Annalise asks, you were supposed to meet me for drinks at the Royal Hotel bar tonight at six.

He typed back a few minutes later.

Jim: I'm way too cheap to pay eleven bucks for a domestic beer.

Bennett: She doesn't know that, jackass. Just cover for me if she asks.

Jim: No, I meant I've wanted to check out that place, and it's too pricey for my budget. So it's gonna cost you. Three drinks there next time we go out. You're paying.

I shook my head.

Bennett: Fine. Good friend you are, making me pay to cover my ass.

Jim: You're lucky we weren't supposed to fake meet for a dinner. Their surf and turf goes for seventy-five bucks.

I tossed my phone onto the dash and started my car. I'd parked on the second floor of the garage, and there was a long line to pay and exit. A sudden urge to get the hell home hit me as I waited. So of course, every person in front of me paid with a credit card, then I hit the light on the corner of the garage before having to stop for pedestrians at every turn. The street to get back to the highway was a one-way, which meant I had to pass the hotel again.

I made the mistake of looking at the door as I passed, and a flash of blonde came through. Only this time, Annalise didn't notice me. Her head was down, and she walked quickly, practically running out of the hotel. Stuck in a line of traffic, I watched in my rearview mirror as she sped up even more, passing a few parked cars before bending to put her key in a door. She swung it open and hopped inside. Then her head dropped into her hands.

Fuck. She was crying.

A horn from the car behind me blared, jolting my attention from watching her in the rearview to looking at the driver's arms waving in the air. The light had turned green, and everyone in front of me had driven off. I gave the asshole the finger even though I was in the wrong and then hit the gas.

Get the fuck out of here, Bennett.

You don't need this shit.

She told you straight out to mind your own damn business.

And yet...

I found myself pulling to the fucking curb.

Annoyed with myself, I threw the car into park and hit my palms against the steering wheel a few times. "Such a dumbass. Just go the fuck home!"

Naturally, I didn't follow my own advice. Because apparently I was a glutton for punishment when it came to this woman. Instead, I got out, slammed the car door shut, and started walking down the block, back toward her car.

Maybe she'd be gone.

Maybe I'd imagined she was crying and instead she was laughing into her hands.

Of course, I had no such luck.

Annalise didn't even notice me as I approached. Her car hadn't been started yet, and she was busy wiping her tears with a tissue. I walked around to the passenger side, leaned down, and knocked gently on the window.

She jumped.

Then looked up, saw my face, and began to cry harder.

Fuck.

Yeah, I have that effect on women sometimes.

I dropped my head back and stared up at the sky, silently berating myself for a few seconds, then took a deep breath, opened the car door, and got in.

"Coming to gloat about being right?" She sniffled.

"Not this time." I leaned in and playfully elbowed her. "Plenty of time for that in the office."

She laughed through her tears. "God, you're such a jerk."

I couldn't argue with the truth. "You okay?"

She took a deep breath in and let it out. "Yeah. I'll be okay."

"You want to talk about it?" *Please say no.*

"Not really." *Yes!*

"He told me he missed me and rubbed my arm."

Okay. So she doesn't get the definition of "Not really."

I inwardly sighed, but outwardly nodded so she could continue if she wanted to.

"I asked him if that meant he was ready to get back together. He said he wasn't ready. Then your words yesterday hit me. '*Saying he misses you isn't committing to jack shit and might just be to lower your defenses and raise your skirt.*'"

I'm poetic, aren't I? "I'm sorry."

She looked down for a few minutes. I kept my mouth shut, trying to give her some headspace. Plus, I had no idea what to say other than *I'm sorry* and *I told you so*, and something told me the latter wasn't a good idea.

Eventually, she looked over at me. "Why did you come?"

"I parked in a garage a few blocks over. You happened to walk out as I passed, and I saw you were upset."

Annalise shook her head. "No. I meant why did you come tonight at all—to the hotel?"

I opened my mouth to speak and she stopped me, wagging her finger as she spoke. "And don't even try to tell me you were meeting a friend. Give me more credit than that."

I toyed with the idea of standing my ground on the lie, but decided to come clean. The problem was, the truth didn't make any sense—even to me.

"I have no fucking idea."

Her eyes roamed my face, and then she nodded like she understood.

That makes one of us, at least.

"Are you hungry?" she asked. "I didn't make it to the entrée. Just had a salad as an appetizer before I left. And I don't really feel like going home yet."

"I'm always hungry."

She looked over at the hotel and back to me. "I don't want to eat here."

"What do you like to eat?"

"Italian. Chinese. Sushi. Burgers. Bar food." She shrugged. "I'm not picky."

"Okay. I know the perfect place. It's about a mile from here. Why don't you drive, and you can drop me back at my car when we're done."

She answered quickly. "No."

"Why not?"

"I don't like to drive with people in the car."

"What do you mean you don't like driving with people in the car?"

"Just what I said. I like to drive alone."

"Why?"

"You know what...just forget it. I'm not hungry anymore."

What the hell? I raked my fingers through my hair. "Fine. I'll drive myself. Do you know where Meade Street is?"

"Yes."

"It's called Dinner and a Wink."

"Dinner and a Wink? That's an odd name."

I grinned. "It's an odd place. You'll fit right in."

chapter 13

Annalise

"This is so good."

I'd been prepared for the worst when we walked in. The place looked like a dive from the outside. Inside décor wasn't much better—bad lighting, dated furniture, and the faint smell of stale beer wafted through the place, compliments of a fan kept behind the bar—although every bistro table and stool at the bar seemed to be filled with couples. And the people were all so happy and friendly. I looked around, and a woman sitting with a man smiled and winked at me. It was the second time that had happened in the half hour we'd been here.

"How'd you find this place? It's off the beaten path and looks terrible from the outside."

"Ah." He brought his beer to his mouth. "I'm glad you asked. I found this place by accident once. I dated a girl who lived a few blocks away and stopped in for a much-needed drink after I broke it off with her. She didn't take it too well. It's a special place."

I looked around again, and a few more people smiled at me. "The food is so good, and everyone is really friendly."

Bennett's smile widened. "That's because it's a swingers' place."

I coughed mid-swallow, nearly choking on my food. "What did you say?"

"A swinger's place." He shrugged. "I didn't know it the first time I came here either. Thought everyone was just glad to see me. Don't worry, they won't approach you. If a couple is interested, they wink. If you wink back, they'll come over and chat."

My eyes bulged. I'd been winked at twice already and could've winked back.

"Why would you bring me here?" I chanced another peek at the people eating. More smiled, and this time, a guy winked at me. I turned my head quickly. "These people think we're a couple and out cruising to swing."

He chuckled. "I know. Thought you'd find it funny, seeing how you told me you got dumped in college because your boyfriend wanted to swing."

"There's something wrong with you." After I said it, I looked around again. It suddenly felt like we were sitting center stage. And apparently we were popular, because I got two more winks.

"The food's awesome, and no one hits on you unless you wink back. It's the perfect place to come when you want to be left the hell alone and grab a bite to eat."

He had a point...I guess. Although he'd thought of bringing me here to poke fun at the story I'd told him.

"So tell me why you don't drive with people in the car," Bennett said. "Are you a nervous driver or something?"

I'd had a drink before dinner, so my guard was down a little. "I do something most people might think is strange when I drive, so I try to avoid passengers."

Bennett dropped the french fry he'd just picked up back down onto his plate and leaned back into his chair. "I can't wait to hear this."

"I shouldn't even tell you. I told you about the swinger's thing, and you brought me to this place. Your sense of humor is a little deranged. God knows what you'll use this one against me for."

He raised his arms up to rest on the top of the booth and spread them out wide. "If you don't tell me, I'm going to start winking at people so they come over here." He looked to the right and wielded a megawatt smile. I followed his line of sight and found a couple who looked anxious for his wink.

"Oh my God. Don't do that."

He lifted his beer to his lips. "Start talking."

I sighed. "Fine. I narrate while I drive. Are you happy now?"

He wrinkled his nose. "Narrate. What does that mean?"

"Just what I said. I narrate. If I'm about to pull up to a stop sign, I say out loud, *Pulling up to a stop sign*. When I see a light turn yellow, I might say, *Slowing down. Light turned yellow*."

He looked at me like I was nuts. "What the hell do you do that for?"

"I had a car accident when I first started to drive, and I was nervous about getting back behind the wheel. I found

116

narrating my moves helped calm me while I drove. It sort of just stuck. So I don't let anyone ride with me, except for my mom and best friend, Madison. They're so used to it, they don't even notice I'm doing it and just keep talking."

"You are *definitely* driving me home. I'll Uber back to get my car tomorrow morning before work."

"What? No!"

He turned his head to the right, but kept his eyes glued to me. "I'm gonna wink."

"Stop it. Don't." I couldn't even pretend to be seriously mad, because the whole situation was absurd.

Bennett set his beer down and lifted up a fry. "Picking up a french fry."

He raised it to his mouth. "Raising it to my lips."

I chuckled. "God, you're a jerk."

He wiggled the fry at me. "You're smiling, aren't you?"

I sighed. "Yeah. I guess I am. Thank you."

"Anytime, Texas. I'm here for your amusement for the next few months." He winked. "Before they ship your ass off to Dallas."

A minute later, a couple appeared at our table. It took us both a minute to realize what had happened. Bennett had winked at me, and some couple took that as their invitation.

⌒

"Have you ever stolen anything?"

Bennett asked me the question just as the waitress came over to check on us. He ordered another beer, and I asked for an ice water. It was his fourth or fifth—I'd lost count. Since he'd decided his car was staying parked outside overnight, and I was driving him home, he'd made good use of being free to indulge a bit.

The waitress stood next to our table, looking at me rather than going to grab our order. I thought perhaps she had been waiting for the rest of my order, so I smiled politely. "I'm good. Just the water for me."

She smiled back. "Oh, I'll grab that beer and water in a jiffy. I'm just waiting to hear your answer to his question."

Bennett laughed. "She looks like she could've been a thief, right? Innocent enough face, but there's a little spark in her eye. Not to mention the wild hair."

"I stole a box of condoms once," the waitress offered. "It wasn't too long ago, either. I was in the drug store, and my mom walked up in line behind me. I had shampoo and Trojans. I slipped the condoms into my pocket to hide them and let her go first, hoping I could take them out after she was gone. But she waited for me. I'm twenty-two years old, but we're Catholic, and she's very religious. The choice was to either break her heart or go to jail for petty theft. I risked it."

Bennett grinned. God, he had a damn sexy smile. "I stole a box of condoms once, too. I was fourteen and broke, and a hot seventeen-year-old girl invited me over. Didn't get caught, but did lose my virginity. Totally worth the risk." He raised his chin to me and wiggled his eyebrows. "Did you steal condoms, or just lube?"

"I never stole anything." I felt my face heat, and Bennett pointed at me. "Holy shit. You're turning red—you're lying. You're a klepto, aren't you?"

Unfortunately for me, over the course of the evening, Bennett had discovered my weakness. *I suck at lying.* Every time I told a lie, my face would flush, or I'd divert my eyes and fidget. As the number of beers he drank increased, he'd created a little game—The Texas Truth. He'd ask me a question, and I'd try to lie about some answers—hence his question about stealing. So far, he'd nailed me on every lie.

I looked at the amused waitress. "I was nine, and I *really, really* wanted the new 'N Sync CD. So I sort of put it down my pants when my mom wasn't looking."

"Niiiice," Bennett said.

The waitress laughed. "I'll be right back with your beer."

When she was gone, he, of course, wanted more details. "Did you get caught?"

"No. But by the time I got to the car, I'd started crying because I felt guilty. I admitted what I'd done to my mom, and she made me go back into the store and give the CD to the manager. He called the cops, who gave me an hour-long lecture, just to scare me some more."

"You know I have a strong urge to change your nickname from Texas after hearing that story, right?"

"To what?"

"Snatch. But I already have problems with HR, so I don't think me yelling *Hey, Snatch* down the hall would go over too well."

I wrinkled my nose. "You're a pig."

The waitress brought our drinks, and he took a long swig from his beer. "When was the last time you actually told a lie?"

I knew the answer to that question without having to think about it. But there was no way I was sharing *that* story with Bennett. "It's been a long time."

I felt my face heat.

Damn it.

He saw it and chuckled. "Spill your guts, Texas."

"If I tell you, you have to promise you'll never make fun of me for it, or even bring it up again."

"Who me? *Never.*"

"Give me your word."

He held up three fingers like a boy scout. "You have my word."

I knew before I started talking that it was a bad idea to share my story with him, yet I was having fun and wasn't ready to call it a night.

"Fine. But when I'm done, I want a story I can torture you about. Something embarrassing."

"Deal. Go ahead, liar."

I smiled and shook my head. "Okay. Well, I live in a co-op. My building has twenty-four apartments. An older gentleman, Mr. Thorpe, lives across the hall from me, and he has two female cats. He shows them in competitions."

Bennett's eyes had dipped to my mouth and now jumped to meet mine. He cleared his throat. "Show cats? I didn't even know that was a thing. But it's fucking weird, if it is."

I sort of agreed. Although that wasn't the point of my story. "Anyway. I have a male cat. He's not a purebred or a show cat, just a regular tabby that I got suckered into adopting. That's a story for another day. Sometimes Mr. Thorpe goes up to Seattle to visit his brother for a day or two, and he asks me to take care of Frick and Frack. If he goes for longer, he boards them at this woman's house who lets all the cats have free roam of her apartment. I've used her, too. Sometimes she has, like, thirty cats, yet it doesn't smell. I have no idea how."

"Okay. Are we getting to the lie soon? I'm not a cat person, and this story's turning boring. Just get to your big, fat lie."

"Stop being so impatient. *Anyway*...Mr. Thorpe's cats are of course indoor cats, so I pretty much just need to run over and feed them twice a day. Six months ago, I was watching his cats and accidentally left my apartment door open when I went across the hall to feed them. By the time I realized it, my cat had run over, and I found Tom humping one of Mr. Thorpe's prized Persians in his bathroom."

"Who's Tom?"

"My cat."

"Named for Tom and Jerry?"

"No. Hardy. I love him. Anyway, I didn't mention what had happened to Mr. Thorpe, assuming his cats were fixed, even though mine was not. A few months later, one of his cats gave birth to eight kittens."

Bennett raised his brows. "And you lied about it?"

"I found out during the quarterly co-op meeting. All the neighbors were there, and Mr. Thorpe had them riled up over how irresponsible some pet owners are. He assumed the cat got pregnant when he boarded her or at the pet park he takes them to for socialization."

I saw Bennett was about to open his mouth to poke fun, so I stopped him. "Yes, he walks his prized cats to a park so they can socialize. *On a leash.* But I'm the horrible person in this story, and I still feel guilty, so no making jokes about Mr. Thorpe or his stupid cats."

"Got it. No making fun of Thorpe. Just your whorey cat and his lying mother."

Bennett bared that boyish smile again, and my belly did an unexpected little flip. I attempted to ignore it.

"Anyway, so I didn't own up to my cat's crime, but I am paying child support. I don't want you to think I'm a total deadbeat."

He perked a brow. "Child support?"

"Once a week, I sneak over to his apartment and leave a case of the expensive food he feeds them at his front door."

Bennett burst into laughter. "And you say *I'm* nuts?"

"What? I'm just ashamed. I can't shrug the financial responsibility."

"Who does he think is leaving the food?"

"I don't know. I avoid him because if he asks me point blank, my face is going to flush when I lie."

"That sucks. I'd be screwed if I didn't have a poker face."

I drank some of my ice water. "Your turn. Give me an embarrassing story."

He scratched at the five o'clock shadow on his chin, which I decided he wore really well. "Let me think. I don't get embarrassed too easily." A minute later, his face lit up, and he snapped his fingers. "Got one. My parents thought I was gay."

I chuckled. "Good start. Go on..."

"I was probably ten or eleven when I discovered masturbation. The Internet wasn't big yet, and materials were scarce. So I used to swipe my mom's magazines. *Cosmo* was my favorite, but she didn't pick that one up too often, so most of my collection was pretty desperate— *Good Housekeeping, Woman's Day, Better Homes & Gardens*. On a good week, one of them would have a bikini shot in it for an article on avoiding swimmer's ear or some shit. But sometimes all I got was a shot of a comfortable bra for an article about avoiding breast-related back pain. Anyway, I stashed them under my mattress when they weren't in use. One day my mom found them when she was changing my sheets and asked me why I had them. I said I liked to read the articles. She seemed suspicious of that answer and asked what the last article I'd read was. The only thing I could think of fast was the one next to the pictures I'd jacked off to—'How to Make Men Notice You'."

I covered my mouth as I cracked up. "Oh my God."

"Yeah. My dad was sent in that night to give me a birds-and-bees talk. At the end, he told me he'd love me no matter who I was."

"Aww...that's so sweet."

"Yeah. But for the next few years, my mom followed me and my buddies around the house whenever I had friends over. I had to keep the bedroom door open when boys came to hang out, and sleepovers were pretty much forbidden. It sucked. But around thirteen I realized it also had an upside."

"What's that?"

"When I brought Kendall Meyer home, I could feel her up in private without worrying about anyone barging in. My mom treated the girls I brought home like a straight kid's male friends. I could close the door and lock it, and she didn't think anything of it."

The two of us spent hours sharing more embarrassing stories. We wound up staying at the swingers' bar until after midnight. On the drive home, as I'd suspected he would, Bennett poked fun at my narration. I was surprised to find we lived less than a mile apart.

"Checking rearview mirror. Pulling to the curb," I whispered as I arrived in front of his building. A few seconds later. "Putting car into park."

When I looked over at Bennett, I saw he had a funny grin. "What?"

"Just wondering if there's anything *else* you narrate?"

"No. Just driving."

He flaunted a mischievous half grin. "I was imagining you narrating sex for the entire drive home. *Taking off panties. Opening legs wide. Pulling down boxers. Attempting to wrap my fingers around—*"

I interrupted. "I get the idea. I think you're going to be splurging on some fresh copies of *Better Homes & Gardens* with that imagination."

Bennett grabbed the door handle. "You have no idea, Texas."

I was glad it was dark, because this time my face flushed for a different reason than lying.

He opened the door. "Goodnight. Thanks for the amusing ride home."

I'd started the evening so miserable and was ending it with a smile. I realized Bennett had given that to me, and I hadn't thanked him. Rolling down my window, I called after him as he rounded the car and hit the sidewalk. "Bennett?"

He turned back. "Texas?"

"Thanks for tonight. Maybe you're not such a jerk after all."

The streetlight illuminated his face enough so I caught his wink. "Don't be too sure of that."

He turned to walk toward his door, but continued to speak loud enough so I could hear. "Bending her over the bed. Wrapping crazy blonde hair around my fist. Tugging hard while spreading legs wide." He opened the front door and stopped for a brief second before going in. "Much better than *Woman's Day* tonight."

chapter 14

Bennett

Three nights in a row.

And now this.

What the fuck? I blinked a few times, attempting to rid myself of another new fantasy. It almost worked, but then Jonas pushed a bunch of file folders around on his desk, looking for something, which caused a stapler to fall off on the side where we were sitting. Annalise leaned forward to pick it up. Her damn hair tumbled forward to one side, giving me a clear view of the creamy skin of her neck. It looked so soft and smooth—my brain jumped to wondering if she was smooth *all over*.

A few days ago, the night Annalise had dropped me at home, I'd jerked off to thoughts of her before going to bed. It was normal, I'd told myself. I'd just had dinner and drinks with a beautiful woman—any guy who didn't come home imagining her blonde hair wrapped around his fist while her sexy ass was perched up on all fours really was buying *Woman's Day* to read the articles.

One-hundred-percent normal. Meant nothing at all. So why not indulge? One night of fantasy couldn't hurt.

Let's face it, it wouldn't be the first time I'd fantasized about a colleague. No one would know. No harm, no foul. But one night had turned into two, and two had turned into three, and then yesterday when I walked into the break room and found Annalise bending over to grab something out of the refrigerator, I'd actually started to get hard. *At work*. In the middle of the fucking day. To visions of the shapely ass of a woman I needed to obliterate, not fantasize about until I ruined a two-thousand-dollar suit with an embarrassing teenage-boy moment.

So I'd retreated over the last forty-eight hours—giving her the cold shoulder yesterday and again this morning. I'd made a mental decision not to allow myself to think about her, except for ways to come out the victor on every pitch. Unfortunately, my eyes didn't get the message. And that just pissed me off. Each time I caught my gaze wandering her way, I reined myself back by harnessing the anger over my momentary lapse in judgment. Which meant I'd been a dick a lot in today's meeting. But it sure as shit wasn't my fault her red skirt showed off a lot of leg and kept catching my eye. Or that she wore skinny, four-inch heels that wrapped around her delicate ankle and begged to pierce the skin on my back.

That shit was all her fault.

Annalise shifted in her seat and crossed and uncrossed her legs. Like white on rice, my eyes were right there.

Fuck me. She had great legs.

I shut my eyes. *Nope, can't look, Fox.*

I counted to five in my head and then opened them, only to notice a cluster of tiny little freckles on her left knee. I had the insane urge to reach over and rub my thumb over them.

Crap.

Pull your shit together.

Annalise moved yet again, and her skirt tugged up another half inch.

Her *red* skirt.

Fitting, because this woman was the damn devil.

We'd sat two feet apart from each other on the other side of Jonas's desk for a solid fifteen minutes, listening to him update us on the status of various things related to the merger. Occasionally, Annalise would chime in and say something and look my way, but I stayed quiet with my head straight ahead, focused on the boss rather than letting my eyes do any more roaming.

"That brings us to the board's assessment of you two. One of the board members, who is also a major shareholder, brought in an opportunity with a potential new account to pitch."

I leaned forward in my chair. "Great. I can handle it."

I felt Annalise's eyes burn into the side of my head. "So can I," she snapped.

"No need to argue. You're both going to handle it. The board has decided this pitch will be one of the accounts you'll both be reviewed on. You'll each get to come up with your own campaign. But you should know, our firm is coming into the game a little late here. Two other agencies are already involved, and we'll have to work on a tight timeline. Pitch is due back in less than three weeks."

"Not a problem," I said. "I do my best work under pressure."

From my peripheral vision I caught Annalise rolling her eyes. "What's the account?"

"Star Studios. It's a new division of Foxton Entertainment—the movie studio. This division will concentrate on foreign blockbusters and remake them here."

I'd never marketed a studio or a film, but I knew from reviewing Annalise's account list that she had managed more than a few. Studios were some of her biggest clients. She definitely knew her way around that marketplace— an unfair advantage for something that could ultimately decide what damn state I lived in.

"I've never worked with a movie studio. But that was Wren's niche." I lifted my chin toward Annalise. "Fifty percent of her accounts are film related. I don't think it's very fair for the board to use a pitch like this to assess our strengths. I have no market experience in this field."

Jonas frowned. He knew I had a valid point. "Unfortunately, we don't have the luxury of picking from too many large proposals. Besides, most of Annalise's film accounts are for individual movies, and this is marketing for a new production company—they want branding and market strategy. Those are your strengths, Bennett."

I looked over at Annalise, and she hit me with an exaggerated I'm-gonna-win-this-one-because-you-don't-know-shit smile. It pissed me off, but not because she had an unfair advantage. It pissed me off because my first thought was *Hey, look at that. She changed her lipstick today*, when it should've been *I'm gonna wipe the floor with you.*

More annoyed with myself than ever, I lashed out at her. "Do you know anyone at the studio? It's a small industry. I just want to make sure you haven't slept with anyone over there making decisions."

Annalise's eyes widened then narrowed to angry slits. "I've never slept with a client. And your comment is offensive. No wonder HR has worn a trail in the carpet from their office to yours."

Jonas sighed. "That was uncalled for, Bennett."

Maybe, but this was total bullshit. "I want to use my own team members, not share so that some Wren employee acting as a mole can leak my ideas to her."

"No one is a Foster Burnett or a Wren employee anymore. We're one team. It's bad enough you two are basically pitted against each other. Your teams are just starting to find their way working together. It will cause a divide if we separate them for this project. You're both going to need to use the full team's resources."

I stewed. Annalise, on the other hand, kissed ass.

"I agree," she said. "We need to keep the team together, not tear them apart."

Jonas opened a file and lifted up his glasses to read the top paper inside. "There's a meeting up in L.A. the day after tomorrow. The studio has invited us for a tour and some backstage insight. You'll meet with the VP of Production and some of the creative talent. Gilbert Atwood, the board member who got us the pitch, is planning on flying up to join you and some of their people for dinner. So it'll probably be a late night, and you should plan to stay over. I'll have Jeanie send you both over the address and contact information so you can make your arrangements."

I managed to mutter an insincere *thanks* at the conclusion of Jonas's little meeting. Not in the mood for talking to anyone, I went back to my office and shut the door behind me. The door abruptly swung open and slammed shut two minutes later.

"What the hell is your problem?"

I was annoyed that she barged in, yet I felt my pulse start to speed up. That only happened on two occasions—when I was about to get into a physical fight, which I'd managed to avoid for at least ten years now, or when I was about to sink inside a woman.

"Sure. Come on in. Don't knock or anything."

"Knocking would be polite, and obviously we aren't doing polite anymore."

I pressed my knuckles into my desk and leaned forward. "What's the problem, Annalise? Competitors aren't supposed to be polite. Football players don't take the spikes out of their shoes before stepping on a man down to get to the end zone. It's the nature of the game."

She took a few steps toward me and planted her hands on her hips. "What happened between the bar the other night and today? Did I miss something?" Although her stance was firm, her voice bent toward vulnerable. "Did I do something to upset you?"

Feeling like the dick I was, I lowered my eyes. When they rose up before I spoke again, they couldn't help but travel over the woman I was about to address. Only along the way, they snagged on something. Annalise's nipples were pebbled and trying to pierce through her black, silky shirt. They looked like two big, round diamonds calling to a poor man—*come and get me, I'm your riches for the taking.*

I swallowed. *What the hell did she just ask me?* I raised my eyes to meet hers and realized she'd just watched the whole thing—what had stolen my attention and made my mouth salivate. Rightly, she looked even more confused. One minute I was accusing her of sleeping with clients, and the next I was ogling her like *I* wanted to sleep with her.

It wasn't just her who was confused. I had no idea what the fuck I was doing.

We stared at each other for a moment. Eventually, I pulled my shit together, remembered what she'd asked me, and cleared my throat.

"It's not personal, Texas. I just think it's better if we don't...if we're not...friendly. There's no way I can relocate, and the last thing I need is to be distracted because I feel badly that I'm kicking your ass."

Annalise's chin rose. "That's fine. But you need to be courteous, at least. I didn't deserve that comment about sleeping with clients, especially not in front of Jonas."

I nodded. "Understood. I'm sorry."

"And if you don't want to be friends, you're going to have to stop following me to hotels."

I liked her sassy much better than vulnerable. It took a lot to keep my smirk under wraps. "Noted."

She nodded and turned to leave. My eyes immediately dropped to her ass. Once a dick, always a dick. Before I could raise them back up, Annalise turned around to say something else and caught me. This time, it was her trying to hide a smirk. "Non-friends also don't ogle non-friends."

She turned back around, then tossed words over her shoulder as she walked through the doorway. "No matter how great her T&A are."

chapter 15

Annalise

"How's the hot guy at work?" Madison asked before biting into a piece of the beef Wellington she'd ordered.

Her nose scrunched up as she chewed. She didn't like it. I felt bad for the restaurant owner. It was the third strike, and we were only just beginning our main course. First, the waiter had brought out the wrong appetizers. Then when Madison had asked for wine and dinner recommendations, he'd recommended the most expensive items. The review was going to be painful.

"Hot guy? Well, he's an asshole. Then he's really sweet, but tries to pretend he's not. Then he's pretty much an asshole all over again. I don't want to talk about him."

Madison shrugged. "Okay. How's everything else at work, then? Do you like the people at the new office?"

I put down my fork. "I just don't understand it. One day he goes out of his way to help me, and the next he's rude and ignoring me."

She picked up her wine. "Are we talking about the hot guy?"

"Bennett, yes."

She smirked and brought the glass to her lips. "Thought you didn't want to talk about him."

"I don't. It's just... He's so infuriating."

"So he's hot and cold to you."

"Scalding and icy would be more like it. Last week, I went to meet Andrew for dinner. Bennett followed me to the hotel because he somehow knew things were not going to end well. And they didn't. Bennett and I wound up getting something to eat together and talking until midnight. The next morning I saw him in the break room, and he gave me attitude—like the entire night before had never happened."

Madison set down her wine glass. "Back up. You met *Andrew* for dinner? I didn't get a midnight call or early morning visit the next day. And now we've been through drinks and appetizers and this was never mentioned?"

I sighed. "Yeah. It's a long story."

She pushed her side of mashed potatoes around with her fork. "My food was delivered cold anyway. Start at the beginning."

I ran her through Andrew asking me to meet, him rubbing my arm at the hotel restaurant while telling me how much he missed me, but then him also backing up as fast as he could when I asked point blank if he was saying he wanted to be together again. I also filled her in on Bennett's thoughts on what Andrew wanted before I went and how he'd showed up to pick up the pieces.

Madison tapped a fingernail to her lips. "So basically you're saying Bennett's an asshole to women, so he's able to foresee what other asshole men are after?"

"I guess. But the thing that doesn't reconcile is, if he's such an asshole to women, why would he try to warn me about Andrew and then be there for me when everything he'd warned me about came true? An asshole wouldn't care what happened to me before or after. He should've been saying *I told you so* the next day at work instead of letting me talk through things that night."

The waiter came by and asked how our meals were. Madison would normally send subpar food back to see how the restaurant handled it, and then give them another chance if they acted professionally. But instead, she fake smiled to the waiter, saying dinner was fine, and ordered another bottle of wine. I had a feeling our discussion was sidetracking her assessment at the moment.

"Sounds like Bennett might have Beast syndrome," she said.

"Beast syndrome?"

"All men fit into one Disney character or another. That guy I went out with a few months ago who had *three* video game consoles and hung out with his friends five nights a week? Peter Pan syndrome. Remember last year I dated a guy who told me he was the VP of Finance for a tech company, only to find out he worked in customer service taking orders? Pinocchio syndrome. That gorgeous French guy I went out with who wanted to do it in his bathroom in front of the mirror so he could look at *himself*? Gaston."

I chuckled. "You're nuts. But I'll bite. What's Beast syndrome? Because Bennett is gorgeous, not beastly."

"Beast syndrome is when a man constantly roars at you to scare you away. Perhaps he was less than magnanimous in his early days, which he thinks defines who he's forever banished to be. So he tries to keep people from getting too close. But he's not really the villain he thinks he is, and every once in a while, a peek of the prince underneath shines through. That usually just makes him roar louder."

"So...like, he was a player, and now he thinks he always needs to be that guy instead of a nice guy?"

Madison shrugged. "Maybe. Or maybe he was mean to an old beggar woman. I don't know the reason, but it sounds like he's afraid that showing too much of his underlying prince will cause him to get hurt."

"I'm not so sure about that. But I do know it's time I move on from Andrew."

"I couldn't agree more. He's been stringing you along for years now—claiming you guys couldn't move in together because he couldn't have distractions while writing his dumb book for three years. Then when the book was finished, he wasn't ready to move on because he'd fallen into a depression because the book didn't do as well as he'd hoped. Guess what? Life sucks. We all have disappointments. You know what we do? We get drunk for a week, then dust ourselves off and get back to work and try harder, not dump the person we love."

"You're right. I'll always love Andrew. But things have changed from what we had in college and after graduation. He's not the same happy, spontaneous person he used to be, and he hasn't been in a long time. I guess I was holding out that he'd magically go back to being the guy who used to show up at my place with a bottle of wine and surprise me with a weekend at a bed and breakfast."

Madison reached forward and covered my hand with hers. "I'm sorry, babe. But on the bright side, maybe the next guy will be more into oral."

I sighed. The night after Andrew told me he needed a break, I'd gotten way too drunk and spilled my guts on some private things—namely, that Andrew only went down on me on my birthday. When I'd tried to talk about it with him, he'd said he just needed to be in the mood. Apparently, that mood never struck.

"I think I'll put that on my match.com profile. Looking for a well-educated, handsome, financially secure man who isn't afraid of commitment or getting up close and personal with my vagina."

The waiter came by and opened our second bottle of wine. He poured two glasses, and Madison didn't bother waiting until he was out of earshot before lifting her glass in toast. "To cunnilingus."

I clicked my glass to hers. Maybe it was the topics we'd just burrowed through, but I found myself thinking... *I bet Bennett would take pride in pleasing a woman, not limit going down on her to once a year.*

I'd intentionally booked a different flight than my counterpart. Our assistant had asked if I wanted to travel with him, and even though I would've preferred to take the seven a.m. flight he'd already been booked on, I chose to take an eight thirty shuttle up to L.A. Our meeting wasn't until one, and it was only an hour-and-a-half flight, but I liked to be early. Now I looked up at the big board and regretted making a business decision based on anything other than business. My flight was pushed back to eleven, and I'd be cutting it close to get to the meeting on time. Meanwhile, Bennett was probably taxiing right about now. *Damn it.*

I took my time at the Hudson News, perusing the latest bestsellers since I was going to have a few extra hours of sitting around. Settling on a popular women's book about learning to accept who you are, I headed down to the gate to read. Only when I arrived, almost every seat in the boarding area was taken. I figured the flight before me hadn't started its boarding yet. When I looked up at the sign over the check-in desk, I realized that's exactly what it was, only the earlier flight was the one that had been scheduled to take off at seven to L.A.— Bennett's flight.

I glanced around the waiting area, but didn't see him.

"Looking for someone?" a low voice rumbled from behind me, and hot breath tickled my neck.

I jumped forward, dropped the bag with my book, and almost tripped over my own carry-on luggage. But a large hand gripped my hip and steadied me.

"Easy. I didn't mean to scare you."

My hand flew to cover my rapidly beating heart.

"Bennett. What the hell? Don't sneak up on a person like that."

"Sorry. I couldn't resist."

I smoothed down my blouse and bent to pick up my book, which had come out of its bag. "Shouldn't you be on the other side of the terminal if you saw me standing here?"

Bennett ran his fingers through his hair. "Probably." He plucked the hardcover book from my hands as I attempted to stash it back in the plastic bag. "But apparently it's a good thing I'm here." He read the cover of my purchase. "*You Do You*. What is this? A self-help book on masturbation?"

I snatched it back and tucked it into the bag. "No. What it is is *none of your business*."

"Boy, you're cranky. I think you really need that book."

"It's a book about accepting who you are and not worrying about what everyone else thinks about you, if you really must know."

He smirked. "That's a shame. What I thought it was about would be a hell of a lot more interesting."

"What's going on with your flight? Do you know what the delay is about?"

"Weather delay in L.A., something about high winds. All the flights are backed up. Originally they said a forty-minute delay; now it's up to two hours."

"I was booked on the eight thirty. Mine's pushed two and a half. I better see if they can get me on your flight."

After a twenty-minute wait in line, the best they could give me was standby. Bennett was leaning against a pillar, scrolling through his phone when I returned.

"I'm waitlisted. Not sure I'll get on."

He winked. "Don't worry. I'll handle it for us if you aren't able to get there. I'll relay what the client's looking for when I get back."

"Yeah. That's a great idea. I'll rely on what you come back with to prepare a pitch for a client you don't want me to win."

"Looks like you might not have a choice."

I looked at the time on my phone—a few minutes after seven. It was a five-and-a-half-hour drive up to L.A. If I left now, I'd have six hours to get back home and get there. "I'm going to drive."

"What? It's over three-hundred miles."

I picked up my bags. "I can make it. It's better than sitting here for two more hours only to find out I can't get on the earlier flight and then missing the meeting."

Bennett looked at me like I had two heads. "It'll take you an hour to even get back home with rush hour traffic now."

He was right. I couldn't go back for my car. "That's true. I'll rent one here. That'll save some time. I'm going to go. Good luck with your flight."

I turned and started to weave my way back through the terminal toward the exit. I dreaded driving half a day on the highway, but I dreaded the thought of living in Texas even more.

Luckily, I caught the Air Tran to the rental car center just as the doors were starting to slide closed. In the center, I picked the agency with no line.

"I need to rent a car for the day for a one-way trip to Los Angeles?"

The woman typed into her keyboard. "What size car are you looking for?"

"Whatever is the least expensive."

"I have an economy available. It's a Chevy Spark."

"That's fine."

"Actually," a deep, familiar voice said next to me, "can we get a full size, please?"

My head swung to find Bennett standing next to me.

He extended his driver's license to the woman behind the counter and graced her with his signature, charming smile. "And put it under my name. I'll be driving. I can't take five and a half hours of listening to her drive."

The woman looked between the two of us and then addressed me. "Would you like me to change it to a full size, ma'am?"

I addressed Bennett. "Did they cancel your flight or something?"

"Yep."

I thought about sharing a car with Bennett. Six hours of him being mean to me or giving me the cold shoulder was worse than driving alone.

I looked back at the rental agent. "I'll take an economy. Mr. Fox can rent a full size if he wants."

"Seriously? I'll pay for half. It'll cost you less than an economy car by yourself."

"It's not a matter of money. The company will pay for it anyway. I just think it would be better if we drove separately."

He looked perplexed. "Why?"

I looked at the agent, who raised her brows and shrugged, as if to say she'd like to know why, too.

"Because you've been a jerk to me. I don't want to deal with that for the long drive. I'd rather be by myself."

Bennett's face fell. If I didn't know better, I would've thought hearing me say that made him feel bad. We stared at each other. I could see the wheels in his head turning as he mulled over his response.

The muscle in his jaw clenched, and his eyes darted back and forth between mine. "Fine. I apologize."

This man ran so damn hot and cold. "And you'll be nice for the entire trip?"

He sighed. "Yes, Annalise. I'll be on my best behavior."

I looked back at the agent. "We'll take a mid-size car."

I caught Bennett's mouth opening to say something in my peripheral vision, so I nipped that in the bud. "It's a compromise."

He shook his head. "Fine."

And just like that, I was about to take a road trip with the Beast.

chapter 16

Annalise

I didn't argue over who would take the first shift driving—only because I really hate driving anyway. But I did use Bennett's wanting to be behind the wheel to negotiate that the passenger had control of the radio.

We'd been on the road for about two hours now, and our conversation had been limited, mostly polite small talk about work. He seemed to be off somewhere else, although I wasn't sure if he was lost in thought or maybe he liked quiet to concentrate when he drove. I figured I would follow suit on the limited talking in case it was the latter.

"There's a rest stop in about a mile," Bennett said. "I'm going to stop to use the restroom. But they also have a Starbucks if you want coffee or anything."

"Oh, that's great. I don't have to go, but I'll definitely grab a coffee. I need more caffeine. Want me to pick you up anything?"

"Yeah, that'd be great. Whatever dark roast they have with cream, no sugar."

"Okay."

At the rest stop, Bennett went to the bathroom while I waited in a long line for coffee and scrolled through my emails on my phone. Earlier I'd emailed Marina to let her know about our change in plans. I knew some airlines canceled your return flight if you didn't show up for the first leg of the trip, so I'd asked her to contact Delta and make sure we stayed booked on our return flights. Her response was interesting.

> Hi, Annalise. You're all set. Since your flight hadn't taken off yet, they let me convert it to a one-way ticket without a change fee due to their delay. Your itinerary number is the same. But since Bennett's flight had already taken off, his return was automatically canceled, and I had to book him a new one way and apply for a refund on his outbound. He has a new itinerary number: QJ5GRL
>
> Hope your trip gets better.
>
> Marina

Bennett had said his flight got canceled. Perhaps Marina was mistaken? I started to write her back, and then something made me check for myself. Calling up the Delta flight status website, I typed in the departure and arrival cities and set the approximate time of departure as 7AM. Sure enough, it confirmed that Bennett's flight had taken off fifteen minutes ago and was due to land at a little after eleven. The page also listed the subsequent flights, so I scrolled down to find mine. The estimated landing time was now pushed to after our meeting was set to start at one.

I'd made the right choice to drive. But why had Bennett joined me?

Not knowing the answer gnawed at me as we drove. I internally debated the reasons Bennett might've lied about his flight being canceled. There were only two I could come up with. He had either been afraid his flight *would* get canceled and I'd show up to the meeting alone... or...he didn't want me to drive alone because he knew how I felt about driving. The logical explanation was that he didn't want me alone with the client. It should've been a cut-and-dried answer requiring no debate. Yet I kept coming back to what Madison had said the other night at dinner.

Beast. Was he a good guy underneath the roar and trying to hide it?

Whatever the reason, I could have just let it be. But that wasn't my strongpoint. No, I had to understand the man next to me, whether he wanted me to or not.

I turned my body toward the driver's side so I could watch Bennett's face as I spoke. "So Marina got back to me about confirming our return flights."

"Good. Any issues?"

"No. We're all set with the same return." I paused. "Except she mentioned something."

"Let me guess, her lunch went missing and she called the cops on me even though I'm not there today?"

I chuckled. "No. She mentioned that she had to rebook yours. It seems they canceled your return because your seat wasn't used on the outbound flight that had already taken off."

Bennett side glanced from the road to me, and our eyes caught. He returned to staring straight ahead and said nothing for a solid minute. I saw the wheels in his head turning.

Eventually he said, "Needed to play it safe. Couldn't have you showing up at the client without me."

I was probably nuts, and I couldn't put my finger on why, but I didn't believe him. For some reason, I was suddenly *certain* Bennett was lying. He'd taken the trip with me because he didn't want me to have to drive alone. It warmed my heart a little, though he clearly didn't intend for *that* to happen. And it made me want to be nice back.

I took a deep breath and stuck my neck out...*again*. "The other night really helped me a lot."

He glanced over a second time. His face was pensive, like he was curious to hear what I had to say, but also didn't think it would be wise to have this conversation.

"Oh yeah?"

I nodded. "I've been thinking about it. I really owe you. If you hadn't set me straight on what you thought Andrew's intentions were before I went, I would have woken up the next morning in a room at that hotel. Not only that, but when I eventually figured out on my own that he wasn't planning on us reuniting for more than one night at a time, it would have been like ripping open a wound that had already started to heal."

"Just told you what I saw happening. Could have been totally off base."

146

"But you weren't. And you were there for me, to help pick up the pieces when I might've fallen apart, even though I'd told you off."

Sitting in the passenger seat while Bennett drove really had a big advantage: I could study his face. Being able to focus and watch the way his jaw ticked, his mouth moved, and his brow furrowed with confusion when he was unsure of how to answer shed a lot of light on Bennett Fox. He struggled for a moment over how to respond to my last comment before deciding on a simple nod.

"So now that you know my sad relationship history, what's your story? The only thing you've given me is that you've never had a girlfriend on Valentine's Day. It's only fair that I know something about your love life. Plus, we're stuck in this car for hours more, so you might as well tell me and get it over with, because I'll get it out of you before we reach L.A. And don't worry—we can go back to being non-friends when we open the car doors."

Bennett stayed focused on the road, but managed a forced smile. "Nothing to tell."

"Oh come on, there must be something. When was the last time you had a date?"

He shook his head.

He did *not* want to be having this conversation. But my need to have it was stronger than his resistance. The man had me curious.

"Was it a week ago? A month ago? Seven years?"

He sighed. "I don't know. A few weeks ago. Right before you vandalized my car."

"What was her name?"

"Jessica."

147

"Jessica what?"

"I don't know. Something with an S, I think."

"So I guess you only went out with her once since you don't even know her last name?"

A guilty smirk dimpled his handsome face. "Actually, I went out with her a few times. I'm just bad with names."

"Really? What's my last name?"

He answered without missing a beat. "Pain in the ass."

I ignored that. "So you went out with Jessica S. a few times. Why did it end?"

He shrugged. "It never really began. We just got along and...were compatible."

"So you were compatible, yet it only lasted a few dates. Why is that?"

"I didn't mean we were compatible for anything long term."

It took me a minute to catch on. "You mean compatible as in you were compatible in the bedroom?"

"It is what it is."

"So you're saying it was a sexual thing only."

"We went out to dinner a few times. Enjoyed each other's company. I just like keeping things simple."

"Really? Why is that?"

"I like my life better without unnecessary complications."

"So you see women as complications, then?"

"Most women are complicated, yes."

I pondered that for a moment. "So how does it work? You meet a woman and ask her if she's interested in a night of sex only?"

Bennett chuckled. "It's not quite that simple."

I teased. "But if it's not that simple, it would be complicated. And you don't do complicated."

He mumbled something under his breath about me being a pain the ass and shook his head—something he did frequently when I spoke.

"No, seriously," I said. "I'm interested. How does it work? Do you use a dating service or something?"

Bennett glanced to me and back to the road a few times. Seeming to realize I had no intention of letting the subject go, he sighed. "It's less sterile than that. If I take a woman out, at some point the conversation inevitably turns to what both of us are looking for in a relationship. I'm honest and say I want to keep things casual. But it's not hard to tell what a woman is looking for before you get to that point. So I avoid the ones that are...complicated."

"You're saying you can tell whether a woman might be interested in a sex-only relationship by just, what, talking to her for a few minutes?"

"Usually."

"That's ridiculous."

He shrugged. "Seems to have worked out for me so far."

I looked out the window, lost in thought for a minute, then asked my next question while watching him in the reflection. "What about me?"

Bennett's eyes completely left the road and his head swung toward me after that. "What *about* you?"

"You've spent some time with me now. Tell me, would I be interested in a sexual relationship only, or am I *too complicated*?"

149

I turned back to look at him and watched as he raised a hand to his chin and rubbed. A wide smile spread across his face when he stopped pretending to deliberate over his answer.

"You're as complicated as they come, sweetheart."

I opened my mouth to argue, then shut it, then opened it. "I am not."

He flashed me a look that said *bullshit*.

"I'm not!"

"You've been on a break with that moron for what, three, four months now? How many men have you gone out with during that time?"

My lips pursed.

"So I take that as a *none*, then?"

"I needed a break."

"From sex?"

"From men." I frowned. "Andrew really hurt me."

"Sorry. But that just proves my point. You could have gone out and had sex if you wanted—a physical release. But you associate that with a relationship."

I guess he was right. I'd had a one-night stand my first year in college and hated the way I felt the next day. I suppose I was complicated.

Now I was the one who wanted to change the subject.

"Have you ever had a girlfriend?" I asked.

"Define girlfriend?"

"A person you dated exclusively."

"Sure. I told you, I'm not big on sharing when I'm seeing someone."

"How long was your longest relationship?"

"I don't know, a few months. Maybe six."

"Have you ever been in love?"

Bennett's jaw tightened. Clearly that question caused some hurt.

He cleared his throat. "You said you owe me one, right?"

I nodded.

"Let's change the subject to talking about business, and we'll call it even."

chapter 17

Bennett

"Annalise? So great to see you."

The guy who had just walked into the room to join the meeting came around and hugged Annalise. I watched his hand travel to just above the crack of her ass as he wrapped his arms around her—debatable whether that would be considered appropriate for a colleague.

"Tobias?" She pulled back from the embrace. "What are you doing here?"

"I'm the new VP of Creative for Star Studios. I left Century Films and started here a week ago. I didn't see your name on the agenda for today until this morning or I would have reached out earlier."

"Wow," she said. "Well, it's great to see a familiar face. How have you been?"

"Good. Keeping myself busy at work. Still perfecting making wine on the side. First full crop came in last week at the little farm I picked up last year. I may have to call your parents for some tips."

"That's great. They'd be happy to help. You'll have to share a taste when your first bottles are ready."

I stood right next to Annalise, watching the entire exchange. While the sommelier, or whatever the fuck you call a winemaker, didn't divert his eyes from the woman in front of him to notice me, Annalise suddenly remembered I was here.

"Oh. Tobias, this is Bennett Fox. Bennett and I work together at Foster, Burnett and Wren."

I shook his hand and sized him up. Tall, not bad looking, shoes shined, a good firm shake.

"Nice to meet you, Ben."

Normally I corrected people if they shortened my name to Ben, although never a client. Clients could call me *dickhead* for all I cared, as long as they gave me their business. But something about an immediate name-shortener always irked me. You aren't my friend. I'm not calling you Toby and asking you to go out for a beer. We just met. It's Ben-*nett*...the extra syllable doesn't cost you more.

"Why don't we have a seat? I think everyone is here," he said.

I waited for all the ladies in the room to take a seat, but apparently that was a little too long. Because before I could sit in the chair next to Annalise—you know, to show a united corporate front—Tobias put his hand on the back of the chair in front of me and pulled it out for himself.

Not wanting to cause a scene, I moved to the next available seat, which happened to be on the other side of the table.

The VP of Production kicked off the meeting, giving a thorough overview of the company's business goals and target audience. I took notes as he spoke and, for the most part, tried to pay attention. But every once in a while, I'd look over at Annalise. Twice now Tobias had been whispering to her while she took notes. The conference table was probably about four feet wide. It made me want to find out if I could reach him with my foot under it.

After the formal presentation ended, each of the Star staff went around and added something. When the floor went to Tobias, he should have kept quiet because he didn't have anything of substance to add. Apparently, the guy just liked the sound of his own voice saying meaningless buzzwords. *And* to have an excuse to touch Annalise.

"So I'm the new guy here at Star, obviously. And the team has done a superb job today of laying out not only who we are, but the brand we foresee ourselves to become in the future. One thing I can add is that synergy is important. Our logo, our marketing message, our team, our strategic alignments—they're just the ingredients to bake a big batch of cookies. Leave out the pinch of salt or the chocolate chips and what do you get? Probably still a cookie—but it won't be as delicious as it could have been. Cohesiveness is the name of the game, and the campaign that wins our hearts will be the one that mixes well with everything else to bake the best cookie."

Womp womp womp. Cookies. Womp womp womp. More cookies. That's what I heard.

He droned on and on, saying nothing really, until he finally concluded with a nod to Annalise. "I've worked with Wren before, and so I'm confident they have the ability to think big and think outside the box to come up with something great." He touched her arm. "We just

154

need to give Annalise and her team the right baking list, and she'll come back with the tastiest batch of chocolate chip cookies we've ever eaten."

Annalise and *her team*. Great. What a dick.

After the meeting was over, Tobias volunteered to give us a tour of the production lots. He offered his hand for Annalise to get into the front seat of the golf cart before walking around to the driver's side. I was relegated to the rear-facing bench seat and had to strain to hear him point shit out as we drove.

After four hours of meetings and being shown around by the president of Annalise's fan club, the three of us went back to his office to talk. By then, his familiar touches had amped up in frequency, and I felt my face burning.

"So what else can I do to help you hit this out of the park?" Tobias looked only at Annalise when he spoke, even though the three of us were sitting at a small, round table.

"I'd love for us to sketch out some rough logo designs and run them past you informally before we get going too far down the road on our full branding pitch to the group," she said.

Tobias nodded. "Done. Send over anything you want me to take a look at. Better yet, come on back down, and I'll arrange a lunch with some of the key players and see if they could give you an early feel."

"Wow. That would be great."

I felt the need to contribute something. Or maybe remind him that I was in the room. "Thanks, Tobias. That would be great."

He acknowledged me with a polite smile and returned his attention to the woman next to him. Again, he touched her arm. "Anything for Anna."

Annalise caught me staring where his hand rested and quickly moved her arm.

Holy shit. That's a guilty face. Did she fuck him? Here I was thinking the guy was just a regular run-of-the-mill asshole who takes advantage of his position. But there was something more going on here.

The two of them spent a while talking about crap they did together at his last studio. Of course, I couldn't contribute to that conversation either, which might have been the point. Luckily, Tobias's assistant eventually knocked to interrupt and remind him he had a conference call soon.

"See if you can push it back, will you, Susan?"

I wanted to get the fuck out of this office. I stood. "That's alright. You've been so generous with your time. We don't want to overstay our welcome. *Right, Annalise?*"

Her brows drew down. "Umm... Of course. Will you be at dinner tonight?"

"I wasn't planning on joining, but I'm going to see if I can move some things around to make it after all."

I forced a fake smile. *Fuck off.* "Great."

After Toby boy got another hug, Annalise and I walked to the parking lot in silence. It felt like a giant knot had taken root at the back of my neck. I opened her car door and our eyes met for a brief second. My face remained stern.

If I spoke right now, I'd definitely explode. We had a few hours until our dinner tonight, so I'd need to hit the gym for an hour or so to help blow off some of this steam—maybe two hours.

After she folded inside, I shut the car door with moderate success at not slamming it hard enough to come off the hinges.

The minute the ignition started, I put the car into drive and began to move through the lot without programming any directions.

"Do you know how to get to the hotel?" Annalise asked.

"Nope. Why don't you figure it out and direct me, considering you're the boss."

Annalise frowned. "What did you want me to do? Correct the client in the middle of his presentation? You know that would be unprofessional."

"Not half as unprofessional as encouraging the client to paw you."

"Are you fucking kidding me?"

Annalise wasn't much of a curser, so I knew before getting a look at her red face that she was pissed. Which was fine. That *fucking* made two of us.

"He's friendly because we worked together before. He's also happily married, not that I need to explain anything to you."

"You can't really be that naïve, can you? To think that a little thing like being married makes a shit of a difference to some men?" I paused, although I should have just ended my rant there. "Oh wait. You *can* be that naïve. You're the same woman who thought meeting an ex at a hotel *wasn't* for a booty call."

If I'd thought her face was hot with anger before, I was wrong. The red shade deepened to a near purple. She looked almost as if she'd been holding her breath. For a half second, I considered getting out of the car for my own safety.

"Stop the car," she demanded. "*Stop the damn car*!"

I came to an abrupt halt.

Annalise unbuckled her seatbelt and whipped the car door open. We were still in the parking lot, and at least there were no other cars or people around to watch as she got out, started to pace while flailing her hands in the air, and shouted about what a dick I was.

Maybe I was a dick. In fact, I knew I was. But it didn't make what had gone on between the two of them all afternoon any less acceptable. So I left her out there to stew while I did my own grumbling inside. After about fifteen minutes, she waltzed back to the car, got in, and buckled her seatbelt.

"Drive to the hotel. We have to pretend to be friendly in front of the client at dinner tonight. But there's zero reason to be nice right now."

I restarted the car. "Fine by me."

One hour didn't help. Two did nothing but make my arms and calves ache.

Not even a half-hour power nap and shower with steaming hot water and a massager setting helped me relax. Every muscle in my body was still tense.

As fucked up as it was, I was *not* dreading dinner. In fact, I looked forward to it. I couldn't wait to see how

Annalise acted after I'd called her out on whatever was going on with that dick.

At quarter to eight, I went downstairs to the bar where we were meeting the crew from Star Studios in fifteen minutes. I was glad our dinner plans were at the restaurant in our hotel so I didn't have to drive and could have a drink or two. God knows I needed it.

The VP of Production and the head screenwriter were already seated at the bar. They extended a friendly welcome.

"What are you drinking, Bennett?"

I glanced at their glasses, both filled with amber liquid. "I'll take a scotch."

The VP patted my back. "Good choice." He turned and ordered another of whatever year and brand the two of them were drinking and swiveled back to me. "We did all the talking today. Tell me a little about you."

"Alright. Been with Foster Burnett going on ten years, started out as a graphic artist and worked my way up to creative director. I spend too much time at the office, try to play a little golf on the weekends, and my assistant hates me because I once ate her peanut butter and jelly sandwich from the refrigerator when I was on deadline and working at midnight."

The last part got a laugh. It was funny to say, and I assumed they thought I was exaggerating. It just wasn't funny that she *actually* hated me.

"Graphic artist, huh? Do you still draw?"

"Does doodling while I'm on the phone with my mother count?"

The men's laughter was interrupted by a woman's voice. "Bennett here is just being modest. He's quite the artist. You should see some of his work—especially the cartoons he creates. He has quite the vivid imagination."

I turned to find Annalise—wearing a blue dress that fit her body and made her tits look fantastic, yet somehow was still appropriate business attire. She looked gorgeous. It almost made me forget the little war we were having, and that she'd just attempted a dig at me for my sexy cartoon doodles.

I sipped my drink. "Speaking of modest...when it's Annalise's turn to tell a little about herself, don't let her forget to mention her car hobby. She can take apart a car like no one's business. Hell, on her second day at the new office, she took care of a windshield wiper problem I didn't even realize I'd had until the day before."

Annalise maintained the broad smile on her face, but I caught the little shiny daggers she shot my way from the slight squint of her eye. I beamed my pearly whites right back, only my amusement wasn't fake. I enjoyed screwing with her. I could've gone on all night like this, trading barbs dressed as compliments. It did more in two minutes to relieve the tension I'd felt than hours at the gym and a shower had done.

After a few more exchanges, where she disguised a knock about my dating life as being dedicated to my work, and I hit her with a knock about her being naïve disguised as her being open-minded, my neck loosened for the first time all day.

Although the pain returned less than five minutes later when her buddy showed up.

"You made it," I said.

I watched his eyes do a quick sweep over Annalise before answering. "It was too important to not make it happen."

Yeah. Sure.

Within a few minutes, the rest of our party had joined us, including the board member who was friendly with the VP at Star and had gotten us the invite to come today and pitch for their business. We moved our discussions to a table over dinner, and I wasn't surprised to see that somehow Annalise and Tobias managed to sit next to each other again.

Although I was lucky enough to be seated next to the board member who would soon decide where the hell I lived, I couldn't focus enough to take advantage of the opportunity to properly talk him up. Instead, I found myself scrutinizing every gesture between the happy-looking couple sitting across from me.

The way she threw her head back to laugh when he said something that was supposed to be funny.

The way her mouth moved when she talked and her tongue wiped the remnants of wine from the top of the glass each time she took a sip.

The feminine way she dabbed the corners of her mouth with her cloth napkin.

The way *the asshole* kept touching her arm and bumping shoulders with her.

By the time we made it to dessert, I'd started to have trouble coming up with anything to say and mostly kept quiet. The fun I'd felt at the beginning of the evening was long gone, and I was anxious for the night to end.

When it finally did, we all stood around in the hotel lobby saying our goodbyes. Annalise waved one last time as the entire Star team exited the hotel, and then it was just the two of us. The smile she'd been sporting immediately morphed into an angry face.

"You are the most unprofessional person I've ever met!"

"Me? What the hell did I do?"

"You spent all night giving me the evil eye and glaring at Tobias."

"Bullshit! I did not."

She stilled for a moment and studied my face. "You're serious, aren't you? You really don't even realize what you were doing."

"I wasn't doing shit."

This woman was nuts. Maybe I'd been quiet, way less social than I'd normally be, but she was also sitting across the table from me.

"You were sitting in my line of sight. Where the hell did you expect me to look?"

"You were pouting and stewing like...like...you acted like a damn jealous boyfriend."

"You're nuts."

"You're impossible to work with." She stormed off before I could say anything more, heading to the elevator.

I stood there a moment, trying to figure out where the hell she'd gotten me acting like a jealous boyfriend from. My adrenaline had spiked, and I knew there was no way in hell I was going to be able to sleep. So I decided to head back to the lobby bar and have a little liquid sleep assistance.

"You acted like a damn jealous boyfriend." Her words kept swirling around in my mind, along with copious amounts of ten-year-old scotch.

After two drinks, I was definitely calmer. But I couldn't shake everything that had gone down tonight. Things had started out well enough—the blue dress, her great tits. I'd been pretty composed when she arrived, even after our blowup in the car this afternoon. Watching her talk, watching her laugh, seeing the man sitting next to her stretch out and rest his arm around the back of her chair during appetizers. I couldn't see his hand, but I imagined him trailing a finger along her back, thinking no one would be the wiser.

Except me. *I knew.*

I rattled the ice around in my glass and then gulped back the rest of my drink.

That fucking finger.

I wanted to break it.

How dare that bastard touch her?

The thing that crossed my three-quarters-of-the-way-to-drunk mind next seemed to come out of nowhere.

Keep your hands off my girl.

What the fuck?

Come again?

I laughed to myself, trying to shake off the ridiculous thought. It's the alcohol talking.

Had to be.

Right?

Or...

Fuuuuuuck.

My head fell back against the top of the bar stool, and I stared at the ceiling for a minute, lost in thought. Everything started to click into place at rapid speed.

I shut my eyes.

Shit.

I *was* acting like a jealous boyfriend tonight.

But why?

The answer should've been obvious, even to someone as thick-headed as me. But it took two more drinks and until the bar started to close down to mull it over some more.

Once I'd figured it out, I decided to do something stupid...

chapter 18

Annalise

Thump thump.

I rolled over and covered my head with the blanket.

A few minutes later, there was the sound again. *Thump thump.*

I ripped the cover down and sighed. What the hell time was it? And who the hell was banging? It didn't sound like someone knocking.

Patting for my cell on the nightstand, I picked it up and pushed the *on* button. Bright light illuminated the pitch-dark hotel room and affronted my sleepy eyes. I squinted a glimpse at the time. 2:11 a.m.

I sighed. Must be people coming down the hall after the bars closed. I attempted to roll over and fall back asleep, but now my bladder had woken, too. On my way to the bathroom, I peeked out the peephole and peered down the hall as much as I could. It seemed to be empty now.

But the moment I climbed back into bed, it started again.

Thump thump.

What the hell? I shoved the covers down and climbed out of bed to check the peephole again. Nothing. But this time, while I was up on my tippy toes peering through, the thumping noise came again—and the door vibrated. I jumped back.

"Hello?"

A low voice said something from the other side of the door, but I couldn't make out the words. I checked the peephole again, only looking *down* through the viewer this time. *Hair.* Someone was sitting in front of the door. My heart started to race.

"Who's there?"

More mumbling.

I dropped down to their level and put my ear to the door. "Who's there?"

I heard the distinct sound of laughter.

Was that?

I rose to the peephole and looked down as much as I could once again. The hair looked like his, too. But I couldn't be certain. So I double-checked the safety chain lock before I slowly cracked open the door.

"Bennett? Is that you?"

"What the fuck?" His voice grumbled clearer through the open space. Looking down, I found him slumped against the door. He'd been using it to keep upright, and fell back when it moved.

I pushed him and the door forward to unlatch the safety chain, then opened the door wide.

Bennett followed right along, his weight pushing the door open until he was sprawled out, lying flat on the floor—the top half of him in my room, his legs outside in the hallway. He went hysterical laughing.

"What the hell are you doing?" I asked. Then it dawned on me that he could be ill and in need of medical attention. "Shit." I leaned down in a panic. "Are you okay? Does something hurt?"

The smell of alcohol answered in the absence of actual words.

I waved a hand in front of my nose. "You're drunk."

He flashed the sexiest crooked smile. "And you're fucking beautiful."

Not exactly what I expected.

I stepped around his body on my carpet and looked up and down the hall. No one else was out there.

Bennett pointed up at me with his entire face joining in for a dirty smirk. "I can see up your dress."

I had on a long T-shirt that barely reached my thighs. And he *was* looking up at my underwear. I pulled the material tight at the hem and pressed my legs closed.

"What's going on? Did you think this was your room or something? You're two doors down, the room next to the elevator, remember?"

He reached up, and his fingers skimmed my thigh. "Come on. Let me see 'em again. They were black and lacy. My favorite kind."

Warmth spread up my legs from the feel of his fingers on my skin. But my heart was smart enough to remember what he'd done earlier. I pushed his hand away. Which he found amusing.

"You don't like me, do you?"

"At the moment, no."

"That's okay. I like you."

"Bennett, do you want something, or do you need help getting back to your room?"

"I came to apologize."

That thawed my ice a little. But he was drunk, so I couldn't be sure he knew what the hell he was sorry for.

"Apologize for what?" I asked.

"For being a dick. For acting like a jealous boyfriend."

I sighed. "What was your problem tonight?"

A goofy grin spread across his face. "Toby boy shouldn't have been touching you. I was angry. I shouldn't have taken it out on you."

More of my guard came down. "It's fine. I guess on some level I can appreciate your chivalry, wanting to stick up for me."

He found that comment amusing, too. "Chivalry. That's something I've never been accused of."

Bennett reached out and put his hand on my bare foot. He traced figure eights with his finger. God, his touch felt good, even there.

He stared down, watching his hand draw, while he continued to speak. "I'm sorry, Texas."

For some stupid reason, the use of my nickname softened me. "It's okay, Bennett. Don't worry about it. Just don't let it happen again. Okay?"

He stopped drawing and covered the top of my foot with his palm. His thumb reached up and stroked my ankle. I felt it between my legs.

"It will, though," he whispered. "It will happen again."

My brain had become distracted by the way his simple touch radiated all over my body, so I didn't follow what he was saying.

"What will happen?"

"I'll act like that again. I can't help it. You know why?"

I wasn't sure I cared as long as that thumb kept stroking my ankle.

"Hmmm?"

"Because I *was* jealous."

My jaw dropped. I had to be misinterpreting what he was saying. "You were jealous about what?"

He looked up from the floor and our eyes locked. "About him touching you."

"But why?"

"Because *I* want to be the one touching you."

I suddenly became acutely aware that I was standing in only a T-shirt.

"I need to put some pants on." The door to my room was still open, with half his body in the hall. "Can you pull your legs in so I can close the door and grab something to wear?"

He managed to bend his knees and lift them enough so the door would shut, but he didn't get up from the floor. He also didn't let go of my foot. The sound of the lock clicking closed rang out extra loud, followed by silence. I remained painfully aware that I was half naked, Bennett was touching my leg, and the two of us were very alone in my hotel room.

I tugged my foot from his hand and hurried to my suitcase to find the sweats I should've put on before opening the door in the first place. Digging them out, I rushed to the bathroom.

Jesus. I scared myself, catching my reflection in the mirror. Bedhead, smeared makeup, puffy, tired eyes with dark circles—I looked like a homeless person. Mascara ran down one of my cheeks and—I leaned forward for a closer look—was that *drool* dried to the side of my face?

I spent the next God knows how long fixing myself. I tied my hair into a ponytail, washed my face, brushed my teeth, put on deodorant, and slipped into sweatpants. Then I had a long conversation...with myself.

"You're fine. He's just drunk. He has no idea what he's saying." I took a deep breath. "Nothing's gonna happen out there. You're just going to help him up, and help him to his room."

But...if he starts to rub my foot again.

"No. Definitely not. This is stupid. Just go out there, already. How long have you been hiding in here anyway?"

The better question is, how long has it been since you were with a man?

"Stop it. You're being ridiculous. This is your nemesis, a man you don't even like half the time."

Tonight doesn't have to be that half of the time...

I pointed a stern finger at the mirror. "No more." Then I took one last look at myself and straightened my posture before putting my hand on the doorknob. *Here goes nothing.*

Literally.

Because I swung open the bathroom door to find...

Bennett snoring on my floor.

I couldn't go back to sleep.

And since I had an early-morning flight, I only had a few hours to kill until I had to leave for the airport. Yet a few hours didn't seem like nearly enough time to replay everything Bennett had done and said last night.

I'd tried to wake him after I'd come out of the bathroom, but it was no use. He'd fallen into a deep, drunken sleep. So I covered him with an extra blanket from the closet, tucked a pillow beneath his head, and left him sleeping right there on my floor.

Even while I'd gotten ready this morning—zipping my suitcase, the sound of the shower, dropping the deodorant on the tiled bathroom floor—nothing made Bennett flinch. I got the feeling he could probably stay that way until this afternoon, and he probably needed to, but then he'd miss his flight. Luckily, his wasn't until three hours after mine, so he didn't need to get up for a while.

I phoned the front desk and asked them to give me a wakeup call at nine, but I wasn't so sure the sound of the phone ringing from the other side of the room would even wake him. So I decided to set the alarm on his cellphone, too. Only I had to get it out his pocket first.

Crouching down, I examined his face, making sure he was still in a deep sleep. Bennett really was one damn handsome man—his complexion had a natural, sun-kissed color even in his drunken stupor, and I knew that if his eyes were to open, they'd be shockingly green against his skin. And what man had lips that full and pink? Of course, unlike me, he slept graciously. His lips were slightly open, showing a hint of his perfect white teeth, while mine would be leaking drool into a puddle on the floor. It almost wasn't fair how good looking he was.

But I had a flight to catch, and so did he. So I couldn't waste any more time admiring him. I needed to try to slip his phone out of his pocket to set an alarm.

Except...

When I went to reach into his pants pocket, my eyes snagged on a significant bulge a little to the left. *Oh my God.* Bennett had a hard-on in his sleep.

Wow. That's...a good size.

I might've stared at it for a minute or two.

I might've taken another minute to close my eyes and imagine what it might feel like in my hands if I unzipped his pants and reached inside.

I might've wondered if he would even know if I opened that zipper.

Or if he woke up while my hands were wrapped around that bulge, what he would do.

This man is really making me lose my mind.

I shook my head and snapped myself out of my insanity. I needed to get on the road and set this damn phone alarm.

My hand shook as I reached into his pocket. With every move I made, I kept checking his face to make sure he wasn't waking up. Ever so slowly, I inched his cell free.

When it was out, I exhaled, realizing I'd been holding my breath. My hands were still shaky as I woke up his phone. I hadn't thought about the possibility of a password—most people had one. But when I pressed the *on* button, no keypad came up. Instead, it booted directly to his home screen, and an unexpected picture of an adorable little boy. He was probably no older than ten or eleven, with shaggy, light brown hair and the biggest, toothy smile. He wore shorts and yellow plastic rain boots, and he stood on a rock in the middle of a stream, holding up a giant fish.

I looked at the photo and then to the sleeping man next to me. Could Bennett have a child? He'd never mentioned one, and he'd said his longest relationship was less than six months—not that you need to be in a relationship. But it seemed like something that would have come up in our conversations by now. I looked between Bennett and the photo a few more times. There wasn't any resemblance that I saw.

I might've guessed he'd have a few dirty pictures of women on his phone, but not a sweet little boy as his background. The man was truly a complete enigma.

Luckily, while staring down at the boy, I caught the time on Bennett's phone.

Crap.

I needed to get out of here. I quickly set an alarm for two hours from now and went into his settings to turn the volume all the way up and make sure his phone would vibrate at the same time. Then I laid it on the floor, right beside his ear. If that didn't wake him, nothing would.

I got up and grabbed my luggage, giving the room one last look for anything I might've forgotten. Then I navigated around the sleeping man and gently opened the hotel room door. He still hadn't budged.

I stole one final look at the bulge in his pants.

Well, Bennett Fox, this has been interesting, to say the least. I can't wait to see how much of it you remember in the office tomorrow.

chapter 19

Annalise

At eight a.m., I'd already been in the office for hours.

On my flight home yesterday, I'd typed up a summary of the information I took away from the Star meetings and sent an email to three staff members—two from Wren and one from Foster Burnett—asking them to read over my notes and meet for a brainstorming session first thing this morning.

When I'd gotten to the office at five a.m., Bennett's door had been shut, although the light was on. After catching up on emails for an hour, I went to get coffee and noticed his door was open and the light was now off. I figured he'd done what he often did—arrived at the office early, did some work, and then went for his morning run after a few hours. We hadn't had any contact since I'd left him passed out in my hotel room yesterday morning, and even though my curiosity about how he'd handle what had happened was eating at me, I had no time to waste today.

Just as my meeting began, Bennett strolled past the bullpen. He took a step back, catching sight of us inside.

His hair was wet, and he held a large Starbucks coffee in his hand.

"What's going on in here?"

"We're just getting started on the Star Studios pitch," I said.

His eyes inventoried the people in the room, and I thought he might be about to question why I'd picked people to work on the campaign with me without discussing it with him first. But instead, when our eyes met, he merely offered a curt nod before walking away.

Me and my handpicked team worked the rest of the morning together. I'd had a dozen loose concepts for Star in mind before we started, and we narrowed my list down to two ideas and then expanded on them, as well as adding two more that the session came up with. Our plan was to spend a little time on our own, each running with all four of the concepts, and see which popped when we met again in a few days.

On my way back to my office, I stopped off at Bennett's. He had his head down, sketching something.

"Did you make your flight?" I asked.

He leaned back in his chair and tossed his pencil onto his desk. "I did. Luckily I had the wherewithal to set an alarm, I guess."

Ummm... No, you didn't.

He continued. "I don't really remember much about the night after we finished dinner. Did I pass out on your floor after walking you to your room or something?"

"You don't remember knocking on my door?"

"Apparently not." His brows furrowed. "Why did I knock?"

175

"To apologize for the way you acted at dinner." *And tell me* why *you acted the way you did.*

"I don't usually have more than one or two hard-liquor drinks. I'm more of a beer person." He grinned. "Hope you didn't try to take advantage of me."

Disappointment hit me. *He doesn't remember.* I'd known there was a good chance the entire night would be a blackout for him, but I hadn't expected to feel hurt that he didn't remember the things he'd said.

But of course, it was better this way. "You got confused which room was yours and passed out when I went to put a sweater on and show you to your room."

I felt my face start to heat from my lie. *Shit.*

"Gotta run. Talk to you later." I abruptly walked away and went to hide in my office with the door locked before he could notice.

Later in the afternoon, I spent some time tweaking Bennett's Bianchi Winery campaign. The copy he'd written needed work to reflect that the winery was family owned and not part of a large corporate conglomerate—something Matteo took great pride in. Other than that, I changed a few colors on the labels for the new line of rosé that Mom wanted brightened up and replaced the proposed late-night radio air buys with evening slots.

I had plans to hit the gym on my way home tonight—to avoid running into Andrew in the morning—so I cleaned up my desk at a reasonable hour and packed files to work on for the Star Studios campaign afterward. I grabbed the revised Bianchi art and copy to drop off at Bennett's office as I passed on my way out. Only my hands were full, and right before getting to his door, a few of the papers from the top of the pile fell. I bent to pick them up and overheard Bennett talking.

"I'm not angry. This is just my face ever since Annalise arrived."

We'd had our share of arguments and name calling, but that was between us, and it'd felt more like a game of cat and mouse—not truly insulting, even when we were flinging insults at each other. But him talking shit about me to someone else felt worse than if he'd said that same thing to my face, for some reason.

"She seems nice enough to me," a man's voice said. I thought it could've been Jim Falcon. "Smart, too."

That made me feel a little bit better.

"Sort of a shame you had to meet the way you did, in competition for the same job and all. If you'd met at a bar, I think the two of you would have hit it off."

"She's not my type," Bennett snapped.

Yesterday, I was beautiful. Today, I wasn't his type. I wanted to be annoyed, but instead all I felt was hurt.

"Yeah. Guess you're right. Smart, nice, and beautiful... what man would want that shit?"

Thanks, Jim!

"Fuck off, Falcon." Bennett's voice turned terse. "If I'd met her in a bar, I'd have kept my distance after spending three minutes with her. Trust me."

I'd never actually been in a fistfight, yet I suddenly knew what a punch in the gut felt like. My insides felt a hollow pain. What had I been thinking? Allowing myself to believe his drunken words were a confession of feelings of some sort and more than incoherent drivel? Worse, I'd let myself start to think that beneath the arrogant Beast was some sort of misunderstood Prince Charming.

Sometimes a beast is just a beast, no matter how many layers you peel back.

The sound of footsteps snapped me out of my momentary pity party. I turned around and started to walk in the other direction. Jim had moved closer to the door, so I could still hear him as I put distance between us.

"It's been a while. Let's do happy hour Friday night. We'll find you someone mean, ugly, and stupid to drag you out of this mood."

The hot-and-cold relationship I had with Bennett took a turn into the tundra by midweek. Only this time it was me doing the instigating.

Jonas had assigned the second account the board planned to judge us on, Billings Media, and we were both in the thick of working on early drafts of our separate Star campaigns. Near the end of our weekly meeting, I mentioned to Jonas that I had an appointment scheduled for next week with one of the VPs from Star. I knew that would piss Bennett off. He glared at me, but said nothing, and I ignored him and continued talking to the boss.

When Tobias had originally offered to look at any early designs, I'd assumed both Bennett and I would take him up on it. But that was back when I was an idiot who thought the playing field should be fair so the true better person could win.

After the crap Bennett pulled in L.A., and overhearing how he really felt about me, I no longer had any doubt that the better person was going to win—*me*.

I'd just returned to my office and picked up the phone to return some calls, when Bennett barged in without knocking.

"The door was shut because I'm busy."

He took an exaggerated look around my neat office. "Don't look busy to me."

I sighed. "I need to make some calls. What do you want, Bennett?"

"Flying to L.A. for a lunch? Let me guess, you're meeting at a hotel?"

"Screw you."

He glared at me. "No, thanks. I told you, I don't like to share. Certainly not with Toby boy."

I stood. "Did you come into my office for any reason other than to pick a fight?"

"Your friend Tobias isn't taking my calls. Is that your doing?"

Tobias hadn't even mentioned that Bennett had called. "Absolutely not."

"I walked over while Marina happened to be making your flight reservations the other day. That's the only reason I even knew you'd decided to go see your friend. Nice teamwork, by the way. I'd almost fallen for your *we're one team* bullshit. When the invite was extended for them to take a sneak peek at our work, I assumed it was a *company* invitation...not a personal Annalise invitation."

I leaned my palms on my desk and put on a saccharine sweet smile. "Me too. Guess we've both learned a lot about each other since L.A."

chapter 20

Bennett

Well, well, well. The night just got a fuck of a lot more interesting.

I sucked back the rest of the beer I'd been nursing for the better part of an hour and motioned to the bartender. "Ever hear of a drink called a sore loser?"

"I think so. Vodka, sweet and sour mix, grenadine, orange juice, and sugar around the rim, right?"

"And a maraschino cherry or two."

The bartender made a face. "Sounds more like a recipe for a hangover, if you ask me."

"Yeah. That's why it's perfect." I motioned down to the other end of the bar, where Annalise had just walked in with Marina, of all people. "See the sexy blonde talking to the crazy-looking redhead?"

He looked down the bar. "Sure."

"Can you whip up one of those drinks and send it to down to her? Make sure she knows the name of the drink and who sent it."

"If you say so."

"And I'll take another beer when you get a chance."

Our unofficial company happy hour had quite a turnout tonight. It was the first time both the Wren and Foster Burnett crew had socialized outside of the office. I'd guess at least thirty people showed up, half of them from the marketing department since Jim Falcon always organized this.

I kept my eye on Annalise while the bartender mixed together the drink and walked to the other end of the bar to deliver it. She smiled and looked down at the fancy glass filled with pink liquid and then followed to where the bartender pointed. Seeing me, her lips immediately soured to a frown. Marina, of course, joined her in shooting daggers in my direction. Too bad I hadn't thought of it earlier; it would've been funnier if I'd had a PB&J delivered for Marina along with Annalise's sore loser—funny to me, at least.

From the other end of the bar, Annalise held up her drink with a frosty smile and tipped her head to me in thanks.

For the next hour and a half, I attempted to mingle. But the more I caught myself sneaking glances at Annalise, the more I got annoyed. She, on the other hand, didn't appear the slightest bit distracted or even to notice that I had grown obsessed with following her every move.

At one point, a guy who didn't work at Foster, Burnett and Wren sidled up to her and started to chew her ear off. The asshole had on a brown tweed jacket with leather elbow pads and worn loafers—probably a writer like her last douchey boyfriend or a professor of some useless subject like philosophy.

Look, if you're thinking I'm jealous, I'm not. Get that shit right out of your head. Jealous is when you want something another has achieved—and Annalise has not and *will not* achieve anything over me—or when someone has something that's yours, and we all know I never have, nor ever will, claim any woman as mine.

I'm just protective by nature, that's all. And while the woman might have worked her way up the corporate ranks to a position equal to mine, she clearly didn't know shit about men.

At some point between throwing her head back in laughter and tossing around her hair, she excused herself from the now half-hour-long conversation she'd been having with Mr. Brown Tweed. My eyes followed her down the corridor I knew led to the bathrooms. I told myself to stay put, not go over there and fuck with her... but...

I wasn't a great listener.

I raised my hand to the bartender, ordered another sore loser, and then walked it over to the ladies' room. I stood outside and waited until she stepped out. She took two strides down the hall and almost crashed right into me.

Her eyes squinted so tightly, it was a wonder she could even see. "What are you doing, Bennett?"

I extended the drink. "Thought you'd like another drink."

"No, thanks." She went to step around me, but I sidestepped in front of her.

"Get out of my way."

"No."

Her eyes widened. "No?"

I grinned. In hindsight, that probably was a dickish thing to do, even for me. "That's right. No."

"Look. Whatever game you're playing, I don't want to play."

"No game. I'm just looking out for you, making sure you haven't drunk so much that you're falling for the lines some random guy feeds you. Clearly your ability to judge a man's character, even when you're sober, is poor."

Her face turned red. A fire danced in her baby blue eyes, and it looked like smoke might start billowing from her nose. I'd seen her pissed. Hell, it had become one of my favorite pastimes over the last few weeks to piss her off...but she'd never looked this angry. I actually took a step back.

And you know what she did?

You guessed it.

She took one forward.

I'll admit, I got a little scared then.

Jabbing her finger into my chest, she started in on a staccato tirade.

"You" *Jab*

"think" *Jab*

"I'm" *Jab*

"a" *Jab*

"bad" *Jab*

"judge" *Jab*

"of" *Jab*

"character?" *Jab*

She actually waited for me to answer. I shrugged like a coward.

"Well, you know what? You're absolutely right. I let Andrew string me along for way too long. Yet somehow, when I found out who he was, it didn't sting half as much as it did realizing how wrong I was about you. I was so sure you were just an asshole on the outside and a good person on the inside. I thought if I dug a little deeper, I'd dig past the dirt and find the hidden gold. But I was wrong. I dug through the dirt and you know what I found? *More dirt*."

Tears welled up in her eyes. I went to say something, to tell her I was only screwing around, and she stopped me with more words.

"And you don't need to worry about me believing the lies of a drunk guy. I already made that mistake once. You know, you were really convincing, too. Telling me how beautiful you think I am and that you were jealous of another man touching me. In fact, you were so good, I stupidly believed the drunk lies you fed me even after you didn't remember saying them. That is, until I overheard you talking to Jim the other day and realized what a complete idiot I was...*again*. Shame on me. But trust me, I've learned my lesson."

Before I could say or do anything, Annalise skirted around me and back into the bar. I hung my head, feeling like an elephant had just sat on my chest.

"Fuck."

What have I done?

The next morning it poured. Not your typical, April-showers-bring-May-flowers type of bullshit rain, but the kind that comes with gray skies and thunder louder than a bowling alley on league night. Couple that with the pounding I had going on in my head, and the last thing I wanted to do was go to a monster truck show this afternoon.

I hadn't even drunk that much last night. Hell, I had my third beer still in my hand when I finally grew some balls and went to chase Annalise after she'd finished chewing me out. I'd thrown it against the outside brick of the building when I found her—just as she pulled away from the bar inside an Uber. Not surprisingly, she didn't make the driver stop, though I yelled after her.

When I pulled up at Lucas's house, I didn't bother to dig the umbrella I kept in my car out of the glove box, so my clothes were soaked after making the short walk from the car to the front door. I knocked and hoped by some miracle he answered today, instead of Fanny. The last thing I needed to go with a pounding headache and rainy-day trip to a loud monster truck show was a run-in with that woman.

The door opened. No such luck.

"I hope you plan on using an umbrella when you walk with Lucas. I can't afford to get sick when he catches a cold."

Shocker, she didn't give two shits that Lucas might get the cold, only that he might pass it along to her. I wasn't in the mood.

"I'll make sure he runs between the raindrops."

She pursed her thin lips. "He can also use some new sneakers."

I ignored her. I'd long ago learned not to expect the monthly check I gave her to go toward anything *Lucas* might actually need.

"Is he ready? We need to be somewhere."

She slammed the door in my face and screamed inside the house, "Lucas!"

I preferred standing out in the rain than talking to her anyway.

The smile on Lucas's face when he opened the door made me smile for the first time since last night. About a year ago, he'd stopped running into my arms. So I'd come up with a secret handshake just for us. We went through the fifteen-second-long hand-slapping, fist-bumping, shake routine.

"Did you buy earplugs?" he asked.

I'd stopped at the store on the way over. Reaching into my pocket, I pulled out two sets.

Lucas frowned. "When am I gonna be old enough to stop wearing these?"

"Old enough? I'm still wearing 'em, aren't I?"

"Yeah. But that's because you're a dork, not because you're old."

I smiled. This kid could make me forget a bad day. "Is that so?"

He grinned and nodded.

"Well, just for that comment, I'm not giving you my jacket to put over your head while we make a run for the car, like I was going to do."

Lucas shook his head again and scoffed, "Jacket over my head. You really are a dork." Then he took off running for the car.

Shit. I had about a half mile to go to get to the arena when I realized I'd forgotten the tickets. They were in the top drawer of my desk at the office, along with the early entry passes I'd bought so Lucas and I could go check out the trucks before the show started.

Luckily, the office wasn't too far, and we were a little early since it never mattered what time our plans were to Fanny—only that I got him out of her hair exactly at twelve every other Saturday.

I pulled into an illegal spot in front of the building and looked around. There wasn't a meter maid in sight, and I'd only be a few minutes. My free pass on parking tickets had expired when I stopped calling the cute meter maid I'd gone out with a few times.

"Just have to run upstairs to pick up the tickets from the drawer in my office."

"Cool! We never come here. Do you still have Ms. Pac-Man in that big room?"

"We do. But we don't have time for a game today."

Lucas pouted. "Just one. *Please?*"

I was such a sucker. "Fine. One game."

There were a few people milling around the office, even though it was Saturday. I was relieved to find Annalise wasn't one of them—her door was shut and no light came from under the doorway. I didn't want another confrontation with her in front of Lucas. God knows I'd worked hard over the years to keep him from seeing the asshole I often was the other six days of the week.

I unlocked my office and went to my desk drawer, only to find the tickets weren't where I thought I'd stashed them. I remembered bringing them here with a batch of bills I needed to pay… I could've sworn I'd tucked them in the top right drawer. After a few minutes of searching my desk, it became clear they weren't here at all. *Shit.* I hoped they were somewhere in my apartment, and I hadn't inadvertently shredded them with my junk mail.

I looked at the time on my phone. If we left now, we'd be cutting it close. But the arena was in the opposite direction of my apartment; there was no way we'd make it if I drove all the way to my place first. Worse, I had no idea where I'd put the tickets, if they were even there.

I sighed. "I don't know what I did with the tickets. I'm going to have to call Ticketmaster and find out if they can send me an electronic version or something."

"Can I go play Ms. Pac-Man while you do that?"

"Yeah, sure. That's a good idea. It could take me a while if I get stuck on hold, and I need to look up the number first. Come on, I'll take you to the bullpen."

As we walked, I kept trying to retrace what I'd done with the tickets after I'd opened the envelope in my office. I remembered looking at the early-admission passes with logoed lanyards and thinking that Lucas would be pumped to wear a badge around his neck. But I couldn't for the life of me recall what I'd done once I'd stuffed it all back in the envelope—which was exactly what I was focused on when I strolled into the bullpen.

And discovered someone was already in there.

Annalise looked up. She started to smile, but then she saw my face and her lips curled to a scowl. Unexpectedly seeing her there had caught me off guard, too, which is why I stopped three steps into the room—and caused Lucas to walk right into me.

188

"What the heck?" he whined.

"Sorry, buddy. Uhhh... It looks like someone's working in here, so it's probably best you don't play and make noise."

Lucas walked around me and looked at Annalise. She glanced at him, then me, then back to him.

Offering a smile, she spoke to my little buddy. "It's fine. You're welcome to play a game while I'm in here."

Lucas didn't give me a chance to argue. He took off running for the Ms. Pac-Man machine. "Great!"

Annalise chuckled as she watched him.

When she looked back to me, our eyes met, but whatever was on her mind was unreadable.

"You sure you don't mind? I need to make a call. I seem to have misplaced some tickets we need."

"It's fine."

I nodded, although she didn't notice because she already had her head down, burying her face in her work.

"Thanks," I said. "I'll just be a few minutes."

Back in my office, I looked up the telephone number and dialed Ticketmaster on speakerphone. While the million prompts to push buttons droned on, I searched my desk again. Still no tickets. And of course, there wasn't a prompt for *I lost my tickets*, which caused me to have to wait for the last prompt to push the dreaded "all other callers, please press seven." That inevitably led to a few more annoying prompts to try to identify the particular problem.

Losing patience, I pushed zero a half a dozen times in an attempt to get switched to a live, customer-service person—but that didn't do anything but restart me at the beginning of the prompt merry-go-round.

After at least twenty minutes, I finally spoke to someone who said they'd reprint my passes, and as long as I had the credit card I'd paid with and picture identification, I could pick them up at the *will call* booth at the arena entrance.

I hung up and immediately began thinking how Annalise was probably going to be pissed at how long I'd left Lucas playing Ms. Pac-Man and think I'd done it just to distract her or something.

To my surprise, she wasn't pissed off at all. In fact, she had a smile on her face and was laughing when I walked into the bullpen. She and Lucas were seated across from each other on beanbag chairs, and they were yelling random things to each other. It wasn't until I walked farther into the room that I noticed Annalise had a phone held up against her forehead. He'd gotten her to play the digital charades game I never let him beat me at.

"It's big." Lucas said.

"The sun!" Annalise yelled.

Lucas laughed and shook his head. "Marmalade."

"Fruit. A big fruit. Cantaloupe. Watermelon."

Lucas made a face like she was nuts. "Scooby-Doo."

Annalise looked totally confused, so Lucas offered another hint.

He pointed to me. "Bennett wanted to be one when he grew up."

It took even me a few seconds to realize the word he was trying to get her to guess. She was never going to get it—not with *those* clues.

The phone buzzed, indicating the time for her turn was up, and she lowered her phone and turned it to read the word Lucas had been giving her hints about.

Her entire face wrinkled up. "A great Dane? What does marmalade have to do with a dog?"

I chuckled and answered for him. "Nothing. He meant Marmaduke."

"The old cartoon strip?"

"Yeah."

"But he said you wanted to be one when you grew up?"

I shrugged. "I did."

Annalise laughed. "You wanted to be a great Dane?"

"Don't knock it. He's king of the canine family."

God, when she smiled it made my chest hurt. But when she smiled and laughed with *Lucas*—even at my expense—it really did something to me. I watched as her laughter died down and her face returned to sadness, almost as if she'd forgotten what a dick I was for a minute.

"I also beat her at Ms. Pac-Man and foosball."

"She hasn't had as much practice as I have. Annalise just started at this office."

Lucas stood. "Did you get new tickets?"

"Yeah. We can pick them up at the door."

"You wanna come, Anna?" he said. "I'll give you my earplugs."

She offered a sincere smile. "Thanks for the offer, Lucas. But I have a lot of work to do today."

He jammed his hands into his pockets. "Okay."

Annalise avoided my gaze, looking down at her phone.

"You ready, buddy?" I asked.

"Yep!" He ran to the door, rather than walking.

The kid had a shitload of energy.

I waited for Annalise to look up, but she didn't. Eventually, I spoke to the top of her head.

"Thanks for hanging out with him."

I wanted to say I was sorry for last night, too. But the timing wasn't right. Plus, I'd apologized for a half dozen other times I'd acted like an asshole already. I wasn't sure she'd accept it this time...or that I even deserved her to.

chapter 21

November 1st

Dear Me,

So far eighth grade sort of sucks. I'm taller than almost all the boys. No one asked me to the Halloween dance, so I went with Bennett. He didn't want to dress up, but I made him be Clark Kent. He wore some nerdy glasses and a dress shirt with a Superman shirt underneath. I went as Wonder Woman. My friends all think Bennett is hot and were jealous. So that was fun.

For my birthday, Bennett and his mom took me to the monster truck show. Mom's new boyfriend, Kenny, sells stuff at the concession stand, so we got free hot dogs and sodas.

The landlord is trying to kick us out of our house again. Mom lost her job at the diner and says we're probably going to have to move. I hope it's not too far.

I love my English teacher, Mrs. Hoyt. She said my poems have a lot of potential and wanted to enter some in a contest. But the entry fee was twenty-five bucks and Mom said we have better uses for our money. Mrs.

we shouldn't

Hoyt surprised me and entered me anyway. She said the school had a fund to help out for things like that. But I have a feeling it was really Mrs. Hoyt's money that paid. So I dedicate this poem to you, Mrs. Hoyt.

Flowers will wither
love blossoms in the warm sun
cold comes way too soon

This letter will self-destruct in ten minutes.

Anonymously,
Sophie

chapter 22

Bennett

I couldn't stop thinking about Annalise all day.

Luckily, Lucas didn't seem to notice since he was busy eating a giant tub of popcorn, two hot dogs, and a soda large enough to fill a sink basin. We had third-row seats, so the roar of the trucks and our earplugs also kept us from talking much. With nothing to do but sit in my seat, I couldn't stop obsessing over Annalise's face when I'd walked out of the bullpen earlier. She'd moved past angry and now settled in on hurt.

God, I'm such a dick.

After the show was over, Lucas and I were walking to the car in the parking lot when my phone buzzed with a text.

Cindy.

Now there's a name I hadn't thought about in a while. It'd been a few months since we'd had any contact. Cindy was a flight attendant I'd met on a business trip last year. She lived on the east coast, and we'd hooked up a few times—twice while I was in New York City and once while she was out here. Apparently she was in town tonight on an unexpected layover and wanted to know if I could go out. *Go out* meant a quick dinner and then *staying in* her hotel room all night.

It was probably exactly what I needed.

A sure-thing good time.

Simple. No complications.

Relief from some pent-up frustrations.

Yet I tucked my phone into my pocket and didn't immediately text back.

I'd call her after I drove Lucas home.

But after I dropped him off, I knew I needed to take care of something before I made plans with Cindy tonight. I owed Annalise an apology, and that should come before my good time. So I drove to the office. It was nearly five o'clock, so I had no idea if she'd still be there. She'd probably come in early this morning to get a jump on the day. It was Saturday, after all. Yet I took the drive over anyway.

The area around the office was commercial and became a ghost town on the weekends, even more so at night. So the closer I drove, and the more empty parking spots I passed, the less I thought she'd still be at the office. Until I hit our street and saw a sole car in the parking lot—one that looked exactly like mine.

The lights were off in the reception area until the motion-activated system flickered them on. A few people had been working earlier today in various departments, but as I passed through the hallways now, the entire floor seemed to have emptied out. Every office was either dark or had the door closed.

Except for one.

Light streaked the hallway carpet from an open door at the far end. But it wasn't until I got two doors away that I heard any sound.

I stopped in place, hearing a voice. It took me a few seconds to realize it was Annalise. She was...*singing*. It was a vaguely familiar country song I'd heard a few times—something about losing your dog and best friend—but, damn, her voice was good, like a sweet angel, with a little vibrato devil soul aching to come out. It made me smile.

I wanted to listen more, but I was even more curious to see what she looked like while she sang. So I walked the few steps to her doorway.

Her head was down, her nose buried in a file cabinet, and earbud wires dangled from her ears. She didn't immediately notice me. I could only see her profile, but it gave me a brief chance to watch her. And I was awestruck by how beautiful she looked.

She had on jeans and a white button-up shirt, and her hair was pulled back into a ponytail. Yet she'd never looked more gorgeous. The lack of a fancy business suit and blown-out hair allowed the focus to be just her. Some people needed all that window dressing. But not Annalise. Her beauty came from the flawlessness of her porcelain skin, the smooth curves of her body, and eyes I knew lit with fire. And that voice...I was completely transfixed.

As I stared, she craned her neck a little more to thumb through some files, and the movement must've caused her to catch a shadow in her peripheral vision.

Her head whipped up, eyes went wide, and singing cut off mid-word.

"Oh my God!" She stood and ripped an earbud from her ear. "You scared the shit out of me."

I held my palms up. "Sorry. I didn't mean to scare you."

She put her hand over her chest and took a few deep breaths. "How long have you been standing there?"

"Not long."

"I guess I had the music too loud, so I didn't hear you."

Or I didn't say anything so I could keep looking at you. To-may-to. To-mah-to.

"What are you doing here?"

"I stopped by to talk to you."

She shut the file cabinet drawer. The initial shock had worn off, and her voice went flat. "I'm all talked out. Just go away, Bennett."

I stuffed my hands into my pockets and took a step into her office. "You don't have to talk then. Just listen. I'll get out of your way when I'm done."

She wore a mask of indifference, but said nothing—apparently this was my opportunity.

I cleared my throat. "I didn't lie in the hotel room. I do think you're beautiful, and I was jealous of that guy's hands on you."

Her jaw dropped. "I thought you didn't remember anything you said that night."

I smiled sheepishly. "Okay. So *that* was a lie. But what I said that night—it wasn't."

"I don't understand."

I took another step toward her. "It was easier to say I didn't remember saying those things and let you chalk up what I'd admitted to drunken ramblings."

She looked down for a minute, and when she looked back up, she seemed hesitant to accept what I was saying.

"Why didn't you want me to remember what you said?"

And there was the million-dollar question. I could've given her a perfectly acceptable answer that made sense and was probably the one that *should've* been true—because we're competing for the same job, and it would've been inappropriate—but that answer would have been bullshit.

I owed her some honesty, so I swallowed my pride. "Because every word I said that night is the truth, and it scares the living fuck out of me."

Her lips parted, and her face flushed a light shade of pink. I loved how she couldn't lie or get embarrassed without showing it. It made me wonder if it also happened when she was turned on. I bet it did.

"Why does it scare you?" she asked quietly.

The questions just kept getting harder. I ran my fingers through my hair and tried to find the right words.

"Because I've never been a jealous person. Might not have had a long-term relationship like you have, but I've dated enough. Sometimes saw the same person every weekend for months. Yet I never asked what she did during the week. Because I didn't care. It was always about the day, the time we spent together. Jealousy is about tomorrow."

She mulled that over for a while, then nodded and asked a question I didn't expect. "Who is Lucas to you?"

"He's not my son, if that's what you're asking."

"In the bullpen this afternoon he mentioned he lives with his grandma and you two spend every other Saturday together."

I nodded. "His mother died, and his father is a deadbeat who doesn't care if he exists. He's my godson."

She turned and looked out the office window. When she turned back, she said, "Anything *else* you need to say?"

Shit. Had I forgotten something? It sounded like she was prompting me for more. I quickly ran back through everything I'd said...I'd admitted I lied, admitted I thought she was beautiful and had been jealous. What else was there?

Seeing the lost look on my face, she tossed me a life ring. "You've been a jerk to me all week. Especially last night at the bar."

Oh. Yeah. That. I smiled. "Did I mention I was sorry for acting like a dick? Because I could have sworn I led with that."

She smiled back. "You didn't mention it, no."

I took a few steps closer. "I'm sorry for acting like a dick."

"*Again*, you mean."

I nodded. "Yes, again. I'm sorry for acting like a dick *again*."

She searched my face. "Okay. Apology accepted. *Again*."

"Thank you." I'd pushed my luck enough with her for the day, so I figured I should take off. "I'll let you get back to work."

"Okay, thanks."

I didn't really want to leave, so I took my time turning around. She stopped me right before I made it to her doorway. "Bennett?"

I turned back.

"For the record, I find you attractive, too."

I grinned. "I know."

She laughed. "God, you're such a jerk. I think that's more the reason you've never had a Valentine than you not wanting candles and romance."

"You want me to be your Valentine, don't you? Probably because you think I'm so hot."

"Goodnight, Bennett."

"'Night, beautiful."

chapter 23

Annalise

The waiter finished refilling our wine glasses. "I'll check on your dinners. Is there anything else I can bring you in the meantime?"

I looked to Madison and then the waiter. "I think we're good. Thank you."

He walked away, and Madison's eyes followed him.

She lifted her glass to her lips. "You should sleep with him."

"The waiter? He's, like, twenty."

"No. *I* should sleep with the waiter. You should sleep with the Beast."

I'd just finished catching her up on the last week of office drama—from our visit with Star Studios and Bennett's subsequent attitude, to the unexpected weekend, office pop-in and this week's flirty banter. My relationship with Bennett changed as often as people changed their underwear.

I nodded. "Yeah, that's a great idea. Sleep with the guy who's trying to steal my job."

"Why not? You know that old saying...keep your friends close and fuck the shit out of your enemies."

I laughed. "That's not exactly the saying."

She shrugged. "Let's be pragmatic about this. You've already admitted you're attracted to each other. It's not like that's going to go away. And you need to get back out there. He's moving in a few months anyway, so he's the perfect rebound guy."

"I love that you've already decided he's the one who's moving and not me."

"Of course. The fact that you're going to win is a given. You can't leave me."

I sighed. "Bennett is not the kind of guy I would date."

"Did I say anything about dating? I said you should sleep with him, not court him as prospective husband material. Fuck his brains out, not go shopping to pick out china patterns together."

"That's..." I trailed off. My gut reaction was to say *crazy*. But I had to admit...the thought was pretty damn appealing.

Madison grinned like a Cheshire cat. She knew me well.

"You're thinking about fucking him, aren't you?"

"No." I felt my skin start to heat. "And before you say anything...it's warm in here."

"Uh-huh." She grinned. "Sure it is."

The next day, I was working on printing a logo using the 3D printer when the damn thing jammed up. I couldn't seem to unclog the nozzle. Bennett walked over when he saw me taking it apart.

"Need some help?"

"It was in the middle of printing something, and then it started to make a clicking sound. I think the nozzle is jammed up with filament."

"Is this the first thing you printed?"

"No. I did two other projects before this, and they printed fine."

Bennett rolled up his shirtsleeves. "Sometimes a heat creep happens. The hot end needs to cool before it heats up each time, or the filament liquifies too much and causes a jam."

I stared down at his forearms. They were corded and tanned, but that wasn't what had my rapt attention—it was the ink peeking out where he'd folded his shirt up.

Bennett noticed where I was focused. "You have any ink?"

"No. Is that your only one?"

He wiggled his eyebrows. "You'd have to do a full-body check to find that out."

I rolled my eyes.

He turned some nobs on the printer, then pulled out a silver tray and reached one arm inside the machine. When his arm came back out, I could see a little more of his tattoo. It looked like Roman numerals with something wrapped around them.

"Is that a vine?"

He nodded. "It's from a poem that's special to me."

Huh. Not what I expected.

Bennett opened and closed a few trays and then inserted the silver one he'd removed back into the printer.

"It's what I thought. You've got a heat creep. The hot end probably didn't have the proper time to cool down. I used it for a few hours this morning, too. Cancel the job and give it an hour. When the filament cools down, it will unclog on its own."

"Oh. Okay, great. Thanks."

"No problem." He began to unfold his shirtsleeve. "If you need it faster, I have a small fan in the bottom drawer of my desk. If you set it up on top of the printer and angle the air blowing down, it will speed up the cool off."

"It's okay. I can wait."

I felt a tad bit guilty that I was printing stuff to take with me to Star Studios in a couple of days, and here he was helping me.

"Did...Tobias ever call you back?" I asked.

The muscle in Bennett's jaw flexed. "Nope. Left three messages." Our eyes met briefly before he looked away. "Let me know if you have any other problems."

I nodded, feeling guilty. He made it three steps away before I caved. "Bennett?"

He turned back. "The lunch is Thursday at one. Marina made my reservation. Come with me. We're one company. We should go together."

It was the right thing to do, even if it wasn't the smartest thing.

Bennett squinted. "Why would you do that?"

"Because I plan to kick your ass based on my work, not because some client might be attracted to me so he isn't calling you back."

"So you're finally admitting that jerk's attracted to you?"

I took a play from Bennett's book. "Isn't everyone?"

I zipped the carry-on bag on the floor shut.

"I'll show you mine, if you show me yours?"

I looked up to find Bennett sporting a dirty grin.

"I meant the presentation you got in that bag. Get your mind out of the gutter, Texas."

I smiled. "I was beginning to think you were standing me up. The flight just began to board."

Bennett set a box down on the seat next to me in the waiting area and held up his hands. They were covered in black dirt and grease. "Got a flat. I had to change a tire on the way to the airport."

"A tire? You drove and parked? Why didn't you just grab an Uber?"

"I did. But we got a blowout halfway here. And the driver was, like, seventy with a bad back. He called AAA to change the tire for him, and they said it would be a forty-five-minute wait. With rush hour traffic, I didn't have time for that. So I changed it myself."

"Oh, wow. That's dedication."

"I would've run here, if push came to shove." He looked over at the line for boarding. "Looks like we have a few minutes. I'm going find a bathroom and try to get my hands clean. Can I leave my presentation with you?"

"Sure. Of course."

"Are you sure I can trust you not to peek and steal my ideas?"

I grinned. "Probably not. But go anyway."

When he returned, the line was just about gone. I stood. "We should get going."

Bennett lifted his own carry-on box and then grabbed mine.

"I can carry that."

"It's fine. I have an ulterior motive, though. I'm *accidentally* going to drop it and kick it around a few times—see how good your 3D model holds up."

Such a wiseass.

When we arrived at the end of the gangway to step onto the plane, I asked, "What row are you in?"

"The same one as you. We're both in aisle seats, across from each other. I told Marina to put us together so we could work if we wanted to."

"Oh. Okay." *I was afraid of that.*

Bennett stored our presentations in the overhead, and we took our seats in row eleven. After I buckled in, I decided to just come out and tell him my little problem.

"Umm... Just so you know, I'm a nervous flyer."

His brows dipped. "What does that mean? You're going to narrate the entire flight? *Taxiing down the runway. Hitting a takeoff speed of a hundred-and-fifty miles per hour. Tucking my head through my legs to kiss my fine ass goodbye...*"

I let out a nervous laugh. "No. I just get panicky on flights, so I use an app that helps keep me calm. It's a combination of meditation, music, and guided breathing techniques. If we hit turbulence, I can push a button, and a therapist walks me through calming exercises."

"You're shitting me."

"I'm not sure how much work we'll actually get done on the flight."

He grinned. "Screw work. This is way better. I can't wait to watch you freak out."

Great. Just great.

Five minutes after takeoff, I opened my eyes and found Bennett watching me with a grin.

I shook my head. "Am I amusing you?"

"You are. And the way you gripped that armrest during takeoff, I'm glad I'm sitting across from you so you don't mistakenly grab for something else if we hit turbulence. You had that thing in a death grip."

I laughed. "Takeoff is the worst part for me. Once we're in the air, I'm not usually so bad, unless it gets bumpy."

"So is it all modes of transportation you don't like, or just cars and planes?"

"Very funny."

"You said you had an accident that made you a nervous driver. Did something happen that made you nervous to fly? Like a bad flight or something?"

I put on my best solemn face. "My dad was a pilot and died in a plane crash."

Bennett looked freaked out. "Shit. I'm so sorry. I had no idea."

I tried to keep a straight face, but the look on his was just too funny. My smile snuck out. "I'm just screwing with you. My dad sells insurance and lives in Temecula."

He laughed. "Nice. You got me."

After we leveled out, it was a short flight over to L.A., and once Bennett and I started joking around, the time flew by. All flights should be that easy on my nerves.

Once we landed, the captain came on the overhead and said we were a few minutes early, so we needed to wait to pull to our gate. I turned off my flying app and took my phone out of airplane mode. Emails began to fill my inbox. Noticing one from Tobias, I opened it.

Crap. I turned to Bennett. "I just got an email from Tobias. He said he had an urgent situation pop up that needs to be dealt with, and he had to push back our lunch meeting."

"Until when?"

I frowned, knowing what he'd think. "He said he had a meeting that got rescheduled, and he can fit you in at five tonight."

"Just me?"

I nodded. We'd blocked him for two hours, planning to each take an hour. "He'd like me to meet him for dinner tonight at eight."

The muscle in Bennett's jaw flexed.

"I know what you're thinking. But even if it were true, I'm a big girl and can take care of myself. And the fact that you're here with me right now should tell you that I want to win this account fair and square, based on my work."

He nodded. We were both quiet as we disembarked the plane. Once we rented a car, I realized I needed to change my return plans. If dinner was at eight, there was no way I'd be catching even the last flight of the day back. I needed Marina to book me a hotel and push my return flight to tomorrow morning.

Bennett was busy navigating through the Hertz rental parking lot, so I broke the ice. "I'm going to have Marina change my travel plans. Do you want me to have her change yours?"

"No. It's okay. I'll handle it."

we shouldn't

He didn't speak again until we merged onto the highway and started to head toward Star Studios. "We have a whole day to kill now. You want to hit a coffee shop and set up to work?"

Neither one of us had brought our laptops, since we had presentation materials to carry on. Although we did have our phones to at least answer emails and stuff. But that wouldn't take up an entire day. Tobias's email had left some lingering tension between the two of us, so I thought maybe a little relaxation might actually be in order.

"I have a better idea."

"What's that?"

I grinned. "Foot massages."

chapter 24

Bennett

She had to be screwing with me.

"What are you doing?"

Annalise's eyes fluttered open. We were sitting side by side in oversized chairs as two women rubbed our feet.

"What?"

"You look like you're about to start moaning."

Her eyes were actually glassy and hooded. She leaned in to whisper to me. "Honestly, I probably could...*you know*...from a foot rub. It's my favorite thing to relax ever."

Jesus Christ. I looked down at her feet. I'd never sucked a woman's toes before, although I hadn't been opposed to it. The right opportunity just never presented itself. But right now, I was absolutely positive I'd totally been missing out. If a little foot rub felt that good to a woman, I might have even been neglectful. I needed to remedy that shit right away, and I knew just where I wanted to start. Wonder what the two masseuses would've done if I'd gotten up and bumped one out of the way, replacing her hands with my mouth.

Annalise shut her eyes and went back to her happy place. I watched her for a long moment and then leaned over to whisper in her ear.

"If that's your favorite thing to relax ever, then the douche did you a favor by breaking things off. I can think of a few things that would leave you feeling spineless."

She laughed. Only I wasn't kidding. And I had the strongest urge to be the one to prove that to her. I tried to relax and enjoy the rest of my rub, but it was too late. The next thirty minutes basically consisted of me fantasizing about all the things I could do to the woman sitting next to me that would make her think a foot massage was child's play. Well, that and thinking of all the disgusting feet with funguses that the woman rubbing my feet had rubbed right before mine. I needed *some way* to keep the constantly threatening hard-on at bay.

After our massages were over, we walked next door to an Asian noodle house for some lunch. Annalise's phone started to buzz while we looked at the menu.

"It's my mom. Excuse me for a moment."

She didn't get up from the table, so I listened to one side of the conversation.

"Hi, Mom."

Pause.

"Yeah, that sounds great. I'll bring dessert."

Pause.

"We just had dinner the other night. She said something about going to her sister's for the weekend. But I'll ask anyway."

Another pause. This time, her eyes jumped to meet mine. "Umm. I doubt it. But I can ask him, I guess."

She talked for a few more minutes and then hung up.

"Everything okay?" I asked.

Annalise sighed. "Yeah. My mother just can't help herself. She's having a private wine-tasting party with the first bottles of the season next weekend. She told me to invite my best friend, Madison, and then she told me to invite you. Once she locks on to the scent of an eligible bachelor for her daughter, she's like a pit bull. I'll tell her you're busy."

"Why? I don't have any plans except work this weekend."

"It would be...I don't know...weird for you to come."

"No weirder than sitting next to you watching a five-foot-tall Asian woman almost give you an orgasm."

She laughed. "I guess you have a point."

"Plus, we both know the truth." I winked. "Your mom inviting me isn't really for her daughter."

"I told her we were competing for a promotion, not to keep our jobs here in California. I haven't mentioned the possible move to Texas because I figured there was no point in making her worry. But if I told her the only interest you have in her daughter was to have me shipped off eighteen-hundred miles away, I think you'd be surprised how much her friendliness changed. She's super protective of me."

Definitely not the *only interest* I had in Annalise. But she had a point, and if her mother knew about Texas or any of things I'd fantasized about doing to her daughter, I was pretty sure she'd be chasing me out with a corkscrew in her hand.

"Are you an only child?"

"Sort of. My sister died when she was eight."

"Shit. I'm sorry."

"Thanks. She was five years older, so I was only three when it happened. She had neuroblastoma—a childhood cancer that's really aggressive. I wish I remembered her more. Although, at least I don't remember too much about her passing. But to answer your question, I don't have any other siblings. My parents started to have trouble with their marriage after that. What about you? Any other full-of-themselves Foxes running around out there I should look out for?"

I shook my head. "Just the one. My dad died when I was three—heart attack at thirty-nine. Mom never really got over it or remarried. Although, she moved down to Florida to be near her sister two years ago, and lately she's been mentioning she goes for walks with some dude named Arthur. Figured I should probably take a trip down there soon, see if I need to be kicking Artie's ass."

"That's oddly sweet."

"Yeah, that's me. Oddly sweet."

The waitress came and took our lunch order. Annalise ordered a soup, appetizer, and lunch.

"You sure as shit can eat for a little thing."

"I didn't eat anything this morning because of my nerves about flying. And I won't be eating until eight tonight, so I figured I better stockpile."

The reminder of her dinner with Tobias tonight ruined my appetite. "So where is this date tonight?"

She frowned. "It's not a date."

"Oh, that's right. Let me rephrase. Where is the business meeting with the guy who wants to get in your pants?"

She folded her arms across her chest. "I don't want to tell you."

"A romantic little Italian bistro with candles? Maybe a corner booth next to the fireplace."

"Jerk."

"French? Maybe Chez Affaire."

"It's at the same place we ate last time. The same exact restaurant where both of us shared a meal and discussed business with the entire team from Star. The same place that seemed like a logical and convenient choice for a meeting just two weeks ago. Yet I'm sure you'll be convinced that now he has an ulterior motive by picking it."

I'd been teasing her, but *fuck,* the thought of the two of them having dinner at the hotel she'd be staying at really yanked me. And I wasn't even going to attempt to convince myself it had anything to do with business. I'd already admitted once that I was jealous. There was no point in exposing my weakness to the competition a second time. So I sucked it up. At least I tried to.

"It is a convenient choice. *Very* convenient."

———

Maybe I hadn't given the guy a chance.

Tobias patted me on the back as we left the office of the Director of Film Acquisitions. He'd raved about the marketing plan I'd come up with, including the new logo and taglines. And now it was the third office he'd walked me around to that seemed to love my ideas.

"I've been here three weeks, and that was the first time I saw Bob Nixon smile. You either hit it out of the ballpark, or that guy started on new meds recently."

"Thanks so much for taking the time to do this. I know you had something come up earlier today, so I appreciate you still fitting us in."

We walked back into his office. "Anytime. Glad I can help. Now that I've seen some of your great ideas, I'm really looking forward to seeing your final concepts when we come up to tour your office in a few weeks. I've heard great things about your work from Annalise, and now I know why."

I was beginning to feel like a total idiot. I'd let my personal feelings get in the way of business—let it cloud my judgment toward Tobias—and God knows I'd ridden Annalise hard about this guy. And here she was building me up to the guy who was going to pick the campaign that would go a long way toward keeping my damn job.

"I'm sure her presentation will be just as on point, if not more so. She's incredibly talented," I said.

Tobias's office phone rang. He picked it up and told whoever was on the line that he needed a minute and then held the receiver to his chest. "Why don't you pour us two celebratory drinks?" He lifted his chin, pointing to a long credenza positioned under the windows. "Middle cabinet has a nice brandy and some glasses."

While he talked on the phone, I took out two crystal highball glasses and a decanter filled with amber-colored alcohol. The top of the cabinet had a bunch of framed photographs, so I perused while I waited. One had a little blond boy and an older girl sitting on a rock somewhere

216

in the mountains. A few were of various celebrities and Tobias at different movie premieres. The last was a photo of a woman with the same two little kids from the first framed photo, only they were older in this shot, and all three had their hands up in the air as they barreled down a drop on a rollercoaster. Their smiles were huge.

I shook my head. I'd been really blinded by jealousy. This guy was obviously happily married, and had a nice little family. I'd totally misread the situation last time.

Or...*maybe I didn't.*

Tobias hung up as I set down the last framed photo.

"You have a beautiful family," I said.

He came around his desk and took one of the glasses of brandy I'd poured, then lifted the picture I'd just set down. Swirling the liquid around in his glass, he stared down at it.

"Candice is beautiful alright. Too bad she's a fucking bitch on wheels. We separated nine months ago. With all the *#MeToo* crap going on, figured it would be better to keep up my façade as a happily married man in public."

He lifted his glass and clinked it with mine. "Speaking of beautiful women, I'm looking forward to seeing what your colleague came up with later."

chapter 25

Annalise

He's such a jerk.

I continued to wear my big, fake, happy face as I said goodbye to Tobias. But the moment he pushed through the revolving door, I pivoted on my heel, scowled, and headed to the bar to look for my stalker. A feeling of déjà vu came over me.

"Excuse me?" I called to the bartender. "I'm looking for the guy who was sitting down at that end of the bar just a few minutes ago?"

He nodded. "Drinks Corona and looks like someone ran over his dog?"

"That would be him."

"Paid his tab and left a minute or two ago. Not sure if he's a guest here since he paid cash. Didn't catch which way he went when he took off."

"Oh, he's a guest here alright," I mumbled and started toward the front desk. "That I'd bet my life on."

The front desk had two employees, and both were helping people already, so I got in line. But while waiting, it dawned on me that they might not give out another guest's room number so easily. So instead, I walked back to the lobby, dug out my cell, and looked up the phone number of the hotel.

"Hi. I'm trying to reach a guest there. He's my boss, actually. He gave me the direct telephone number to his room for a conference call we're about to have, but I seem to have misplaced it."

"I can connect you. What's the guest's name?"

"Ummm... Could you possibly just give me the direct number again? He gave it to me because I'll be calling with a few other people on a conference line, and for privacy reasons, he doesn't like to give out the name of the hotel where he's staying. The operator says the name of the hotel when she answers at the main number. He's going to kill me for losing it."

"Sure. No problem. What's the guest's name?"

"It's Bennett Fox."

When I'd given my direct-dial phone number to Marina earlier today, I'd noticed that my room number was the last four of the phone number. Either that was one hell of a coincidence, or they all worked that way.

I heard her clicking some keys before returning to the line. "That direct number would be 213-555-7003."

"Thank you very much."

"No problem. Have a good evening."

I swiped to end the call. *Oh, I'm going to have a good evening alright—chewing out the asshole in room 7003.*

Was it possible that blood could actually boil? I started to sweat on the elevator ride up to the seventh floor. It felt like heat was pouring from my pores—I was that pissed off.

Not only had I made sure the jerk had a chance to present his ideas to Tobias, but I'd never said one bad word about him, never tried to manipulate my friendship with Tobias to gain an advantage. And what does the jackass do? He makes up lies about me so I look like a dumbass talking to the client.

The elevator doors slid open, and I marched down to room 7003. Without taking a minute to calm myself, I banged on the door. When it didn't open in three seconds, I banged some more—this time louder. The door swung open mid knock.

"*What the fuck?*" Bennett roared.

If I hadn't been so pissed off, I might've been distracted by the sight of a shirtless Bennett Fox standing on the other side. But I was furious, so seeing he had chiseled abs only made me angrier.

Of course he also has a perfect body. What a dick.

I marched right past him, into his hotel room.

He stood there blinking for a moment, seeming confused as to what the hell was going on. Eventually, he shook his head and let go of the doorknob still in his hand.

"Come on in. I wasn't in the middle of getting undressed or anything."

"You have some nerve."

220

"I have lots of nerve. You'll need to be more specific about what crawled up your ass."

His playing dumb made me lose my cool. Not that I'd been too much in control before, but I snapped.

I got right in his face and jabbed my finger into his chest. "I'm in a committed relationship with *Marina*? What the hell is wrong with you!"

"Oh. *That*."

"I've done nothing but right by you, and how do you repay me? You go and tell the client I'm having an affair with a woman in the office, so I look completely unprofessional!"

He raised his hands as if he were surrendering. "No. No. That's not what I meant to do at all."

"Oh really? So you *accidentally* told our client I was sleeping with our assistant and meant to what? Make me look professional?"

Bennett ran a hand through his hair. "I wasn't thinking."

"Bullshit. You knew exactly what you were doing!"

"The guy's a dirtbag. I was trying to keep things professional. I said it so he wouldn't hit on you."

"You're so full of shit that I think you actually start to believe your own lies, and that's what makes your ridiculous excuses so believable. You're a master of manipulating things to screw with people when they're feeling vulnerable."

I made a pout and mimicked his sorry-ass apologies. "I'm sorry, Annalise. I was jealous. Oh no, I was trying to protect you from the big, bad client."

Bennett's jaw clenched as he stared at me. "I wasn't manipulating you."

Frustrated, I turned to walk out. But then I thought better of it and went back for one last question. "Why are you even still here, Bennett?"

It pissed me off that he was playing games. His nostrils flared like *he* had reason to be pissed off.

"Answer me!"

In the blink of an eye, my back was up against the door, and Bennett was all around me. His face ducked down to line up with mine, and his forearms pressed firmly against the door on either side of my face. His bare chest heaved up and down so close to mine, I could feel the heat radiating from it. Fire turned the soft green of his eyes to a near gray.

"I'm here because I can't fucking keep away."

My jaw dropped. "I don't understand."

"Well, that makes two of us."

Nothing made sense. One minute we got along great, and I saw slivers of a person I really liked. But then...

"Why do you keep hurting me?"

Bennett hung his head for a moment while I tried to take in what was happening.

When he looked up, his eyes were filled with remorse. "I don't mean to hurt you. I just...you make me crazy. In thirty-one years, I've never wanted a woman like I want you, and of course, you're the one woman I can't have."

I swallowed. My heart felt like it was ricocheting against my chest. "I don't believe you," I whispered.

His eyes dropped to my mouth, and he groaned. The sound shot straight between my legs, and my lips parted with a tiny gasp I hoped he didn't hear.

But the wicked grin spreading across his face told me he'd most definitely heard it.

"You don't believe me? What should we do about that?"

"Bennett, I—"

He reached out, wound his fingers tightly into my hair, and tugged me flush against him. His lips crashed down on mine, swallowing the rest of my words. I was shocked at how I felt it all over—my body lit up like a Christmas tree from just one simple connection. His hands slid up to cup my cheeks, and he tilted my head, dipping his tongue inside my mouth. My purse and portfolio carrier fell to the floor. Everything else around us ceased to exist.

I wrapped my arms around his neck and dug my nails into his hair. He groaned again and reached around to my ass, squeezing two handfuls while lifting me off my feet. My legs wrapped around his waist. *God, I love skirts.*

With me open to him, Bennett pressed his body against mine. I felt the hard length of him meet my heat, and he growled.

"Fuck. You feel so damn good."

I whimpered when he deepened the kiss, digging my nails into his back and clinging to him. Our kiss was desperate and needy, down and dirty, and I could feel a heart beating a million miles an hour, although I wasn't sure if it was his or mine. When we finally came up for air, we were panting, and I felt dizzy.

Bennett nuzzled into my neck while I attempted to catch my breath. He kissed his way from my collarbone up to my ear.

"There are so many things I want to do to you."

I loved the gravelly sound of his voice.

"Like what?" I whispered.

I felt his lips curve into a smile against my neck. "I want to taste you everywhere." He gave a slight, unexpected yank to my hair and exposed more of my neck while he kissed his way back down.

"Yes."

"I want to bury my face between your legs until you scream out my name."

"Yes."

"I want you on all fours so I can be everywhere, so you can't think or feel anything but me. One hand playing with your tits, the other one fingering your ass. My cock rocking deep inside of you." He ground his erection against my exposed center, and my eyes rolled into the back of my head.

Oh God. It felt so good. My body began to vibrate. I started to think I might be able to come from just the feel of him against me and the sound of his sexy voice telling me what he wanted to do.

Things between Andrew and me had never been like this, not even at the beginning.

Bennett lifted and carried me from against the door into his room. I expected my back to hit the bed, but instead he set me down on my feet next to it and took a slight step back. His glazed eyes raked up and down my body, and for a few heartbeats, I thought he might be rethinking what was happening, what was about to happen.

"Undress for me."

The assertive tone and strained sound of his voice showered goosebumps all over my body. Sometimes his confidence made me want to smack him. Apparently other times it made me want to strip naked.

I unbuttoned my blouse and looked up at him. There'd been so many times when I was unsure whether to trust him or not, but the kind of desire I saw in his hooded eyes now couldn't be faked.

"I haven't been able to focus on anything since the day you walked into the office," he said. "You've starred in all my fantasies, even when I tried to hate you."

I slipped my shirt from my shoulders and let it fall to the floor.

"Take off the skirt."

It was easy to feel bold the way he was looking at me. I reached back, unzipped my pencil skirt, and shimmied it down to the ground. I was grateful I'd worn a pretty, lacy bra and thong that helped my confidence. I stood tall, wearing just my lingerie and heels.

Bennett flicked open the button of his trousers. His happy trail made me pretty damn happy. He removed his pants, and my eyes went wide at the bulge in his tight boxer shorts.

Damn. Now I know where the cocky confidence comes from.

He lifted his chin. "Bra."

I unfastened the clasp and tossed it aside. My nipples were already hard, but they grew painfully swollen as I watched him lick his lips.

"You're incredible."

I loved the way he demanded things, but I wanted to show him I was right there with him. So I took a deep breath, hooked my thumbs into the sides of my panties, and slipped off my last shred of clothing without him telling me to.

Bennett smiled like he knew exactly what I'd communicated. His eyes did a slow sweep over me and darkened, yet they sparkled with a mischievous glint.

He motioned to my heels. "Those stay on."

He guided me to sit on the edge of the bed and dropped to his knees. The sight was pretty damn spectacular. Bennett Fox was always handsome, but half naked, with every ripped muscle on full display, while kneeling before me was an all-new level of sexy. He looked into my eyes as his hands pushed my knees open as far as they could go.

I gasped when Bennett leaned in and licked one long stroke. Unlike the strip of our clothes, there was nothing slow or teasing as he buried his entire face between my legs. It wasn't soft and gentle. It was rough and desperate. He alternated between sucking on my clit, pushing his tongue inside of me, and licking me with long strokes that made me want to hold him there and never let him come up for air.

My head fell back, and it became difficult to keep upright. "Oh God."

My cry made him growl and push that much farther. I began to writhe as my body trembled from the inside out and ripples of pleasure throbbed between my legs. I yanked at Bennett's silky hair and moaned as intense waves of ecstasy hit me hard. Tears welled up in my eyes, my emotions needing to escape in some form, and I fell back on the bed, unable to withstand the weight of my own body any longer.

Through the fog of my sated brain, I heard the faint sound of foil opening. Next thing I knew, I was being hoisted up from the bottom of the bed to the headboard, and Bennett climbed over me.

I expected the frenzied pace to continue, but this was a man who'd surprised me at every turn since the day I'd met him. He brushed the hair from my face and gently leaned in and kissed my lips.

"You good?"

Not sure I could speak yet—or maybe ever again—I responded with a big grin and nodded. He smiled down at me as he pushed inside. Our gazes stayed locked, our shared smiles morphing into something more serious as we both felt the intense connection. He worked slowly—short, tempered thrusts as he eased in and out of me. Once my body had accepted his girth, he went a little deeper, pushed a little harder, until eventually he ground down, filling me completely.

Together we found our rhythm—him pumping and me meeting each thrust until our bodies were coated with sweat, and the sound and smell of sex filled the air around us. Bennett cupped behind one of my knees and lifted my leg, changing the angle of his strokes ever so slightly, but he'd found my tender spot.

"*Bennett...*"

His jaw flexed, the same way it often did when I'd pissed him off. Only now I realized his muscle tensing wasn't so much an expression of anger, but rather him trying to hold something back. And this time he was trying to hold back finishing for me.

I moaned as my orgasm began to take hold, and my eyes fluttered shut.

"No way, sweetheart. Open up and give it to me."

Bennett sped up his thrusts, and I held onto his gaze for dear life. My body trembled as I clenched down around him. The need to hide from the intensity of his watching me was strong, but I pushed through and gave him what he wanted.

He smiled down at me as my orgasm began to ebb, and then every muscle in his body hardened, and he started really fucking me—hard and wild with punishing strokes that ended in a roar that shook the room.

After, he buried his face in my hair and kissed my neck as he continued to glide slowly in and out at an unhurried pace. Neither one of us seemed to want the moment to end, so we lingered as long as we could, keeping the connection. But eventually he had to get up to deal with the condom.

Bennett climbed from the bed and went into the bathroom, leaving the cool air to hit my sweat-soaked skin and cause a chill. The jolt of cold made my mind reel at what had just transpired.

Never in my life had I been fucked like that. And I had a feeling that whatever this was between us, I was going to be fucked in a way that wasn't half as much fun soon enough.

chapter 26

Annalise

We were both quiet, lying side by side in the dark room.

I wondered if he already regretted it. "What are you thinking right now?" I asked.

He blew out a deep breath. "Truth?"

"Of course."

"I was thinking about how I could manage to start the audio recorder on my phone without you noticing before I go down on you again. I need to capture that sound you make while you come to use for jerk off material after you toss my ass to the curb in a half hour."

I laughed and turned on my side toward him. "What sound?"

"It's sort of a cross between a moan and a scream, but it's really throaty and fucking hot."

"I don't scream."

"Oh, you so do, babe."

I honestly had no idea what had come out of my mouth tonight. It was kind of an out-of-body experience that I had no control over.

"And what makes you think I'll toss your ass to the curb in a half hour?"

Bennett turned to face me. He wiped a wisp of hair from my cheek. "Because you're smart."

I had no idea how what just happened would play out. Unlike my usual self, I hadn't thought about the consequences of my actions. Instead, I went with what felt right in the moment. And God knows what had felt right in the moment turned out to feel pretty damn amazing. So I kept with that mindset, not letting myself overanalyze anything just quite yet.

"Andrew didn't... He wasn't really into oral sex. So I think the sound you heard might have been the cork coming off some really tightly bottled champagne."

Bennett propped his head up on his elbow. "What the hell does that mean? He wasn't *really into* oral sex? Are you saying he sucked at going down on you?"

"No. I'm saying it didn't happen often. Like...pretty much never."

"But you like it?"

I shrugged. "He didn't."

"And therein lies the problem in your relationship in a nutshell. I'm not just talking about sex, either. Any guy who doesn't get over himself to do something he might not love to please his woman has an issue that goes a lot deeper than sex."

Sadly, Bennett was one-hundred-percent right. Things with Andrew were always about what Andrew wanted and needed. He needed quiet to write his novel, so we put off moving in together. I liked a new restaurant and he didn't, so we didn't go back. He needed space, and I gave it to him. Yet when he wanted to go skiing on vacation and I wanted the beach, I dug out my winter clothes to make him happy. And the worst—God, I'd really missed out—Bennett was right. I *do* like oral sex.

I sighed. "You're right."

The room was dark, but I could see him smile. "I'm always right."

Bennett brushed two fingers along the length of my arm from shoulder to hand. I seriously felt it all the way down to my toes, and it caused me to quake with a little shiver dance.

"Your body is so responsive."

I reached out and flattened my hands to his abs, letting them feel their way around the hard plains. "And yours is so...*hard*."

He chuckled and captured my wrist in his hand, dragging it a foot or so south.

"Oh. Wow. You're...."

"Hard everywhere."

"Indeed. That's not very much downtime, you know."

Bennett did some stealth move, scooping me up and rolling onto his back to lay me on top of him. "Gotta make good use of the time before the blood rushes back to your brain and you smarten up." He lifted his hips and nudged at my opening.

"Feels like the blood hasn't rushed back to your brain yet either."

"How about we make a pact?" He traced his finger along my spine, slowing, but not stopping as he came to the crack of my ass. "Neither one of us thinks about anything until the sun comes up tomorrow."

I brushed my lips with his. "Finally, something we can agree on."

⁓

I slipped from the bed and tiptoed into the bathroom. On my way, I picked up my purse from where it had dropped near the door last night and dug out my phone. Six thirty. My flight was at nine. I scanned my emails to see if Marina had copied me on Bennett's itinerary like she had him on mine. Sure enough, she had sent me his while I was at dinner last night. So I opened it to see if we were on the same flight. We weren't. His was at eleven, for some reason. The thought of not having to travel with him, not having to face him in the light of day, made me feel an odd combination of bereft and relieved.

I tied up my hair and took a quick shower. When I washed between my legs, I felt an ache that made me smile. How many times had we had sex last night? Four? Five? Was that even possible? Whatever it was, I knew for certain it was my personal record. Andrew and I had never gone at it like that. In the beginning, there might've been a night or two that we'd done it twice, but once a week was more our average over the last few years.

My clothes were still on the floor where I'd stripped last night. Although when I put them back on, it looked more like I'd slept in them. But I couldn't find my underwear. So I collected the rest of my things, put in for an Uber, and shook out Bennett's clothes, thinking maybe my panties had gotten mixed up with them during our frenzy last might.

I jumped at the sound of his groggy voice. "Looking for something?"

"Shit." I dropped my purse to the floor. "You scared me. I thought you were sleeping."

"I was. But I woke up when you started rummaging through my clothes."

"I wasn't rummaging through your clothes. I'm looking for my underwear."

He lifted an arm out of the covers and held up my panties, dangling from one finger. "Oh. You mean these?"

I laughed. "How the heck did you wind up with them?"

"I got up to go to the bathroom an hour ago, right after you fell asleep, and I scooped them up on my way."

"They're your color, but not sure they'll fit."

I went to swipe them from his hand, but he pulled back and clenched them in his fist.

"What are you doing?"

He cupped his hands together and brought them to his nose, taking a deep whiff of my thong. "Ah. I love the smell of your pussy."

My eyes widened. "That's a little twisted, even for you, Fox. Now give me back my panties. I have a flight to catch."

"No can do."

"You expect me to fly home wearing a skirt with no underwear?"

He reached out and slipped his hand under my skirt, grabbing a handful of ass. "You should come to work like this every day."

I chuckled. "Seriously, I'm going to be late for my flight."

"You could change your flight and get on the later one with me."

I'd thought of that, but I needed some time away from this man to screw my head on straight. Before I could think of an excuse, Bennett used the hand on my ass to hook my waist and pull me down to him.

"I know you need some headspace," he said. "The thong is my insurance policy. I'm keeping them until you're ready to talk to me. Then you'll get them back."

"What if I decide I don't want to talk about last night?"

He kissed my lips. "Then Jonas gets your underwear."

"You're out of your mind."

"Maybe. But I bet the thought of him sniffing them while *he* jerks off freaks you out a little more than me doing it."

I shook my head. "I don't have time to argue with you. However..." I walked over to his pile of clothes and fished his wallet out of his pocket. I dug out a Visa and let the leather billfold fall unceremoniously to the floor. "...there's a Victoria's Secret at LAX. I'll pick up some new ones...and some other things while I'm at it."

Bennett smiled broadly. "Have at it. Maybe something with garters and cutout panties so you don't have to take it off while I fuck you on your desk next week."

Bennett

Not her.

I stuffed my cell back into my pocket and tried to pretend I wasn't disappointed that one of my buddies had texted to see if I was up for drinks tonight.

But you can't bullshit yourself now, can you?

The afternoon we'd returned from L.A., Annalise was already gone when I got to the office. On Thursday, I had a morning meeting out of the office, and by the time I arrived, she was gone again. Marina said she'd taken a last-minute appointment.

Then on Friday, I saw the same Audi I drive pulling away from the front of our building at ten minutes to seven in the morning, so I texted her. A few hours later, she sent back a short response saying she'd come in early to get some files and was working from home.

It wasn't unusual for staff to work from home a day or two each week—we had flexible hours and site location. But Annalise hadn't taken advantage before now, and I was starting to feel like she might be avoiding me.

By Friday afternoon, it was eating at me, so I sent her another text asking if she wanted to have drinks. She never responded.

Now it was Saturday afternoon, and I was checking my phone like a high school chick each time it buzzed.

I watched Lucas check the price on the bottom of the sneaker he'd been eyeing and put it back on the shelf.

"Do you like those?" I asked.

"Yeah." He shrugged. "They're cool."

"So why don't you try them on? You need new sneakers before our Disney trip in a few weeks."

"They're a lot of money."

"Are you paying for them?"

"No?"

"Then what the hell are you checking the prices for?" I picked the sneaker up and motioned to the kid in a striped Foot Locker uniform who didn't look much older than Lucas. "Can we see these in a nine?"

"Sure thing."

"Hang on," I said to the kid. "Anything else you like, buddy?"

Lucas didn't respond.

"Lucas?"

Still nothing, so I followed his line of sight to what had captured his attention. I chuckled and spoke to the kid waiting on us. "Just that one for now, please."

The cute little blonde Lucas couldn't keep his eyes off of looked up and caught him watching her. She got flustered and gave an awkward wave before turning in the other direction to look at the wall of shoes on the other side of the store.

I leaned over to Lucas and whispered, "She's cute."

"That's Amelia Archer."

"You like her?"

"Everyone in sixth grade likes her."

"Thought you were switching up your strategy and only going to like the ugly ones?"

"She's pretty *and* nice. But she doesn't want anything to do with any of the boys."

"Well, you're only pushing twelve. Kids start to notice each other at different times. She might not be there yet."

"No, that's not it. A month ago, she told Anthony Arknow she liked Matt Sanders, and Anthony spread all these rumors about her. He did it because he liked her, too. Now she doesn't talk to any of the boys anymore."

The joys of middle school. "She'll come around. Why don't you go say hi? Show her the sneaker you're looking at and ask her if she likes it."

"You think I should?"

I picked the sneaker back up from the shelf and held it out for him. "Definitely. You gotta make the move. The good ones aren't alone for long. Just be her friend. She probably needs to see that not all boys are jerks." I smiled. "I mean, we are, but do your best, anyway."

Lucas took the sneaker from my hand and debated. I had a proud-uncle-type moment when he sucked it up and walked over there. I watched as the initial awkwardness of his approach wore off, and his shoulders relaxed a bit. Within a minute or two, he had her laughing.

He came back, smiling from ear to ear. "She's really nice."

"Looked like she liked you going over to talk to her."

He shrugged. "Maybe. Girls are confusing."

This kid was a hell of a lot smarter than I'd been at that age. I thought I had them all figured out until I was eighteen and realized I didn't know shit.

I nodded. "Damn straight they are."

Lucas wound up getting the hundred-dollar Nikes. And we also picked up a few T-shirts and some art supplies he said his grandmother refused to buy because she said the school should provide that stuff, and then he asked for some hair gel crap and Axe deodorant.

Hair gel and Axe—he'd definitely found girls.

"Are you waiting for a call?" Lucas asked as we walked through the mall parking lot on the way to the car.

I looked down at the phone in my hand. "No. Why?"

"Because you keep checking it."

I shoved the phone back into my pocket. "Didn't realize I was."

The little shit grinned. "You're waiting for a girl to call you."

It was hard to contain my smile. I clicked the car-unlock button, and it chirped. "Get in the car, Casanova."

"Who?"

"Just get in."

My phone buzzed just as we pulled up to Lucas's house. Without giving it any thought, I pulled it out of my pocket and checked the name. Lucas must've read my face.

"You're totally waiting for a girl to text you." He grinned.

There was no point in lying. "Yeah. Sorry if I've been distracted."

He shrugged. "Why don't you just call her?"

"It's complicated, bud."

Lucas grabbed his shopping bags out of the backseat and opened the car door. He'd told me to stop walking him to the door last year, so now I just sat in the car and made sure he got in okay.

He climbed out of the car and leaned his head back in, one hand on the top of the door. "You gotta make the move, dude. The good ones aren't alone for long."

The little shit had tossed my own words back at me.

=

chapter 28

May 1st

Dear Me,

We did it! Our first boyfriend. It only took sixteen years. But Nick Adler is totally gorgeous. He always wears a backward baseball hat, and his messy hair sticks out all over from underneath it. We've been together for two weeks now. And...we made the first move! Well, technically Bennett made the first move for us. Whatever.

We usually eat lunch with Bennett and a bunch of other kids. Nick sits at the table across from us. Bennett kept telling us to just go sit with him—to make the first move, but we were too chicken. One day, when we were looking over at Nick, Bennett yelled, "Hey, Adler. Soph's gonna sit with you guys today, alright?" Nick shrugged and said sure. We wanted to kill Bennett. We were so nervous when we had to walk over there. But things worked out. Nick and us even hung out with Bennett and Skylar—his newest girlfriend—last weekend. Bennett's girlfriend is in college already and really pretty. She was nice, I guess.

Oh...and we had to move again. Mom and Lorenzo broke up. Our new apartment is really small. But at least it's not too far from the last one.

Today our poem is dedicated to Nick.

> *My heart has four walls.*
> *He tried to climb but fell down.*
> *For you, they crumble.*

This letter will self-destruct in ten minutes.

Anonymously,
Sophie

chapter 29

Bennett

Fuck it.

I jumped off the highway at the next exit.

I swear, I'd showered and dressed with every intention of meeting my buddies for drinks downtown. But halfway to O'Malley's, I decided on a change of plans.

And now that I got closer, I started to second-guess myself again. Bianchi Winery wasn't just her parents' place—they were also clients.

Then again, that seemed par for the course. Annalise was the last person I should be chasing. So why not track her down at a client's house? What could possibly go wrong?

Everything.

Anything.

But......fuck it.

I was invited. Annalise had told me herself that Margo had extended an invitation to me. At least I wasn't crashing the party.

I pulled down the long dirt road just as the sun started to set. A dozen or so cars were parked along the front of the winery, including my car's twin. I parked and checked my phone one last time. It was going to suck if she was here with a date. But I couldn't imagine she was the type of woman who'd be out on a date a few nights after sleeping with another guy.

Hell, I *was* that type of guy, and I couldn't have done it after the night we'd had.

I walked into the retail store just as Margo Bianchi came up from the wine cellar.

"Bennett! I'm so glad you're feeling better and decided to join us after all."

Feeling better? I went with it. "Turned out to be just a twenty-four-hour thing."

"Annalise and Madison are downstairs. I'm just going to grab another tray of cheese. Go on down. Everyone's loving the new harvest."

"Let me give you a hand with the tray first."

"Nonsense. You go enjoy yourself. I'm sure my daughter is going to be delighted to see you."

I wouldn't be so sure of that. "Okay. Thank you."

The wine cellar had four alcove tables on one side and a long, stone bar on the other. I scanned the tables and saw faces I didn't recognize. But I definitely recognized the exposed back of a woman sitting on the second-to-last stool at the bar. Facing away from me, she had no warning I was here.

I blew out a deep breath and started toward her. The woman sitting next to her caught my eye and watched me approach. I held one finger up to my lips as my other hand touched Annalise's back.

I leaned in to whisper near her ear. "I was feeling better, so I thought I'd join you after all."

She spun around so fast she wobbled and nearly fell off her chair. "Bennett?"

The woman next to her raised a brow. "Bennett? As in the hot guy from the office?"

I extended my hand. "One and the same. Bennett Fox. Nice to meet you. I'm guessing you're Madison?"

"I am." Madison looked back and forth between the two of us. "Well, this is a nice surprise. I didn't realize Bennett was joining us tonight."

Annalise looked frazzled. "I didn't either."

Madison smirked and looked to me for a response. I went with the truth.

"She's been avoiding me for two days. I also have a pair of her underwear in my pocket I thought she might like back."

Her friend laughed and leaned in to kiss Annalise on the cheek. "I like him. I'm going to go find my date. You two play nice."

I slipped into Madison's seat beside Annalise, keeping my hand on her back. "So you talk about how hot I am with your friend?"

"Don't let your head swell any bigger. It was the only compliment I gave you."

I leaned in. "Really? Even after the other night?"

Her cheeks turned pink. God, why did I love that about her so much? "I like your dress."

"You don't even know what it looks like. I'm sitting."

I ran my knuckles along the exposed skin of her back. "It lets me touch your skin without having to sneak my hand up your skirt. So it's one of my favorites already. Seeing the front will just be icing on the cake."

Her cheeks darkened. God, I wanted to fuck her in broad daylight so I could watch every color her skin turned. I bet it was better than fall foliage.

"What are you doing here, Bennett?"

I took the glass of wine in front of her and drank from it. "Margo invited me. You told me that yourself the other day at lunch, remember?"

"Yes. But you didn't mention you were coming."

I held her eyes. "I would have, if you'd returned my call."

She looked away.

Matteo noticed me for the first time and made a big fuss about my arrival. He set me up with a flight of different wines from this year's harvest and stuck around talking for a while, until Margo pulled him away with a big smile—claiming to need his help with the icemaker upstairs.

Annalise traced the rim of her glass with her finger. "We don't even have an icemaker."

I chuckled. "Seems like I'm not the only one who thinks we need a few minutes alone to talk. Your friend disappeared the minute I got here, and your mom is trying to give us some privacy."

She lifted her glass to her lips. "Maybe your presence just repels people."

I smiled. "Maybe. But what does my presence do for you?"

Annalise swiveled her chair to face me. She looked around—I assumed to see how private our conversation would be—then leaned closer.

"I had a really good time the other night."

245

I'd used that opening line enough times to know where this conversation was going. "But…" I said for her.

"But…we work together. Or actually, we're pretty much competitors working in the same company."

I leaned in to whisper in her ear, even though I knew no one could hear us. I just wanted an opportunity to get closer.

"Are you afraid I'll fuck your trade secrets out of you?"

She mimicked my move and leaned in to whisper in mine. "No. Are you?"

I chuckled. I probably should've been afraid. Because I was pretty sure I'd show her whatever she wanted in order to get her to come home with me tonight.

"Look, I'm gonna put all my cards on the table. I haven't been able to stop thinking about being inside of you for two days. You're still getting over the asshole. I'm not looking for anything serious. We have an expiration date in our future whether we like it or not—one of us is getting shipped off to Texas. We can either spend the next month or so being frustrated and pissing each other off at the office, or we can spend that time being pissed off at Foster, Burnett and Wren for putting us in this situation while taking our frustrations out on each other in a productive manner at night. I vote for the latter."

She sucked in her bottom lip while she kicked it around for a minute. "So during the day, if a client we're both pitching gave me some inside information on the direction they wanted to go, and then you found out I didn't share that with you…you wouldn't be pissed?"

"Hell yes, I'd be pissed. But that's the beauty of our situation. I'd be pissed as shit that you got an advantage over me. So the next morning, you might have a little trouble walking from me taking out that frustration on you. Let's face it, it would give me an excuse to paddle that ass I've been dreaming about paddling since the first day I saw you. But I'm competitive, not an asshole. So you can bet I'd make it work for you, too."

Annalise swallowed. "And if the situation were reversed? If I find out something you did that upsets me?"

"Then I'll lick you until you're not pissed off anymore. And probably try to piss you off again the next day."

She laughed. "You're making this sound so simple. But it's way more complicated than that."

I took her hands in mine. "Well, there is one catch."

"What's that?"

"It's going to be difficult for you not to fall for me."

"God, you're such an ass."

I leaned in. "An ass that you have a shitload of chemistry with, like it or not. So whadda you say? By day we fight like enemies, by night we fuck like warriors?"

She looked me in the eyes. "I really hope I don't regret this."

My eyes went wide. I hadn't expected her to say yes, though I was prepared to wear her down. "At the end of the day, we only regret the things we missed out on doing. So I'll make sure we do it *all*."

Annalise's friend walked back over. "You two look cozy."

"Now you come interrupt? Where were you five minutes ago when I had a temporary lapse of sanity and agreed to the crazy deal this lunatic just proposed?"

Madison smiled at her. "You need a good dose of insanity. Plus, we're running out of stuff to talk about after twenty-five years of friendship. This will give us all new material for our weekly dinners."

Annalise leaned over and kissed Madison's cheek. "It certainly will."

———

I'd wanted Annalise to myself from the moment I'd walked in. Not that I didn't have a good time—because surprisingly, I did. Her friend Madison was a straight shooter, and her date was a decent guy, too.

But now they'd just said goodbye, and Annalise and I stood outside the winery, just the two of us, as they pulled away. The dirt that kicked into the air from the tires hadn't even settled yet when I had her face in my hands. I kissed her softly at first, but I couldn't stop myself, and it didn't take very long before it turned hard and heated.

She moaned into my mouth, and I had to force myself to pull back before it was too late and I ended up fucking her against a tree for her parents to walk out and see.

I brushed my thumb over her swollen lips. "Come home with me."

"I can't." She frowned. "I told my mom I'd stay over tonight. Tomorrow morning I take the ride with her to go deliver free bottles of the new season's wine to some of her biggest customers. Matteo cooks a huge brunch, and all the pickers and workers come to eat. We started doing that the first year they bought the place, and it stuck as a tradition."

That sounded nice, but I was selfish, so I couldn't even hide my pout.

"Awww..." She stroked my cheek. "You look like I used to at Christmas when I opened all my new toys and then my mom made me put them away because company was coming over."

I locked my hands behind her back. "I definitely want to play with my new toy."

"I think we should establish a few ground rules anyway," she said.

"Uh-oh. Rules always get me in trouble."

She smiled. "I bet they do. But I think we need a few."

"Like what?"

"Well, like I don't think we should make it public at work that anything is going on between us. Not even to our friends."

I nodded. "Makes sense."

"And when we're together outside of the office, no talking about work projects where we're competitors."

"Agreed."

"Okay. Well, that was easy. You're not usually so agreeable."

"I also have a few of my own ground rules I'd like to establish."

Annalise raised a brow. "You do, do you?"

"Yep."

"Okay..."

"Unless one of us ends things before the expiration date, we're monogamous."

"I guess that was a given for me. But good, I'm glad you put it out there anyway. Anything else?"

"Are you on the pill?"

"I am, yes."

"Then let's get rid of the condoms. I had my annual physical a few weeks ago. Clean as a whistle. If it feels that good inside of you wearing them, I need to find out what the hell it feels like without."

She leaned in and pressed her breasts against me, looking up.

"Bare...okay."

"What time is brunch over tomorrow?"

"Probably by three."

"Come straight to my house after. I'll make us dinner and eat you for dessert."

She looked up from under those long eyelashes and ran her tongue across her top lip. "What about my dessert?"

I groaned. "You're killing me, Texas."

Annalise

I stood with my mouth hanging open, looking out at the view.

Since Bennett and I didn't live far from each other, I'd assumed he also lived in a five-hundred-square-foot apartment and sacrificed space for the nice neighborhood. But West Hill Towers—at least the apartment I was currently standing inside of—didn't sacrifice anything. His open kitchen and living room area was probably twice the size of my entire apartment. And when I looked outside my window, I saw the building next to me. Bennett had a million-dollar view of the Bay and the Golden Gate Bridge with the mountains as a backdrop.

He brought me a glass of wine and stood alongside of me as I gawked at the sight. "Umm... Do you rob banks on the side?"

The corner of his lip twitched. He lifted his wine glass to his mouth. "I'm too pretty to go to prison."

"Sugar momma?"

He shook his head.

"Win the lotto?"

More head shaking. He could have just told me what the deal was. He knew me well enough to know it wasn't likely I'd be letting the subject go without an answer.

"Rich parents? You do wear some expensive suits and shoes."

"My father was a postman. My mom was a secretary at a law firm."

"I know that on average, men tend to make more than women in the same jobs, but this…" I held up my hands toward his view. "…this would be a little insane."

Bennett set his wine down on a nearby bookcase, then took mine out of my hand and set it next to his.

He hooked both arms around my waist. "You didn't kiss me hello."

"I guess I got distracted by the view."

His eyes raked up and down my body. "I'm pretty distracted by the view at the moment."

My stomach got that squishy feeling.

He leaned in. "Kiss me."

I rolled my eyes as if it were a burden to plant my lips on this beautiful man, and then leaned in for a quick peck hello. Only when I went to pull back, Bennett tangled his hand in my hair and didn't let me. My hasty kiss turned into way more than hello. Bennett's other hand slid down to my ass, and he pulled me flush against him. I felt the prod of his erection against my belly.

Well, hello there.

He broke the kiss with a tug of my bottom lip between his teeth. I was breathless.

"Hi," I said.

His mouth curved into a smile. He pushed my wayward hair behind my ear. "Hey, beautiful."

We stared at each other, grinning like two goofy teenagers who just made out for the first time. Bennett used his thumb to wipe smeared lipstick from my bottom lip. "I had an accident a long time ago. Got a big settlement. Invested part of the money to buy this place."

It took me a second to realize what he was even talking about. His kiss had left me dazed.

"Oh. I'm sorry to hear that. I hope no one was too hurt."

Bennett handed me back my wine. "I better check on the pasta."

While he went back to the kitchen, I snooped around. The floor-to-ceiling windows in the living room were the decoration in his apartment, so he didn't need much else. His furnishings were nice, dark and masculine, and he had a gigantic curved-screen TV in the living room.

The only real sense of who Bennett Fox was had to come from his bookshelves. I perused the titles—an odd mix of political nonfiction, hardcover thrillers, and some well-worn comic books. There were four small, framed photos, two of which were Lucas—one in a soccer uniform with half of his front teeth missing in his smile, and one that looked more recent of him and Bennett on a boat. They seemed to have a very strong bond.

There was another of Bennett and an older woman on what looked like his college graduation day. I turned and found Bennett watching me from the open kitchen.

"Your mom?"

He nodded. "Graduate school graduation."

I looked more closely at the photo and could see the resemblance. "You look like her. She looks very proud here."

"She was. I went off the rails for a year the month I started grad school. Dropped out. I'm pretty sure she never expected I'd get back on track and finish."

"Oh, now I'm curious. I expect to hear more about that crazy year at some point."

Bennett's face turned solemn. "It's not a year I'm proud of."

Feeling the need to change the subject, I put the photo of his mom back and picked up the last frame. It was a girl, probably about seventeen or eighteen, leaning against a car and smiling. She was pretty.

"Your sister?" I asked, even though I remembered he'd once mentioned he was an only child.

Bennett shook his head. "Friend. Lucas's mother."

He'd said Lucas's mother died a long time ago, so I didn't push. Instead, I looked down and studied the photo. Her son looked exactly like her.

"Wow, he's like her little mini-me."

Bennett dumped water into the sink from a steaming pot. "He's becoming a little wiseass just like her, too."

I set the photo back down and walked to the bar stools tucked under the living room side of the kitchen counter to watch him cook.

"Are you any good?"

He arched a brow. "You tell me."

"Get your mind out of the gutter, Fox. I was referring to your cooking."

"My mother's Italian, so I can make a few things. Growing up, she worked full time. When I was little, she would pre-make five different meals on Sundays for me to stick in the oven during the week since she worked a lot of overtime. I hung around and helped her. Eventually, she stopped having to spend a full day in the kitchen every weekend, because I picked up how to make some stuff and started to cook for us after school."

"That's sweet."

"But my forte is dessert. I can't wait to feed you what I have planned for later."

And...that sweet didn't last very long. Although I loved his unique combination of sweet and dirty.

When we sat down to dinner, it smelled delicious. My mouth actually watered, even though I'd eaten a full brunch not that long ago. I figured it would be good. Bennett wasn't the type of man who did anything half-assed. But I hadn't expected him to be modest. His spaghetti carbonara was out of this world.

"This is...orgasmic." I pointed my fork at my plate after swallowing my second mouthful. "Madison would give you five stars if she ate here."

He smiled, rather than gloat like he normally did at every opportunity. "Thank you."

I got the feeling I might discover that Bennett outside of the office was very different than the man I'd gotten to know at work—different in a good way. And for some reason, that made me nervous. It was easier to imagine having a fling with the hot jerk I worked with. I didn't need to find things to like about him, other than his body.

"So how were your deliveries this morning and the brunch?"

"Good. Except I was trapped in a car for hours with my mother, and the only thing she wanted to talk about was you showing up at the tasting last night."

He grinned. "She has good taste."

I sighed. "At least she's stopped asking if I've heard from Andrew."

Bennett's fork had been on the way up to his mouth, and he froze. "Have you?"

"He sent me a text the night after we met for dinner at the hotel, but I didn't respond, and he hasn't bothered again."

Bennett shoved a forkful of pasta into his mouth. "Fuck him. Douche."

I couldn't help but smile. I loved how defensive he'd been about Andrew from the get go. "Anyway. How was your day?"

"Had trouble falling asleep last night, so I got a late start. Just went to the gym and then worked until right before you got here."

"Do you usually have trouble falling asleep?"

He looked up from twirling his pasta. "Only when I have blue balls."

That *had* been some kiss last night. "Couldn't you just..."

"Jerk off?"

"Yeah, that."

"Didn't help."

The thought of him pleasuring himself because of the effect I had on him gave me a burst of feminine confidence.

"Tell me about it. I slept at my mom's. My hand doesn't work half as well as my vibrator."

Bennett dropped his fork with a loud clank. "Are you saying you masturbated while thinking of me last night?"

I gave him a teasing smile and nodded.

Five seconds later, I was up and out of my seat. Bennett tossed me over his shoulder, fireman style. "It's time for dessert."

I giggled. "But we didn't finish dinner yet."

"Fuck dinner. I'll fill your mouth."

"This is even delicious cold," I said with a mouthful of pasta.

I had no idea what time it was, but the sun had long disappeared. We'd spent the entire evening in bed, and now we were passing a bowl of cold pasta back and forth while naked in his bedroom.

"You're easy to please." He wiggled his brows. "And I mean that in a few different ways."

It *did* feel like Bennett had no problem pleasing me. My body had never been so responsive. Don't get me wrong, I hadn't been with that many men to experiment. In fact, I could count them all on one hand—including the man sitting next to me—but you'd think that after all the years with Andrew he'd have been better at pushing my buttons than a guy I'd only spent two nights with.

"Do you... Is sex always good for the women you're with?"

He stopped with the fork halfway to his mouth. "Are you asking me if I'm good in bed? Because let's face it, no guy is going to say *no* to that question, even if he needs a roadmap to find a clit."

I laughed. "I just meant, is sex always like that for you?"

He set the pasta bowl on the end table and finished chewing. "You want to know if sex is always good for me because you're not sure if it's me, us, or whether that moron you wasted eight years with is just a useless dud in bed?"

"Sort of... I guess."

"It's all of the above. I haven't had any complaints. But I enjoy a woman feeling satisfied as much, if not more, than satisfying myself. So I'll put in the effort—watch her, figure out what makes her tick."

"Oh. Okay." I felt sort of crestfallen for some reason.

Bennett put two fingers under my chin and lifted so our eyes met. "You didn't let me finish. But there's a difference between good sex and whatever the hell happens when I'm inside of you. We've got chemistry, Texas. And no amount of paying attention or hard work can take the place of that. So, my answer is, yeah...I like to think sex has been satisfying for me and the women I've been with. But what we've got going on? No, it isn't always like that."

My heart did a little flutter. "Okay."

He leaned in and kissed my cheek. "And to answer the last part of your question, you've been deprived, sweetheart. I don't know much about douche boy, except that he was planning on using you and doesn't like to go

258

down on a woman who clearly enjoys it. And those two things are enough to tell me the dickhead is selfish, and yeah...he wasn't good in bed at all. So you were deprived. Easy to please after that idiot."

Bennett got up from the bed, and for the first time, I got a good look at his naked body from head to toe. His shoulders were broad and thick, his muscular arms sculpted even without flexing, and he had more like an eight-pack than a six. *And* I finally got a good look at the tattoo I'd seen peeking out that day in the office—IV II MMXI with a dark vine snaking around the letters. I knew the Roman numeral I translated to one and V was five, so five minus one would be the fourth month—April 2nd eight years ago. Obviously the date was important if he had it permanently inked on his body.

Bennett turned and picked up the bowl of pasta we'd shared, and I spotted a long scar running down the left side of his abdomen. It ran from under his ribcage to just below his belly button. His skin was naturally tanned, so I almost didn't notice it.

"I need a drink," he said, completely oblivious to my following what felt like a trail of clues all over his body. "You want a water or soda or something? Wine, maybe?"

"I'd love a water. Thank you."

I guzzled half the bottle when he returned. All that heavy breathing must've dried out my throat. We hadn't spoken about sleeping arrangements, so I hadn't brought any clothes. And I'd been up late last night helping my mom clean up after the party, and then up early this morning to get on the road for her deliveries. Apparently, my mind and body were in sync, because I yawned.

"I should probably get going soon."

Bennett had one hand behind his head, casually lying in bed as if he were fully clothed rather than stark naked with everything on display. He reached out with his free hand and pulled me over to him, positioning my head on his chest. "Stay over. I know you're probably tired. I promise to let you sleep. But we can shower together in the morning."

I smiled with my cheek against his breastbone. "I don't have any clothes."

"You're not going to ever need any here." He stroked my hair. "In fact, I'd say it's a pretty safe bet you'll mostly be naked when we're at my place."

"I meant for work tomorrow."

"I can take you home now to pick something up, if you want. Or if not, go home early tomorrow morning and get dressed for the office. I'll go for a run while you do that so you don't feel like I have an unfair advantage getting to the office before you."

My head wanted to argue. It would probably be best if we just fooled around and didn't start slumber parties. But my body was in total disagreement.

"I guess I could do that—stop at my house in the morning, I mean."

"Good. Then it's settled. I'll set the alarm extra early for a nice, long shower."

My body started to relax, and his seemed to, too. I'd been scraping my fingers along the smattering of hair on his chest, and I started to trace the scar on his abdomen. Bennett's muscles tensed when he realized what I was doing.

I tilted my head to look up at him. "Is this from your accident?"

He nodded. "My spleen was removed. Ruptured from impact."

"Wow. That must've been some accident."

The muscle in his jaw flexed. "Yeah."

"How old were you?"

"Twenty-two."

I leaned my head down and kissed the scar, intending to trail a line of kisses from top to bottom. But Bennett's curt voice stopped me.

"*Don't.*"

I froze. "Okay."

Settling my head back on his chest, I suddenly felt really awkward.

"Sorry. I didn't mean to upset you. I was just thinking of something my grandmother used to say. 'Scars are the maps to the story of where we've been.'"

He stayed quiet for a long time. When he finally spoke, his voice was low. "Not every scar leads to a story with a happy ending, Annalise."

"Okay," I said softly. "I'm sorry."

For the next hour or so, neither of us said a word. I wondered if he regretted asking me to stay. Even though I was exhausted, I couldn't fall asleep. I thought it might be better if I just went home. But if he'd fallen asleep, I didn't want to wake him.

"Bennett?" I whispered.

He didn't respond, so I carefully pulled back the covers and tried my best not to make the bed jiggle around so he wouldn't wake. I'd gotten as far as sitting up when his voice startled me.

"Where are you going?"

"Shit. You scared me. I thought you were asleep."

"You were going to try to sneak out?"

"No. Ummm... Yeah. I thought maybe it would be better if I went home."

He pulled me back down to his chest, hugging my shoulder tight to him. "It wouldn't."

"Are you sure?"

"You're a nice girl. A nice woman. I like you here. But if I tell you that some of my scars aren't healable on the inside, you're going to try to heal me."

"And something is wrong with that?"

"Some scars don't deserve to be healed. But that doesn't mean I want you to go home. Get some sleep, babe."

chapter 31

Bennett

"The board has selected the last of the accounts that the two of you will be reviewed on," Jonas said. "It's a new account to both of you, so I think you'll be as happy as you could be under the circumstances."

"That's great. What kind of an account is it?" Annalise asked.

At the same time, she also uncrossed and recrossed her legs, so I lost track of the conversation. It didn't help that I knew she had no underwear on under that skirt. After an hour-long fuckfest in the shower this morning, I'd gone for a run while she went home to get dressed. We happened to pull up for work at the exact same time, and both of us had to park in the lot down the street rather than the usual spots we snagged near the building when we were early.

She'd texted me from her car, asking me to walk ahead so people wouldn't suspect anything when we walked in at the same time. I'd thought it was overkill, but I'd soon realized she was full of shit and why she really needed the minute alone.

263

The doors to the elevator I'd entered had started to slide closed when Annalise strolled into the building lobby. Instead of letting it go and taking the next car, she waved and yelled from the door. "Hold the elevator, please!"

There were a few other people in the car already, and a woman from accounting pressed the *open* button.

"Thanks." Annalise rushed in and stood next to me. Trying to follow her request that no one at work find out about us, I acknowledged her with a simple nod and faced forward. She, on the other hand, went out of her way to address me in front of people.

"Bennett." She held out a brown paper bag. "I think you might've dropped something getting out of your car in the parking lot." Her face didn't give anything away, but I caught the twinkle in her eye.

What the hell was she up to? I took the bag, even though I hadn't dropped it. "Yeah, I did. Thanks."

At our floor, she exited the elevator first, giving me a fine view of her swaying ass as I followed her down the hall. Curious, I walked into my office and ripped open the brown paper bag. A note sat on top of balled-up red, lacy fabric. The thong was still warm.

Don't let these distract you today.
Or the fact that I took them off in the car.

I'd laughed, thinking she was being cute. But now I realized I truly was fucking distracted. Was it me, or did she look even more fuckable today than usual? How far was the closest motel from the office? I wondered if she'd be up for a quickie at lunch.

That thought had been still rolling through my head when Jonas had given the name of the new account— Pet something or other. But the change in Annalise's tone brought me back from fantasyland. She sounded apprehensive.

"Pet Supplies & More? The online company based in San Jose?"

"That's the one," Jonas said. "Are you familiar with them?"

She side-glanced over at me and then back to Jonas. "Yes, I am."

I squinted. "You've pitched them before?"

Annalise shook her head and spoke to Jonas. "Trent and Lauren Becker, right?"

Jonas nodded. "Yes, that's them. Have you worked with them before?"

Something about Annalise's reaction was off. She didn't seem excited that she knew them, when that could be a clear advantage.

"No, I haven't. How did the RFP come in?"

"Our CEO got a call from their CEO."

"Oh. Okay. Lauren may not even know I work here with the merger and all. But I can give her a call."

"Why you?" *What kind of a game is she playing?*

"Because I know her."

I straightened my tie. "Obviously not that well if she didn't call you for the RFP and doesn't even know you work here."

"I'll make the call, Bennett. Don't worry your pretty little head. I won't try to exclude you from getting information. But we both know it's better for someone with a relationship to take the lead than someone without one."

"I guess that depends on who is more competent."

Annalise gave me the evil eye, then spoke to Jonas. "I've been to quite a few functions with Lauren and Trent."

"If you know them so well, why haven't you pitched them before?"

"Because it was one of those things that, at the time, I thought it was best not to mix business with them."

What the hell was she being so shady about? "At the time? And now it's okay to mix business with them? What's the deal, Annalise?"

She sighed and caught my eye before turning to Jonas. "Lauren is my ex's sister. The company was actually started by Lauren's grandparents sixty years ago. But she and her husband mostly run it now. I know them pretty well. Andrew and I were together for eight years."

"Great. So we're being judged on three accounts. One, the new creative director wants to get inside her pants, and another, the brother of the owner has already been there."

"Bennett!" Jonas scolded. "You're walking a fine line. I know this job is important to you, and in a perfect world, the only advantage in landing an account would be that someone's pitch is better. So I'll cut you some slack for being upset. But I will not sit here and listen to you speak about Annalise in that way."

I stood abruptly. "Fine. Then I'll leave. It sounds like Annalise will be heading this pitch with *the Beckers* anyway."

"You've got to be kidding me!" The door shook as it slammed shut behind Annalise.

I scrubbed my hands over my face and growled. "Go back to your office. I'm not in the mood to argue, and I have work to do."

She marched toward my desk. "You're acting like a child. I clearly had no idea this account pitch was coming in. I don't know what you're so angry about. I've proven that I play fair when it comes to clients I have a relationship with."

"A relationship, huh?" I scoffed. "Thought you didn't have that relationship anymore."

Annalise's brows drew down, and then a look of understanding crossed her face. She moved closer to me. "Is that what this is about? Andrew? I thought you were mad I had an advantage at work."

Unfamiliar feelings rattled my cage, making me feel like a locked-up lion. My first instinct was to strike out of the hold.

"*Who* you fuck isn't any of my business, unless you're fucking me over at the same time."

She looked hurt. "Who *I fuck* isn't any of your business? I thought we'd decided neither of us would be fucking anyone else."

I didn't want to feel bad. I was pissed. *Fucking Andrew.* If she wasn't in on it, that douche was playing some sort of a game. This wasn't a coincidence.

"He might not be good at going down on you, but I found out this morning you're a little pro at giving head.

I'm sure you can take one for the team and drop to your knees to help land the account."

She reared back and went in for a slap across my face. Only I caught her wrist before it landed.

"Screw you," she seethed.

I flaunted a smug smile. "Been there, done that."

Her other hand came up, and she attempted a lefty smack. That one was even easier to catch.

"You're an asshole." She glared at me, her chest heaving.

Looking down, I noticed her nipples pointing through her shirt. I let my eyes linger so she would notice what had snagged my attention, and then raised them to meet hers.

"You must like assholes, then."

"Go to hell," she hissed.

"I'm already there, sweetheart."

She looked back and forth between my eyes, and a wicked smile tugged at the corner of her lips. "At least *fucking* Andrew might lead to something productive. I don't know what I was thinking wasting my time with you."

I took a deep breath and felt like a bull letting steam out of its nose. Annalise was waving a red cape in the damn air, challenging me. That thought—the thought of a red cape—reminded me what she'd given me this morning. Moreover, what she wasn't wearing.

I leaned in to her, nose to nose. "Do you enjoy screwing with me? Are you wet for me right now?"

Yup. I'd lost it. My dick hardened, and I needed to touch her, no matter how insane it might seem.

Her eyes went wide. Still holding her wrists, I tugged them up and lifted her arms into the air. Then I transferred both wrists into one hand and slipped the other under her skirt. Her pussy was warm and soft. If arguing with her was hell, this was heaven.

I couldn't give her a chance to screw her head on straight and stop me. So without any warning, I went for it. I slipped two fingers inside her, and she gasped. My mouth came crashing down on hers, and I swallowed the tail end of a moan as I pumped my hand three quick times.

When she arched her back and pushed into me, I assumed it was safe to let go of her wrists. I guided her to lean against the edge of my desk and dropped to my knees. I needed to taste her so badly. It wasn't lost on me that we'd just been fighting about her anti-oral ex, and I'd chosen to go down on her.

I just didn't give a fuck what, if anything, that meant at the moment. The only thing important to me right now was that I needed her to come. In. My. Mouth.

I went at it like a storm—licking and sucking, burying my nose so deep inside of her, she started to ride my face. Some men say the sexiest thing a woman can do is to talk dirty or to submit to them, but they obviously haven't had their hair pulled and face ridden by a woman who currently hates their guts.

Nothing. Fucking. Sexier. In. The. World.

When I slid two fingers back into her and sucked hard on her clit, she started to get loud. Thankfully one of us remembered where we were—obviously I didn't give a fuck since I was eating a woman on my desk with an unlocked door—but I was with it enough to at least use my other hand to cover her mouth.

After she went slack, I slowed my pace but stayed on my knees to enjoy a few more leisurely laps of her sweetness. Then I abruptly stood and wiped my face with the back of my hand.

Annalise blinked a few times as if she was returning from another place, but she didn't attempt to budge. Clearly she hadn't heard the noise the first time.

I yanked her to her feet and pulled down her skirt in one swift motion. She looked confused...until she heard the second knock at my office door.

chapter 32

Annalise

Shit!

Bennett had pulled down my skirt, righted my blouse, and smoothed my hair before I even realized what the hell was happening. But he was so busy fixing me, he hadn't noticed what *he* looked like.

Panicked as the door started to creep open, I picked up the nearest thing I could find and tossed it at the offending situation.

Only...it happened to be a large coffee.

As it connected with my target, the top came off and the entire contents splashed all over Bennett's pants just as Jonas walked in.

"What the fuck?" Bennett yelled.

"I'm sorry. It...it was an accident."

Jonas frowned and shut the door behind him. "The two of you knock it the hell off. The entire office can hear you going at it. You sound like two cats fighting."

Bennett opened his top drawer, grabbed a wad of napkins, and blotted at his pants.

271

"It's not what you think," I said. "We were arguing initially, yes. But then we...we found a mutually beneficial way to work through it. We were just about to call the client together when I knocked over Bennett's coffee reaching for his desk phone."

Jonas squinted. He looked like he didn't believe a word I said. But then Bennett backed me up, still wiping his soaked crotch. "We got this, Jonas. I apologized for the stuff I said in your office, and we...kissed and made up. The coffee was an accident."

He looked back and forth between the two of us, still not seeming entirely convinced. "Maybe you two should take this out of the office. Go have a drink or eat something. Make friends. It's on me."

"*Eat* something." Bennett nodded. I caught the twitch at the corner of his lip, but luckily Jonas didn't seem to. "Great idea. Thanks, Jonas."

Our boss grumbled something about being too old for this shit and left us alone in Bennett's office again. He even shut the door behind him.

"What the fuck?" Bennett pointed down to his drenched slacks.

"You had a wet spot."

"What?"

"A giant wet spot. You know, the drizzle before the downpour. And an erection."

"So your answer was to throw a full coffee at my dick rather than, I don't know, hand me a file to cover myself?"

I started to laugh. "I panicked. I'm sorry."

"Guess I should be glad it wasn't hot anymore."

I covered my mouth, but couldn't contain my smile. "That was...absolutely insane."

Bennett's smile was smug. "That was fucking hot."

"That can never happen again."

"That's most definitely happening again."

"You acted like such a dick."

"Next time we fight, I'm going to push you down to the floor and *feed you* my dick. Right here in this office. Door unlocked."

My stomach fluttered nervously. I had no doubt he would do it. And as insane as it was, the thought excited me. But I couldn't let him know that.

I smoothed my skirt and took a step back. "You owe me an apology for the things you said this morning."

He smirked. "I thought I just gave you an apology. But I'm game to give you another one."

"I mean it, Bennett. You can't act like a jealous boyfriend in the office."

"I wasn't jealous."

He seemed genuinely confused by my comment. Did he really think what had just transpired was anything other than good old alpha-male, jealous behavior?

"You weren't jealous? So what were you all pissed off about then?"

He tossed the napkins he'd used to wipe down his pants into his wastepaper basket. "It was about work. The playing field should be level for us."

I studied his face. God, he really had no idea. "*Uh-huh.*"

His desk drawer was still open from when he'd taken out the napkins. I reached in and helped myself.

"New superhero?" I arched a brow.

"Give me that." Bennett tried to swipe the notepad full of doodles from my hand, but I pulled it from his reach.

"Looks sort of familiar." His latest artwork featured a caricature with big hair and giant breasts. She looked exactly like me—with a cape, of course.

He stepped closer and removed the pad from my hand. "You know what superpower this one has?"

"What?"

"The power to drive people fucking nuts."

I flaunted a goofy smile. "You think I'm a superhero?"

"Don't let it go to your head, Texas. I draw plenty of cartoons."

I pointed to the doodle with the superhero leaning against a desk, her legs spread wide in a power stance. The only thing missing was Bennett's head between them.

"Yes. But not all of your fantasies get to become reality."

I'd debated inviting Bennett to join me all day.

What if my competition had been a sixty-year-old, happily married man instead of a thirty-one-year-old, insanely sexy single guy who'd just happened to give me three orgasms this morning—two in his shower and the other on his desk?

Would I play fair? Or was I giving away more than I should because I had a soft spot for Bennett Fox? (And maybe liked his hard spot, too?) Did I care how I won the battle, as long as I won?

Unfortunately, I did care. And I knew I was the minority. In a cutthroat competition like this, most people would use every advantage to win the war. But it was important to me to win fair and square. It's just who I am.

So at five minutes to four, I walked over to Bennett's office. He was nose-deep in artwork, which he'd spread all over the table in the corner of his office.

I knocked on the open door. "Do you have a minute?"

He wiggled his brows. "That depends on what you have in mind."

"Just come to my office in five minutes."

I turned and walked back down the hall, but he appeared at the doorway of my office right on time.

I motioned to the door. "Shut the door. I need to make a call on speaker."

Bennett smirked. "Sure you do."

The dumbass thought I'd invited him for a booty call. Rather than explain, I hit the speakerphone button and dialed.

The assistant answered on the first ring. "Lauren Becker's office."

I looked at Bennett. His eyebrows rose.

"Hi. This is Annalise O'Neil calling for Lauren. We spoke earlier today, and I scheduled a call for four."

"Yes. She's waiting for your call, Annalise. I'll put you right through."

"Thank you."

She put the call on hold, and my gaze locked with Bennett's. "I'm going to beat you because I'm good at my job. Not because of anything else."

Bennett stared at me, his face unreadable.

Lauren came on the phone two seconds later. "Anna?"

I picked up the receiver. "Yes. Hi, Lauren."

"How are you? God, it's been too long."

"It has. I don't know if you're aware or not, but I work at Foster, Burnett and Wren now. The two companies merged."

I looked up at Bennett while I listened to her answer.

"Oh." I said. "Okay. Yeah. I wasn't sure Andrew had told you. Thank you. I appreciate you including us on the RFP."

Bennett's jaw flexed, and I stifled a sigh. I had no control over how the business had come our way, but I did have control over how I managed it. Lauren and I caught up for a minute, and then I cleared my throat.

"I hope you don't mind, but I invited a colleague to join me on this call. He just walked in. His name is Bennett Fox."

After she said she didn't object, I put the phone back on speaker. The three of us then talked for a half hour about the RFP and what she was looking for. Toward the end of our call, I suggested we get together for dinner to discuss things further next week.

"That would be great. I know Trent would love to see you, too." She paused. "What about Andrew? Should I see if he'd like to join us? He mentioned things had been tough since the merger and thought it might be a good time for us to finally work together."

Bennett looked as uncomfortable as I felt. "If you don't mind, I'd prefer if you didn't. We aren't... I wasn't even aware he'd spoken to you about my change at work or asked you to include me in the RFP."

Lauren sighed. "Yeah, I understand."

I had no idea what to expect from Bennett when I hung up, but what I got, I knew was sincere.

"Thank you for including me."

I nodded. "You're welcome."

He took a few steps toward my office door and then turned back. "Why?"

I wasn't sure I understood the question. "Why what?"

"Why do you want to win fair and square? Is it because of what's going on between us?"

"I actually thought about that earlier." I smiled. "Don't flatter yourself. I'd be going about things the same way even if you were a sixty-year-old, happily married man."

"Wow." He shook his head. "And here I was thinking you were just a good person. But you'd let a sixty-year-old, married dude go down on you in his office?"

"That's not what I meant!"

Bennett winked. "I know. But let's pretend so I don't have to admit you're a fuck of a lot better person than I am."

chapter 33

Bennett

"Do you like *Star Wars*?"

I hit mute on SportsCenter and looked over at Annalise. She had three different newspapers spread out in sections all over my bed. I preferred my news in the form of CNN or ESPN, but over the last few weeks, we had settled into a Saturday-morning routine I liked.

We'd have early-morning sex, and then I'd go for a run while she made us breakfast. On the way home I picked up three different newspapers, and after we ate, I'd watch SportsCenter while she read the papers for hours.

Did I mention she cooked and read while wearing one of my T-shirts with no bra or underwear underneath? Yeah, so that's my favorite part.

I slipped my hand under the hem of the white tee she had on and rubbed her thigh. "I like *Star Wars*. I'm not one of those freaks who walk around dressed up as Yoda or Chewbacca at an annual convention of freaks, but I go see the movies. Why?"

Annalise shrugged. "No reason."

But something about her response—maybe it was too fast or too curt—told me she was full of shit. "You're not one of those freaks, are you?"

Her cheeks shaded pink. "No, I'm not."

I pointed to her face. "Don't even try it, Texas. You're halfway to tomato already."

She put down the paper. "Fine. I used to like to dress up as Princess Leia." Her voice lowered. "And maybe sometimes Aayla Secura and Shaak Ti."

I laughed. "Who?"

"Forget it."

"Oh, no. You opened this can of worms. Now that I know you're a *Star Wars* dork, I want to know what I'm dealing with. Are we talking Halloween costumes only, lunchboxes, and you have the entire Klingon language memorized, or full-on crazed fan who dresses up and goes to conventions?"

"Klingon is *Star Trek,* not *Star Wars.*"

"The fact that you know that tells me a lot."

Annalise rolled her eyes. "Why do I share anything with you?"

I laughed. "Okay. I won't tease, my sexy little dork. What made you ask?"

She pointed to an article in the paper. "I'm reading about movie merchandising that outperformed box office sales. *Star Wars* has had almost thirty-five *billion* in merchandising."

"Guess you have a lot of potential buddies out there in dorkland."

She whacked my stomach with the back of her hand. "Shut up."

"You know there's a new land coming to Disneyland soon: *Star Wars: Galaxy's Edge*."

"*Duh*. I know. I can't wait."

This afternoon was my annual trip to Disney with Lucas—his birthday weekend was the only overnight trip Fanny allowed me. Every year, we drove down on Saturday afternoon and spent the night and the entire next day going on rides. Lucas always wrote up a list of the rides that were new each year, and this time one of them was *Star Wars*-themed.

"Do you go on rides at Disney?" I asked.

"I used to. But I haven't been in years."

I hadn't mentioned my trip with Lucas, yet I'd been toying with inviting her all week. "I'm actually driving up to Disney with Lucas this afternoon. It's his birthday this week, and we take an annual trip."

"Oh. That's awesome. You do such fun things with him."

I'd never really brought women around Lucas, mostly because the relationships I had didn't seem to fit with my weekly visits with him. I took women out to dinners where they wore nice dresses, and then I took them home, not fishing or go-kart racing. But Annalise and I were different. We spent hours working together every day, and when we weren't fighting or make-up fucking, we actually had a pretty good time sitting around doing nothing on mornings like this.

Even though it had only been about a month, I'd gotten to know her far better than anyone I'd dated for six months. Plus, she'd like the new *Star Wars* ride they'd put in. So now I felt almost obligated to invite her. It was the right thing to do.

I clicked the muted TV off. "Why don't you come with us?"

She looked as surprised as I was that I'd invited her. "To Disney? With you and Lucas?"

"Yeah. Why not? You can get your dork on at the new *Star Wars* ride, and Lucas will have someone to go on spinny shit with."

"You don't go on spinning rides?"

"Nope. In eighth grade, I was dying to make out with Katie Lanzelli. I took her to the town fair and had planned to suck her face on the Ferris wheel. Right before we went on, I went on the Gravitron. Puked my guts out after I got off. Couldn't very well subject her to kissing me after that. So I quit spinning rides that day."

Annalise chuckled. "Your perversion knows no limits. It even affects your trips to Disney."

"What do you say? Wanna come?" I let my hand on her leg travel higher and stroked the sensitive skin on the inside of her thigh, right next to her lips. "I'd have to get you a separate room because of Lucas, but maybe I could get one next door so I could slip out after he falls asleep and slip inside of you."

"See? *Pervert*. All roads lead to and from sex." She smiled. "I'd love to go. But are you sure? I don't want to interrupt your time with Lucas."

The more we talked about it, the more I liked the idea of her coming. "Positive. He'll be glad to have someone other than me to talk to. Trust me." I looked at her. "Plus, I want you to come."

Annalise lit up, practically glowed, as she nodded her head. Then she climbed on top of me, and I lit up, too.

"What composer scored the songs in the movies?"

"Easy. John Williams." Annalise wiped sprinkles off her lip with a napkin.

Lucas looked down at his phone and swiped again. He'd been quizzing her with all the online trivia he could find since we'd gotten in the car this morning.

"What color was Luke Skywalker's light saber in the first two movies?"

"Blue."

"What about in *Return of the Jedi*?"

"Green."

I shook my head. "Why would they change the color of the light saber? And, a better question, why do you know the answers to all this crap?"

Annalise licked a drip from her ice cream cone, and my dick twitched—*in the middle of fucking Disney.*

"He lost the blue one in a duel with Darth Vader in Cloud City. There was a big uproar over the reason his light saber was green in *Return of the Jedi*. The original movie posters had him holding a blue saber. Some people say they changed the color because the fight scene background was a blue sky, while others think there's a deeper meaning—like the filmmakers trying to show Luke had become his own man."

I chuckled. "Ah, got it. So they wanted to sucker parents into buying more light sabers by changing the color."

Lucas was fascinated with Annalise's *Star Wars* trivia capability. Me, I didn't mind sitting around just watching the two of them—as long as she kept licking that ice cream cone. I was damn happy we'd gotten those adjoining rooms now.

After we finished our dessert, we hit a few more rides before calling it quits for the night. It had been one long-ass day—sex twice this morning, a long run, driving up to L.A., then going on a shitload of rides when we got here. But while I was wiped, Lucas and Annalise seemed to still have plenty of energy.

"Can we go in the pool?" Lucas asked as we got off the tram at our hotel stop.

I looked at my watch. "It's almost 9:30."

"So?" He frowned.

"Annalise probably didn't even bring a suit."

She grinned. "Actually, I did."

"Please?" Lucas shot me puppy-dog eyes.

"I can take him if you're too tired."

"No. It's fine." I pointed at Lucas. "A half hour. That's it."

"Okay!"

I grumbled to Annalise as Lucas ran ahead to the hotel's front door. "It better at least be a bikini if I have to go into a Disney piss bucket."

Her smile sparkled. "Complain all you want, but I see the truth in your eyes. You'd do anything that kid asked you to, and you love every minute of watching him enjoy himself."

She wasn't exactly wrong. Without thinking, I slid my hand into hers and finished the walk to the hotel lobby hand in hand. The screwed-up thing was, I had no idea I'd even done it. It just felt...right. Annalise didn't seem to notice either, or if she did, she didn't say anything.

Just the same, I let go to open the door and shoved my hands into my pockets after that.

———

"He's a great kid."

Annalise and I sat across from each other in the bubbling hot tub, twenty feet away from the pool. A bunch of kids had been organizing a water volleyball game when we came outside, and they'd asked Lucas to join in. So we'd gotten a reprieve from getting into the cold piss bucket and came to soak in the designated over-eighteen hot tub. Lights lit up the pool area, so we could still keep an eye out from a distance, yet we were far enough away to not look like we were babysitting him.

"Yeah. Despite the whack job who's raising him, he's turned out to be a really good kid. He's got his head screwed on pretty well."

"He really looks up to you."

The hot tub had been helping to relax my muscles, but that comment made them tense again. "Yeah."

Annalise went quiet, and I had an idea what she was pondering.

"Do you mind me asking how old he was when his mom died?"

"He was three."

"Wow."

"Yeah."

"Was she...sick?"

I held her gaze. "Car accident."

Her eyes dropped to my torso. She was smart enough to put two and two together. And I knew she was debating asking.

It was the last thing I wanted to talk about. I stood. "It's getting late. Why don't I grab us some towels?"

Lucas was snoring by the time I got out of the shower. The day had been pretty great, but the mention of the accident had brought my head down. I sat on the bed across from Lucas, watching him sleep. He looked just like his mother now. It was hard to imagine that in only a few more years, he'd be the same age she was when she'd given birth to him. Which made me think...I needed to have a talk about condoms and birth control with him. Fanny wasn't going to do it. Hell, I'd had the talk with her daughter, too.

A lotta good that did.

My phone vibrated on the end table, so I swiped to check my messages.

Annalise: Sorry if I was being nosy. You got quiet after I asked about his mom. I didn't mean to upset you.

I attempted to put her mind at ease.

Bennett: You didn't. Just tired. The long day must've caught up to me.

I doubted she'd bought it, but at least she wouldn't push.

Annalise: OK. Well thank you for letting me tag along today. I had a great time. Goodnight.

Bennett: Goodnight.

I tossed my phone back on the end table. In the eight years since that night, I had never spoken to anyone about the accident—except for the cops and the lawyers. Not even the shrink my mother had sent me to could pry that vault open. For a long time, I just figured the less I thought about it, the easier it would be to move on. Until recently.

Sophie's journals had stirred up a lot of things inside me. I was starting to wonder if keeping it in had let me move on at all, or if maybe letting it out might be the only thing to set me free.

chapter 34

January 1st

Dear Me,

We're sad.

Bennett has been gone two months now. He's only a few hours away at UCLA, but it might as well be halfway around the world. We miss him. A lot. He has a new girlfriend. Again. He said this one's a marketing major, too, and they hang out all the time like we used to.

We're still dating Ryan Langley, but sometimes when we're kissing him, we think about Bennett. It's really weird. I mean, he's Bennett, right? Our best friend. But we can't seem to stop it.

College isn't so great. I thought it would be different. But it feels like just another year of high school when you live at home—only without Bennett here. There's even a bunch of kids in my classes who were in my classes back at RFK High.

Everything is the same, yet so different.

We got a job at a hair salon answering the phones. The people there are really nice, and it pays pretty good.

we shouldn't

We're hoping to save money and get our own place. Mom's new boyfriend Aaron is a jerk and is always home.

This month's poem is dedicated to no one.

She glances backward,
afraid to move forward now.
Why aren't you here?

This letter will self-destruct in ten minutes.

Anonymously,
Sophie

Bennett

How bad did I want the job?

Annalise had left for her weekly dinner with Madison a few hours ago. Since I had an early-morning appointment out of the office tomorrow, and my bed would be empty tonight, I'd stayed extra late to finish things for my full pitch to Star Studios, which was coming up soon. This week had been busy as hell, even though it was only Wednesday. And we still had dinner with douchebag's sister on Friday.

I grabbed the key to Annalise's office from Marina's top drawer to leave some sketches on her desk. At lunch today, she'd mentioned she was stuck coming up with a logo for a kid's magic marker company that was expanding into a line of professional artist markers. An idea had come to me while I worked on shading in a different project, and I thought it might work for her client.

Annalise had brought the account with her from Wren, so we weren't in competition—I had no reason not to help.

Only when I went to put my drawings on her desk, I found the entire concept for her Star pitch laid out there: storyboards, 3D-logo models, and a thick, red expanding-file folder labeled RESEARCH. I stared at the banded folder—there had to be three inches of damn research. Way more than I'd done. What could she have in there? Shit that could give her an edge, that's what.

I set my drawings on her seat and picked up the folder. The thing had weight.

Fuck.

I shouldn't.

But what if I've missed something?

I knew two things with absolute certainty. One, it would be a pretty scummy thing to do. And two, if the shoe was on the other foot, and it were Annalise finding my desk with all this shit, she'd turn around and walk the hell out.

But there was no fucking way I could move to Texas.

I wouldn't be doing it for myself. I'd be doing it for Lucas.

There was an exception for shitty behavior when the end justified the means, right?

What the hell could she have in here? Seriously, this thing had to weigh three pounds. Maybe there was a brick inside? Or a book? A hardcover of *Marketing for Dummies*? I could at least check that, couldn't I? It might set my mind at ease to know I wasn't missing research.

I pulled the red rubber band off the file folder.

God, I'm a fucking asshole.

Setting it down on the desk again, I stared at it some more.

What if this weren't Annalise?

She'd said herself that she'd tried to take the person out of the equation when deciding how to act. A sixty-year-old, married man—I was pretty sure that's who she pretended her competition was.

What would I do if I'd found this file of potentially helpful information, only the competition I'd been pitted against was a sixty-year-old dude instead of Annalise?

I'd like to think figuring out the answer to that question required some debate.

But...we all know better, right?

I'd already be at the copier photocopying the crap out of this file.

That, in a nutshell, summarized the difference between me and Annalise. When she walked through a *how would I act* scenario in her head, she always came out on the right side of what was ethical. I, on the other hand, came out on the right side of what would bring me closer to what I wanted.

So what the hell was stopping me?

Annalise and her goddamned ethical bullshit had me feeling guilty.

Groaning, I picked up the file folder, wrapped the rubber band back around it, and set it where I'd found it. I swiped my drawings from her chair, pulled the door shut behind me, and then squatted down to slip the artwork under the closed office door. She'd find them in the morning without ever knowing I'd been inside.

I grumbled my way back to Marina's desk to replace the key. While I was there, I figured I'd leave her a note that I'd be out tomorrow morning since my appointment had originally been in the afternoon.

I found a pen and looked around for something to write on. Next to her phone was one of those message pads that had three little carbon copy tear-off message slips on each sheet. So I grabbed that and started to write on the bottom one.

But the carbon that remained from the message above caught my attention because it had Annalise's name on it.

DATE: *6-1*
TIME: *11:05AM*
FOR: *Annalise*
CALLER: *Andrew Marks*
PHONE: *415-555-0028*
MESSAGE: *He's returning your call. Call anytime.*

"Is something wrong?" Annalise leaned her hip against the counter in the break room.

"Not a damn thing," I said, pouring my second cup of coffee.

She crossed her arms over her chest. "So just a general piss-poor mood then?"

"It's been a busy week."

"I know." She looked toward the door and lowered her voice. "That's why I thought I'd be nice and make you dinner at my place last night. Only you didn't answer my text, and this morning when I saw you in the hall, you looked like you might bite me."

I picked up my mug. "You're the one who wanted to make sure we were discreet in the office. Should I have stopped to feel you up?"

She squinted. "Whatever. Don't forget dinner is at six tonight with Lauren and Trent at La Maison."

I scoffed. "Can't wait."

Annalise rightly read into my sarcasm. She sighed and turned to walk out of the break room.

Near the door, she stopped and turned back. "Thank you for the sketches, by the way. They were exactly what I needed and couldn't come up with."

I looked up from my mug and our eyes caught. *Fuck it.*

"I went into your office to put them on your desk last night. I saw it was covered with your work on the Star campaign, so I left and slipped it under your door."

She cocked her head to the side and searched my face. "You didn't look at anything?"

After I'd found the message from her ex, I'd contemplated going back in. But I fucking couldn't. *Wussy.* I shook my head.

Her eyes lost focus for a minute, and I got the distinct feeling random shit was spinning around in her head as she tried to click together the pieces of some puzzle.

She zoned in on me again. "Are you annoyed with yourself that you *didn't* rummage through my things?"

I folded my arms across my chest. "I asked myself if I would've walked out if it were someone other than you."

"And..."

"I wouldn't have."

Annalise's eyes softened. "Well, thank you. Is that why you're all grumpy? Because you didn't treat me like the enemy."

"It wasn't—until I went to put back the key in Marina's drawer and caught a message she'd left you that someone had called you back."

Her face fell. "It's not what you think."

"So you know what I'm thinking now?"

"When I called Lauren the other day to confirm dinner for tonight, she told me Andrew was planning on joining us. I called him to ask that he didn't. That's why he called me back."

I walked toward the break room door. "Whatever."

Annalise exhaled loudly. "Next time just come to me if something's bothering you."

I stopped in the doorway where she stood. "Or maybe next time, I'll grow some balls and gain an edge on the competition."

⌒

"Sorry about that. I figured those two needed a few minutes alone. My wife likes to meddle in shit where her nose doesn't belong. But I'm a beaten-down man, so I don't fight it." Trent Becker held up his glass and tipped it to me. "My answer is always 'Yes, dear.' *And a good scotch.*"

I raised my glass. "Sounds good to me. Doesn't even matter what the question is."

Annalise and I had arrived at the restaurant from the office at the same time. Lauren and her husband showed a few minutes later. Since the hostess said our table wasn't ready yet, Trent had asked me to go to the bar and get drinks, while the ladies immediately dove into talking.

"Lauren and Annalise have a personal history."

I sipped and looked over the rim of my glass at Trent. "Andrew. I know."

Trent raised his brows. "So she's told you."

"She has."

He nodded. "Makes sense. Especially since he's the one who facilitated this get-together."

This was a business meeting. I had to keep my opinions to myself, but with the door open to peek inside, I couldn't resist. "Odd timing. Annalise has been working in marketing for years. Yet she said you guys had never discussed her pitching for your business."

Trent looked around, then leaned in. "Lauren thinks the sun rises and sets on her brother. But between us, I think he's a bit of a pompous, selfish dick."

This time my brows jumped. Maybe this dinner wouldn't be so bad after all.

"Sounds like you're right, from what Annalise has shared. But like you, I'll keep that to myself." I raised my glass. "And swallow my thoughts down with this scotch."

Trent chuckled. "Annalise is great. I'm glad we should be able to throw some business her way. I just hope it doesn't help my dear old brother-in-law worm his way back in. Let him stay with the Swedish stewardess he's been seeing off and on behind her back the last few years."

Shit.

Figures.

I knew that guy was a douche.

Eight years and still no commitment told me he'd been jerking her around; I just hadn't known the reason. *What a dumbfuck.*

The bartender brought two glasses of wine, and Trent and I argued over who paid the tab. After I won, we walked the drinks over to the ladies, who were huddled on a bench near the hostess station.

"Thank you." Annalise stood for me to pass her the glass. She leaned in with an apprehensive smile. "All good?"

Mine was genuine. "Never better."

Dinner with Lauren and Trent turned out to be surprisingly enjoyable. We talked a lot about their business, and they were open about their ups and downs and seemed to have a good grip on the market they wanted to reach. They also shared the hefty budget they'd allocated to web and television advertising, which justified the board rewarding the campaign responsible for landing the account.

"So who does what?" Lauren asked neither of us in particular. "Is one of you web and one of you TV or something?"

I let Annalise take the lead on that one. How she chose to spin it was her call.

"Not really. We have team members who specialize in things like art, copy, and market research. We'll use them to jointly come up with two different campaigns to present to you."

"Oh, wow. Okay." Lauren smiled. "I'm sure I'll love whatever you come up with. We've always had such similar taste."

Yet again, Annalise could have screwed me. All she needed to do was mention that we'd each do *individual* pitches and they'd be picking whose they liked best. No doubt that would give Lauren a good pre-sell on which one to choose. But Annalise presenting it like it was a team effort really leveled the playing field.

I glanced over, and she glinted a sweet smile.

So fucking beautiful. And that shit was contagious, because I smiled back, and I sure as shit am not a damn smiler. I'm more a pissed-off-face kind of person—mostly because the majority of people piss me off. In fact, I'd venture to guess that the corners of my lips have been tilted up more since I met Annalise than in the first thirty years of my life.

I let my eyes drift back to her for another look. She was just so fucking moral and good. It made me want to do immoral things and make her bad later.

I used my napkin to wipe my mouth and then *accidentally* let it fall to the ground. Bending over to pretend to grab it, I slid my hand up Annalise's dress under the tablecloth and watched her jump when my thumb stroked over the warm center between her legs. Her reaction was to immediately slam her thighs shut, and I almost lost my balance when she closed my arm between her legs with a yank. I coughed and tugged my hand free, trying hard not to laugh.

Is there some way I could finger her right now and watch her attempt to talk business to douche's sister at the same time?

She looked down at me with warning in her eyes. "Are you okay, Bennett?"

I righted myself in my chair and dropped my napkin on the table in front of me. "Just a slip of my hand."

My hand discreetly *slipped* a few more times before the end of the night—the last time to squeeze her ass while we walked to the restaurant door behind our potential new clients. Their car pulled up just before mine did, so we said goodnight and watched them pull away.

If they'd looked, Lauren and Trent could probably still have seen us in the rearview mirror as I pulled Annalise into my arms.

"You were so bad tonight." She pressed her palms against my chest.

I brushed my lips with hers. "I can't help myself. I want to do bad things to you. Come home with me. I missed you in my bed last night."

Her eyes softened. "I missed you, too."

I couldn't remember ever missing anyone, except for Sophie. And that was totally different, because she was really gone. Yet I hadn't just fed Annalise a line. I'd actually missed her. After one night apart. And as much as the thought freaked me out, the thought of not having her in my bed tonight actually freaked me out a little more. So I ignored the warning bells blaring that I was taking things too far.

The valet pulled up in Annalise's car.

"I'll follow you," I said.

"Actually, could we stay at my place tonight? I ordered a new chair for my living room two months ago, and it's being delivered tomorrow morning sometime."

"Yeah. Of course." I kissed her forehead. "As long as I fall asleep and wake up inside of you, doesn't matter where we are."

chapter 36

Annalise

"Shit-take." Madison shook her head.

"Umm... What?"

"Did you not just hear the waiter? He pronounced the shiitake mushroom special as *shit-take* and asked me how I wanted my baked lobster cooked. Umm...*done*?"

I chuckled. "Sorry. I guess I zoned out for a few seconds there."

Madison brought her wine to her lips. "Probably exhaustion from getting laid every night by your new boy-toy.

I sighed. "Can I ask you a hypothetical question?"

"Of course. If it makes you feel better to pretend it's not about you, go right ahead. Shoot."

"It does." I paused and thought about how to word it. "If a woman is involved with a man—one who's been very upfront from the beginning that he doesn't want a long-term commitment—would it be insane for said woman to walk away from a good job with a shitload of stock options and money at stake on the off-chance the guy might come around and want something more?"

Madison frowned and set down her wine glass. "Oh, honey. You were only supposed to use him as a rebound."

I ran my finger through the condensation on the base of my wine glass. "I know. And it should have been the perfect arrangement. I mean, he's a narcissistic, commitment-phobic, chauvinistic, arrogant ass."

Madison threw her hands in the air. "Well, of course you fell for him!"

We laughed.

"Seriously though, one of us is going to be reassigned to Texas in a few weeks. Would I be nuts if I looked for another job so the two of us could have a chance?"

"How much money are we talking about here?"

"Well, I have stock options that vest over the next three years. Basically, they give me the opportunity to buy 20,000 shares for a set price of $9. So it depends on what the stock is worth when they vest."

"What's it worth now?"

I winced. "$21 a share."

Madison's eyes bulged. "That's what...almost two-hundred and fifty grand profit?"

I nodded and swallowed.

She guzzled the rest of her wine. "You like him that much."

I nodded some more. "Don't get me wrong, he's all those things I originally thought, but there's so much more underneath. Like, he has this childlike quality to him, but at the same time, he's so committed and responsible with his godson. Plus, he makes me laugh, even when I'm pissed off at him. And he has a good heart, but he doesn't want anyone to know. Not to mention—he has the goods and knows how to use them."

"How does Bennett feel about all this?"

I shook my head. "We haven't spoken about it."

"Well, I think that's a conversation you need to have before you consider tossing your career and that much money aside."

"The thing is...I don't think we're there yet. And I can't imagine him being okay with me giving anything up for a chance that he'll come around. In fact, I'm pretty sure he'd fold himself right back into the little box he stays locked up in most of the time if he knew what I was thinking. Something has him gun-shy about relationships. But I don't know what."

"Don't you think that's a red flag in itself? That you don't even know what made him anti-relationship?"

"Of course I do! And I know the entire thing sounds ludicrous to even consider. But...I really like him, Mad."

"You know, sometimes it's hard to see things clearly in a rebound relationship. People often seek the security and comfort of what they just lost—and it can cause attachments that are more to the *relationship* than the actual person."

"I've thought about that. I have. But I don't think I'm trying to replace Andrew or what we had."

Madison didn't look convinced. I'd expected her to tell me I was insane for even considering giving up a great job and money for a long shot at a man—at least, at first. But now that she wasn't on board or excited about my idea, it put a damper on my enthusiasm, too.

I changed the subject and tried to enjoy the rest of my night. Although, there was a reason the woman had been my best friend for more than twenty years: she saw through my bullshit.

When we were leaving the restaurant, she hugged me extra long.

"If you love a narcissistic asshole, I'll love him, too. If you decide to quit your job and take a chance on love, you can sleep on my couch and come to my work dinners four nights a week with me when you're broke. I'm here for you, no matter what. I didn't mean to shoot down your feelings. I was just being protective of you, my friend. I trust your judgment. You can make more money and find a new job."

She pulled back and cupped my cheeks in her hands. "You have time. You'll figure this out."

I felt my eyes well up and pulled her in for another hug. "Thank you."

I'd decided not to text Bennett before showing up. But now that I stood in front of his building, looking up at his dark window, I wondered if this was a bad idea. It felt like a booty call, something I'd never done. In fact, in the eight years Andrew and I had been together, I hadn't once even considered showing up unannounced. We just didn't have that type of relationship—which had never seemed odd to me, until tonight.

But here I stood; so screw it. No point in rethinking what I'd felt comfortable doing before I started overanalyzing things and comparing them to my last relationship. I took a deep breath and opened the door to his building. Pressing the buzzer labeled Fox, I waited while tapping my nails on the metal of the built-in mailbox underneath.

I jumped when his voice came through the intercom. "Yeah?"

He was so grumpy; I couldn't help but smile. "Delivery for a Mr. Fox."

I heard the smile in his words. "Delivery, huh? Whadda you got for me?"

"Whatever you're in the mood for."

The buzzer buzzed, opening the door before I'd finished the last word. I chuckled, feeling giddy.

But as the elevator climbed, *other* feelings started to take over. My body started to tingle, and my heartbeat sped up. *My first booty call.* No wonder people made such a big deal about it.

When I stepped out of the elevator, Bennett was waiting in the hall, shirtless, leaning against the doorframe of his apartment. He was the picture of confident and casual, and his eyes glittered as he watched me walk toward him.

He took a piece of my wayward hair between his thumb and pointer and played with it. "*Whatever* I'm in the mood for? That's a pretty big statement for a little girl." His voice was so damn thick and gruff—I loved it.

I shifted restlessly, feeling electricity crackle in the air all around us. Attempting to pull it together, I straightened my spine and looked up at his imposing frame.

"I'm here, aren't I?"

Bennett's mouth curved into a slow, wicked grin. "You most certainly are."

I yelped when he lifted me off the ground. Yet my legs seemed to know what to do before my brain caught up. They wrapped around his waist and locked behind his back as he carried me inside his apartment. His lips sealed over mine while one hand balled up a fistful of my hair, and he used it to tilt my head where he wanted it.

Completely lost in the kiss, I had no idea we'd even been moving until my back hit the soft mattress behind me. Somehow we managed to strip out of most of our clothes while never breaking contact. Bennett dragged my thong down my legs, and my breaths were wild and jagged.

He brushed the hair from my face. "One last chance... *Whatever* I'm in the mood for? You're sure?"

I nodded, though now I was a little nervous.

His wicked grin returned as he reached over to his end table and grabbed something out of the drawer. He held up a bottle of lube. "Full. Brand new. Bought it on the way home tonight in case the opportunity arose. We must be on the same page, sweetheart."

His head ducked to capture one of my nipples between his teeth. He tugged until my back arched off the bed, and then closed his lips over the swollen peak and sucked gently. By the time he lifted his head to align with mine again, I was panting like a wild animal.

He shifted from on top to next to me, taking his body warmth and letting a cool breath of air hit my body. Goosebumps broke out in places I didn't even realize could bump. The sound of the cap popping open on the bottle of lube made me jump.

"I'm assuming you're an anal virgin. Am I right?"

My eyes widened. I nodded because forming words would've been completely impossible.

He kissed me gently one more time, then wrapped one arm around my waist and flipped me over like I was a ragdoll. "Up on all fours, beautiful." His arm lifted and guided me.

The sound of my ragged breaths filled the air around us. Bennett positioned himself on his knees behind my propped-up ass. I felt like I might explode from nerves and anticipation. He bent and trailed a string of kisses from the top of my ass, up over my spine, onto my neck, and then nibbled his way to my ear. His body wrapped around mine, and I felt his cock nudge at my rear.

"We'll go slow. I won't hurt you. Trust me."

I'd unknowingly been tense, and the warmth and concern in his voice helped my body relax a little.

Bennett rose to his knees behind me, and I felt tiny beads of warm liquid begin to fall at the top of my ass. Each drop intensified my anticipation. Traveling painstakingly slowly, they followed the natural path between my ass cheeks. It was the single most euphoric feeling I'd ever experienced in my life. My toes started to tingle.

"Jesus Christ," he groaned. "That's fucking hot."

When the lubricant reached my lips, Bennett rubbed it into me, massaging my clit and teasing at my opening. He hunched over my body and used his other hand to turn my head for a kiss at the exact moment his fingers pushed inside me. Heat spread through my body when he murmured, "I want to be inside every part of you at once."

He shifted his hips and replaced his fingers with his cock. The lubricant and my arousal slipped him inside with ease. He rocked his hips a few times, sinking deep, before lifting back to his knees behind me.

When I felt the tip of one of his fingers circling over my anus, my body immediately clenched in reaction.

"Relax. I won't push you. This is all I'll try tonight. I promise. Trust me."

I closed my eyes and tried to unfurl the coil of tension inside me with a few deep breaths. Bennett gave me a little space and slowly glided in and out of me a few times before trying again. The second time, it still felt foreign, but I accepted it and let it happen. He massaged and pushed the tip of his finger slowly inside, in unison with his hips. Eventually I relaxed and started to move with him, even pushing back and meeting his thrusts. I was shocked at how good it felt.

I became lost in the feeling of being full, and in giving something so special to this man. My arms and legs started to shake, my body quivering in anticipation of the tsunami that had started to roll through me.

"Bennett..."

He pumped harder and faster, at the same time withdrawing his finger and then sliding it all the way back in. When I relaxed enough, he added a second finger. That was enough to set me off. I came hard and loud—sounds coming from me that I didn't even recognize. When I thought I might collapse, Bennett hooked one arm around my waist to keep me steady and pumped into me harder. With a voracious growl, he leaned over, buried his head in my hair, and spilled inside of me.

We were both soaked with sweat when we collapsed on the bed. Bennett, aware of his weight, quickly rolled off my back, and the two of us struggled to catch our heaving breaths.

My hair was plastered to the side of my face. Pushing it off, I rolled over to my back. "Wow."

Bennett pushed up on an elbow and stared down at me. He leaned over for a gentle kiss, then rubbed my bottom lip with his thumb. "Thank fuck that ex of yours is a dumbass and had no idea what you liked."

I smiled a goofy smile. "I don't think I knew either."

He kissed me again. "It's my absolute pleasure to help you figure that out."

"I just did my first booty call." I wiggled my eyebrows.

Bennett laughed. "Pretty damn appropriate name right about now, don't you think?"

chapter 37

Bennett

Content.

For the last half hour, I'd been lying here trying to figure out the last time I'd felt this feeling. If someone had asked me a few months ago, I would have said I felt it every time I had sex—that post-orgasmic relaxation that takes over your body. But I would've been wrong.

That was *sated*. I hadn't realized until now that there was even a difference between feeling *sated* and *content*. But there is—a damn big one. *Sated* is that satisfied feeling you get after a good meal when you were starving. Or when you're horny as shit and you get a release that drains the life out of you. Sure, I was drained right now; don't get me wrong. And I also felt satisfied. But I wasn't *sated*. *Sated* satisfies a hunger that always comes back. *Content* makes you feel like you don't need anything more. *Not ever.*

And that's fucked up.

Yet at the moment, I didn't give a crap how screwed up it was that I felt this way. In fact, for the last half hour,

I'd had to take a piss. But I didn't, because I was afraid when my feet hit the floor, this feeling might be gone again.

Annalise's head rested on my chest, as I stroked her hair. Her fingers traced a small circle around my abdomen.

"Can I ask you something?" Her voice was low.

"Yeah. I can go again. Just move your hand down a little farther south for a minute."

She giggled and play-smacked my stomach. "That's not what I was going to ask." She paused, and her voice turned serious. "But could you really do it again? We did it twice already since I got here."

I took her hand and pushed it down to my cock. I was still semi-erect after the last go-round.

"Ummm... I think you might have a problem. It's supposed to deflate once in a while, you know."

"Well, now that we're talking about my dick, he knows it, and he's even more awake, so if you had a real question, you better get to asking it pretty quick. Your mouth is gonna be too full to speak in a minute."

Annalise propped her head up on her fist, which rested on my chest. "What do you think would happen if we didn't have an expiration date?"

I froze. "What do you mean?"

"What if we just worked together and one of us wasn't relocating soon? Do you think we'd be doing this a year from now?"

I didn't want to hurt her feelings, but I needed to be honest. Words normally came from my brain, but it felt like this one ripped and tore its way up from my heart.

"No."

She closed her eyes and nodded. "Okay."

Fuck.

She turned her head and rested it back on my chest. A few minutes later, I felt wetness on my skin.

Fuck. Fuck.

She was crying. I closed my eyes and took a few deep breaths. Then I rolled us until she was on her back and I could speak to her face to face. I wiped a tear with my thumb. She looked over my shoulder instead of at me.

"Hey. Look at me."

I hated that her eyes were filled with pain when they met mine. Pain I'd caused.

"The answer has everything to do with me, and nothing to do with you. You're..."

I was rarely at a loss for words. But I didn't have any to accurately describe what I thought of her. Yet I knew it was important that my message get through. She'd just come out of a shitty, long-term relationship, and she needed to know what she was.

"You're *everything*, Annalise. I've met two types of women in my life: every woman out there. And you."

"Then I don't understand..."

"You asked me if things were different, if we would be doing this a year from now. I'm being honest. We wouldn't be. But I don't want you to think it's because I wouldn't be the luckiest son of a bitch if I got to keep you in my bed for that long. Because I would. But some people just aren't cut out for long term."

"Why not?"

The truth was *because they don't deserve it*. But I couldn't tell Annalise that. She'd spend every last minute of the time we had left together trying to prove me wrong.

I looked away, because I couldn't look into her eyes and lie. "Because I like being single. I like my freedom and not having to answer to anyone or have any responsibilities. You want candles and flowers on Valentine's Day, and you deserve to get what you want."

She swallowed and nodded her head. I decided it was about time I answered nature's call. "I'm going to go to the bathroom and get something to drink. You want something?"

"No, thank you," she whispered sadly.

Unfortunately, I hadn't been wrong. By the time my feet hit the ground, my feeling of contentment was long gone.

⌒

She avoided me for days after that.

And I let her. We weren't fighting or pissed off at each other. When we passed in the hall, we put on fake smiles, and she made up some excuse about an appointment she had to run to that I knew from stalking her calendar she didn't have. Yet I didn't call her out on it. There was no point.

It was starting to feel like our relationship had run its natural course, and the best night of sex of my life had turned out to be our swan song. It was probably for the best—put a little space between us, and it would make things easier. Our presentations to Star were next week, and Pet Supplies was scheduled for the beginning of the week after that. What was the point of keeping things going?

Yet I couldn't stop myself.

Her door was shut, but I knew she was still in there. We were the only two left in the office at almost nine o'clock on Thursday night. I was also fucking starving.

I knocked on her office door after rummaging through the refrigerator.

"Come in."

I held up a tin-foiled sandwich in my hand. "You hungry? I'll split with you."

She sighed. "Starving, actually."

I walked to her desk and handed her half a PB&J.

Annalise licked her lips and took it, though she stopped with it halfway to her mouth. "Wait...this is yours, right?"

I grinned. "Just eat it. I'll come in early in the morning and replace it."

She glanced longingly down at the sandwich and back to me. "This is Marina's, isn't it?"

I bit half of my half off in one gigantic bite and spoke with my mouth full. "Mmmmm. It's so fucking good."

The corners of her lips twitched, but she bit into her half anyway. "You're corrupting me."

"I thought you were enjoying me corrupting you." I tilted my head. "But you seem to have been too busy for that the last few days."

Annalise's smile fell. "Oh. Sorry. I've been... swamped."

I glanced over her desk. Her laptop was shut, and a stack of files had been neatly piled up.

"Looks like you're just finishing up." I caught her gaze. "So does that mean you're free tonight?"

She stared at me for a few heartbeats and then raised one hand to cover her mouth while she opened it for an obvious pretend yawn. "I'm really wiped out. Maybe another night."

I knew she'd lied even before her skin started to blush, yet I let her off the hook anyway.

I nodded. "Yeah. Sure. I'm tired, too."

⌒

I hadn't been lying. I was tired.

Yet I didn't go home.

Instead, I hit up the shithole bar closest to the office and ordered a double scotch. And then another one. And then another. Until the bartender told me he'd give me one last drink only if I handed him my cell phone.

I tossed it on the bar and slurred my words. "That's an expensive drink. But go ahead...keep it. Just give me the damn thing."

The bartender took my phone in one hand and poured me a drink with the other. He raised a brow. "What's her name?"

"Annalise." I laughed maniacally. "Or Sophia. Take your pick." I tipped my glass toward him, and half of it sloshed onto the bar. "And she looks fucking great in a cowboy hat."

"Which one we talking about? Annalise or Sophia?"

"Annalise. Beautiful, man. Just beautiful." I swallowed a big gulp of my drink.

"I'm sure she is. I'm calling you an Uber. Where you heading after that drink?"

"She thinks I'm a dick."

The stoic bartender sighed. "Pretty sure she might be right about that. What address you going to, buddy?"

"I don't deserve her."

"I'm sure you don't. What about that address?"

I knocked back the contents of my glass. "Are you married?"

He held up his left hand. "Sixteen years."

"How'd you know you loved her?"

"If you give me an address to call this damn Uber, I'll tell you how I knew."

I rattled off the address. He typed into my phone and then slid it across the bar to me. "You know that saying *if you love something, set it free, and it will come back to you*?"

"Yeah."

He shook his head. "Well, that's a crock of shit. If you love someone and you set her free, she might come back with herpes. So get over yourself and lock that shit down before you get an STD." He paused. "Your Uber will be here in four minutes, so you should start walking your drunk ass to the curb right about now."

"We're here."

The driver's voice jolted me awake. Slumped in the backseat, I must've dozed off on the short ride home.

I nodded. "Yeah. Thanks, man."

It took me a few tries, but I managed to find the door handle and open the damn thing. I even stumbled out without falling on my face. The Uber driver mustn't have been as impressed with how well I'd done, because he didn't stick around to watch me make it to the door. He had his foot pressed to the floor to get the hell out of there before I could even finish swaying enough to walk the three steps to the curb. But I waved goodbye anyway.

Somehow I made my way to the front door. Luckily, when two-hundred-and-twenty pounds leans forward on the verge of falling over, it also propels a lot of momentum. I spent five minutes trying to get the key in the lock, but the damn thing wouldn't work. I'd started to think someone had come to my place and changed the fucking lock.

I took a step back and squinted at the door, attempting to get a good look at the lock. But then the door swung open.

What the fuck?

Stumbling back, I blinked a few times.

"What the hell are you doing?" Fanny pulled her robe tight.

I'd gone to the wrong house?

Fuck.

Maybe I didn't.

"I didn't mean to hurt her." I swayed back and forth. "I didn't know how she felt."

"It's after midnight. I should call the goddamn police."

I looked down and swallowed the lump in my throat. "I'm sorry. I'm so fucking sorry."

I'd said the words so many times eight years ago. They did nothing for either of us back then. But what did I expect? Forgiveness? Forgiveness doesn't change the past.

"You want me to tell you it's okay? It's not. Lucas told me about the girl you brought to Disney. You want me to accept your apology so you can move on without a guilty conscience? Is that what this is about? My daughter doesn't get to move on, does she?"

No, she doesn't. I shook my head. "I'm sorry."

"You know what sorry does?"

I looked up and met her angry eyes. "What?"

"Nothing."

The door slammed in my face before I could say another word.

December 1st

Dear Me,

We're pregnant.

Not exactly what we'd planned, huh?

It's a long story, but it happened when we went to Minnetonka with Mom two months ago. Remember the cute guy we met at the bar when we snuck out after Mom went to sleep?

Yup. That's him.

He seemed like such a nice guy.

Until we showed up at his house to tell him we were pregnant two weeks ago, and...

...his wife answered the door.

His wife! The jerk had said he didn't even have a girlfriend!

We haven't told Mom yet. She's not going to be happy.

The only person in the world who knows is Bennett. The day after I told him, he drove home for the weekend to make sure we were okay. We pretended to be. But we're not, really.

we shouldn't

I secretly wish we were carrying Bennett's baby. He'd be so good to us and such a good dad. I really do love him—different than the way best friends should love each other.

This poem is dedicated to Lucas or Lilly.

Thunder breaks above
dark clouds gather in the sky
sun will shine someday

This letter will self-destruct in ten minutes.

Anonymously,
Sophie

Bennett

It felt like a marching band had taken up residence inside my skull.

The dull pounding ratcheted up to full-on percussion jam session anytime I attempted to raise my head from the pillow.

What the hell did I drink last night?

And what time is it?

I felt around my nightstand for my phone, but it wasn't there. Rolling over, I pried one eye open and met a stream of light coming in through the blinds.

God. I shielded my eyes. *That fucking hurts.*

I forced myself from bed, went to the bathroom, and grabbed three Tylenol from the medicine cabinet, swallowing them down dry. On my way back, I found my cell on the floor in the bedroom, next to the clothes I'd worn yesterday.

8:45. *Shit.* I needed to haul my ass into the office. Yet I climbed back into bed. The Tylenol needed to kick in before I could do that. I swiped my phone with the intention of shooting off an email to Jonas to let him know I'd be late, but instead I found a bunch of missed calls.

Two from Fanny this morning, and three from Annalise last night.

What the hell does Fanny want? It was never a good thing when she called.

I was just about to hit ignore when pieces of last night started to creep back, little by little.

Too much scotch.

Uber.

Showing up at Lucas's house and groveling to Fanny.

Calling Annalise from the curb in front of Fanny's.

I shut my eyes. *Jesus Christ.*

I'd woken her up to apologize.

And to tell her I thought she was beautiful.

And smart.

And funny.

And...

That I'd wanted to fuck her wearing a cowboy hat and heels since the first time she stomped her sexy little ass into my office and pushed back.

Fuck.

I spent the next few minutes taking some relaxing breaths that didn't work, and then hit *Call Back* on Annalise's missed call. I needed to apologize before I dealt with Fanny.

She answered on the first ring. "How are you feeling this lovely morning?"

I groaned. "Like I got run over by a steamroller and the bastard refused to back up and finish the job."

She laughed. "Well, I'm glad you're okay. I was starting to get worried. I figured you wouldn't be much in the mood for your morning run, but nine o'clock is like mid-day for you."

"Yeah." I rubbed my free hand over my face. "Listen. I'm sorry about last night."

"It's okay. No biggie. I booty-called you last week. You're entitled to a free drunk dial or two."

I half smiled. "Thanks. Can you do me a favor and let Jonas know I'll be in late? Say I'm working from home this morning to finish up the Star presentation or something."

"Sure. Of course."

"Thanks."

After I hung up, I listened to the voicemail from Fanny. Not surprisingly, she wasn't half as understanding as Annalise seemed to be. But I needed to get my ass-kicking over with. So I hit *Call Back* on her name next, hoping maybe she wouldn't answer.

No such luck.

Fanny bawled me out for a solid five minutes without taking a breath.

"You want to apologize to someone, apologize to Lucas."

I shut my eyes. "I woke him?"

"You sure did. And apparently the little sneak was listening. He wanted to know what you'd done wrong that you were apologizing for."

Fuck. "What did you tell him?"

"I told him to go back to bed and we'd talk about it after school today."

"You can't, Fanny. That can't come from you. He needs to hear it from me."

321

"Then I guess you'll be having a conversation with him real soon."

I raked my fingers through my hair. "He's too young. It'll hurt him too much."

"Should have thought about that eight years ago, shouldn't you? Maybe you would've paid a little more attention."

"Fanny..."

"I'll let him know you'll be having a talk with him when you see him next weekend."

"But—"

She interrupted again. "And if you don't, I will."

Click.

chapter 40

Bennett

"Good luck."

Annalise had her hands full, so I opened the conference room door.

"Thanks." She set her presentation materials down on the long table. "Even though I'm sure you don't really mean it."

I smiled a genuine smile for the first time in days. I actually did mean it, even though I wished I didn't. Shit would be a hell of a lot easier if I didn't want to see her succeed.

I'd just finished my final presentation to Star, and their team had taken a break while I cleaned up my stuff and Annalise set up for her turn.

"How did it go?" she asked.

I'd hit it out of the park, but I didn't want to rattle her. Instead of gloating like my normal obnoxious self would, I shrugged. "Okay, I guess."

She squinted at me. "Just okay?"

I looked at the clock. "They're not coming back for another twenty minutes. You want to do a dry run on me?"

"You mean show you my concepts?"

"Sure." I shrugged. "My turn's over. I can't steal any of your ideas, even if I wanted to."

Annalise chewed on her bottom lip. "Sure. Why not? I'm not usually so nervous, but for some reason, this one is freaking me out a little."

She set up her boards and walked me through her presentation. I looked on, mesmerized by how she started out with such visible nerves, yet managed to plow through to deliver a kick-ass presentation. My gut told me her concepts weren't going to go over as well as mine had, but I wanted to boost her ego, not shred it, so I complimented her.

"Nice job. Your colors brought in a familiarity from their parent company, yet you created an entirely new identity for Star."

She stood a little taller. So I kept going.

"And I like the tagline. The play on the words is smart, too."

"Thank you." Annalise started to look suspicious, so I scaled back the flattery to something more my usual style.

"Your ass also looks phenomenal in that skirt."

She rolled her eyes, but I caught the little grin she tried to hide. I'd done my job here. Her shaky confidence had been firmed.

Jonas walked into the conference room. "You all ready, Annalise?"

She looked over at me, and then to Jonas, with a smile. "Sure am."

On the way out of the conference room, I leaned over to whisper some parting thoughts to my nemesis. "How about a little wager? I win, you'll bend over my desk later. You win, you'll get on your knees under mine."

"Gee, what a prize for me."

I smiled. "Good luck, Texas."

Later in the day, Jonas knocked on my open office door. "Got a minute?"

I tossed my pencil on the desk, glad for the distraction. My concentration had been shit all afternoon. "Come on in."

He closed the door behind him—not something Jonas did often. Taking a seat in the chair on the other side of my desk, he let out a big sigh.

"How long have we known each other now? Ten years?"

I shrugged. "About that."

"In all that time, I've never seen you as stressed as you've been the last week or two."

He was right about that. My damn neck ached from tension, even when I woke up in the morning.

"There's a lot at stake." *Way more than this competition was ever supposed to be about.*

Jonas nodded. "That's why I'm telling you this in confidence today. I owe it to you to put you out of your misery as soon as possible, after how hard you've worked for me all these years."

What was he getting at? "Okay..."

He smiled half-heartedly. "I spoke to the team at Star before they left a little while ago. They're going with your campaign. It was the unanimous choice of the entire team."

I should've felt like high fiving and celebrating, but instead the victory felt hollow. I forced a happy smile. "That's great."

"That's not the only good news. Billings Media has also unofficially told me they plan to run with your pitch. They also reached out to our CEO and let him know they'd been impressed with your work over the years. I didn't ask them to do that, either. They did it on their own because you work hard."

"Wow. Okay."

"I don't think I need to tell you what this means. The board is going to formally vote on all of the senior management staffing restructures and terminations, but it's just a formality at this point. You've won two out of three, so the third isn't even necessary. You're staying put, Bennett." Jonas slapped his knee and used it as balance to get up. "Annalise will be transferred to the Dallas office. But we'll wait until after the Pet Supplies presentations to break the news."

I rubbed the knot at the back of my neck. "Thanks for letting me know, Jonas."

He left the door open behind him on the way out.

I'd won.

Everything I'd wanted two months ago was mine for the keeping. Yet I couldn't have felt more damn miserable. It made me question whether I ever really knew what I wanted to begin with. Because now I couldn't imagine wanting anything that took Annalise a thousand miles away.

An hour later, I was still staring off into space when Annalise came by with her jacket on. "Thank you for the dry run this afternoon. It made my presentation come off smoother."

I nodded. "No problem. Glad it went well."

Her lips curved in a dubious smile. "Sure you are. Anyway, I'm heading out to meet Madison at some Nepali restaurant—whatever that is. Are we still on for dinner tomorrow night?"

I'd completely forgotten she was supposed to make me dinner at her place.

"Sure. Sounds good." *It might be one of the last nights we have.*

Annalise dug her keys from her purse and tilted her head. "You okay?"

"Fine. Just tired."

"Well, get some rest tonight." She smirked. "Because you won't be getting any at my place tomorrow."

chapter 41

April 1st

Dear Me,

> *It's time.*
>
> *These last few months since Lucas and I moved in with Bennett, I've been happier than I've been in my entire life. But this morning, watching Bennett laugh and play with Lucas finally made up my mind. We were already like a family in so many ways. Maybe he could love me back the way I love him?*
>
> *He just got a promotion at his new job—after only a year of working there. He's more settled now.*
>
> *I have to at least try. Tell him how I've felt for so long now.*
>
> *What harm could it do?*
>
> *I can't remember the last time I was this excited. Hopefully when I write next month, something life changing will have happened between Bennett and me.*
>
> *This poem is dedicated to Bennett.*

Two vines growing tall
one wraps around the other tight
Entwined or strangled

This letter will self-destruct in ten minutes.

Anonymously,
Sophie

chapter 42

Bennett

I couldn't sleep again.

Do you remember "The Tell-Tale Heart" by Edgar Allan Poe? You probably read it in high school. No? Well, let me give you the short version. A dude kills another dude and stuffs his body under his floorboards. He keeps hearing the dead guy's heartbeat from beneath the floor because of the guilt his conscience lays on him. Either that, or the guy is just nuts—I was never sure.

Anyway, that's me—with a slight modification. I'm living "The Smell-Tail Heart" by Bennett Fox. I tossed and turned half of the damn night, the scent of Annalise so heavy on my pillow that after two hours of trying to fall asleep, I got up and stripped the bed. I also grabbed a spare pillow I'd had stuffed in the back of my closet—one Annalise had never laid a finger on—and tossed the offending linens into the hall.

Sniff-sniff

Thump-thump.

Lying on a bare mattress, using a pillow with no case, I *still* fucking smelled her. It couldn't even be physically

330

possible. But her scent hadn't dimmed one bit. I beat the pillow with my fist to fluff it up.

Thump-thump.

Eventually, I got out of bed and searched the goddamn room. She had to have left a bottle of perfume somewhere. I pulled everything out of the nightstands, took a whiff of the bottle of odorless lube, and checked under the bed.

No damn perfume.

Sniff-sniff

Thump-thump.

The next morning, my ass dragged. At least it was Saturday so I didn't have to go in to the office. Although I would have preferred that to the thought of talking to Lucas today. I had to be a sadist, or was it a masochist? I always confused those two. Regardless of what you called it, the timing seemed to be a fucked-up coincidence. I was about to hurt the two people in my life I actually gave a shit about.

Fanny met me at the door with a scowl. I couldn't have been more thrilled when she said nothing, slammed the door in my face, and screamed upstairs in her usual friendly manner.

Lucas was his normal, happy-go-lucky self. He walked out, and we did our customary handshake.

Then his nose scrunched up as he looked at me. "Are you sick or something?"

"No. Why do you say that?"

He hopped down the two steps of the porch in one giant leap. "You look like crud. And you showed up at the house in the middle of the night the other day, and you didn't sound so good."

"Yeah. Sorry about that. I didn't mean to wake you up."

He shrugged. "Grandma said you wanted to talk to me about something."

I took a deep breath and let it out. "Yeah. We have to talk for a little while today."

After we loaded into my car and buckled, Lucas turned to check out the backseat. "No fishing rods?"

I shook my head. "Not today, buddy. I want to take you somewhere."

He frowned. "Okay."

During the drive over to the boat harbor, I attempted to make small talk, but it all felt forced. My palms started to sweat as I parked. Maybe it wasn't such a good idea to talk to him about his mother after all. He was still pretty young. Fanny probably had a price to keep her mouth shut. It might take the contents of my bank account, but at the moment, it seemed like a good investment. *Putting it off would be best for Lucas—he's still too young.*

Just as that thought crossed my mind, Lucas stretched his arms over his head in a giant yawn. His armpits were covered in hair.

Yeah. Nice try. This was a discussion he'd probably deserved to have years ago, but I'd been too selfish.

We pulled into the parking lot, and Lucas looked out the window at the Bay and nearby jetty. A few people were fishing off the rocks.

"Where are we?" he asked. "Why didn't we bring a pole?"

"Because today is about listening. Come on, I want to show you some place."

We walked down the jetty. As we approached our destination, I started to hear the sound and smiled.

"You hear that noise?" I asked.

"Yeah. What is it?"

"It's called the Wave Organ. This was your mom's favorite place to go when we were teenagers. She used to drag me here all the time."

The Wave Organ was a wave-activated acoustic sculpture located along the Bay. Made mostly from the rubble of a demolished cemetery, it looked more like ancient ruins than an art and music exhibit. Twenty-something PVC and concrete organ pipes were located throughout the carved granite and marble pieces, creating sound that came from the water movement beneath.

Lucas and I took a seat on broken rocks across from each other and listened to the subtle sounds.

"It's not really music." His face wrinkled up.

I smiled. "That's what I used to tell your mother. But she told me I didn't listen well enough."

Lucas concentrated for a minute, trying to hear something other than the sound holding a seashell up to your ear made. He shrugged. "It's okay. Would be better with a fishing pole."

I agreed with his sentiment.

I'd always been *a spit it out, say what's on your mind* kinda guy, but I couldn't figure out how to dive into the conversation I'd brought him here to have. Apparently, Lucas knew something was on my mind.

He picked up a small rock and tossed it into the water. "Are we gonna have the birds-and-the-bees talk or something?"

I chuckled. "I wasn't planning on it today. But if you want to, we can."

"Tommy McKinley already told me all about stuff like that."

"Is Tommy the pimply kid who smells like a hamster that we took to the movies a few months ago? The one who tied his own shoelaces together and fell over."

Lucas laughed. "Yeah, that's Tommy."

Oh, we definitely needed to have that talk. "I'm guessing Tommy's experience with girls is pretty much zilch. So why don't we have that talk next week. I wanted to talk to you about your mom today."

"What about her?"

I suddenly felt lightheaded. How did I tell this kid I adored that I'd ruined his life? My mouth went dry.

"You know that your mom and I were best friends, right?"

"Yeah. Even though that's weird. Who wants to be best friends with a girl when you're a kid?"

I wilted a smile. There wasn't an easy way to confess to this kid. I'd rather a giant wave wash over the rock I was sitting on and take me out to sea than finish this conversation. But I looked over at Lucas waiting.

Like a coward, I looked down. "You know your mom died in a car accident."

"Yeah." He shook his head. "I don't remember it, though, really. Just a lot of people kept coming to our house."

334

I nodded. "Yeah. A lot of people really loved your mom."

When I got quiet again, he asked, "Is that what you wanted to tell me?"

I looked up and found Lucas's eyes so full of innocence and trust—trust he'd had in me for eleven years, trust I was about to shatter.

"No, buddy. I need to tell you something about the accident."

He waited.

There was no putting the cork back in the bottle after this. I took one last deep breath.

"I should have told you this a long time ago. But you were too young, or I was too afraid to tell you, or maybe both." I looked away, then back at Lucas to deliver the blow. "I was the one driving the car the night of the accident. Your mom and I, we'd just had a big argument and... It had rained a lot. A big tree needed to be cut back and was partially covering a stop sign. I didn't see it until we were almost on top of it. I hit the brakes, but the ground was wet..."

The expression on Lucas's face changed immediately. It seemed to take forever for him to swallow what I'd said, to allow it to fully register. But when it finally did, he stood.

"Is that why you spend all this time with me?" His voice was full of hurt, and the more he spoke, the louder he became. "You feel guilty for killing my mother? That's why you come visit me every other week and pay off my grandmother?"

"No. That's not it at all."

"You're a liar!"

"Lucas..."

"Just leave me alone!" He took off running down the jetty.

I called after him a few times, but when he stopped down the path to pick up rocks and hurl them into the water, I thought it might be better to give him some headspace. He didn't usually get upset talking about his mother, but what I'd told him was a lot to absorb and probably opened a lot of old wounds, along with creating new ones.

Lucas didn't speak to me for the rest of the afternoon. But he also didn't ask me to take him home early. So I didn't. Instead, I stopped at the store and picked up a cheap rod and some tackle and took him to a lake to fish. If I asked something, he growled a one-word answer. I found a certain amount of comfort in knowing that even when he was upset and angry, he still didn't completely ignore me.

As we got close to his house, I knew he wouldn't leave me any time to talk to him once we arrived. He'd hop out the minute I stopped and slam the door behind him. Hell, I would've done the same at his age. Which is why I eased up on the gas and said my piece during the last five minutes of the drive.

"I understand you're upset with me. And I'm not looking for you to talk to me right now. But I need you to know that none of the time I've spent with you was borne out of guilt. Do I feel guilty about what happened and wish it had been different? Every damn day of my life. But that's not why I come visit you. I come visit you because I loved your mother like she was my sister." I started to get choked up, and my voice broke. "And I love you with all of my heart. You can hate me if you want for what happened. I deserve that. But there's nothing more honest in my life than what I've got with you, Lucas."

We pulled up in front of his house, and I turned my head to try to hide wiping my tears. Lucas looked over at me, stared into my eyes for the longest time, and then turned and got out of my car without a word.

chapter 43

Annalise

"You sure you're okay?"

I took Bennett's plate from in front of him. He'd barely eaten anything.

"Yeah. Just tired." He rubbed at the back of his neck.

"Did you not like the chicken?"

"No, it was great. I...umm...ate with Lucas earlier. I wasn't thinking. Sorry I didn't finish when you went to all that work."

I set our plates in the sink and prompted Bennett to pull his chair back from the table a little. Sitting on his lap, I stroked his hair. "It's fine. I don't care at all. You just seem...somewhere else tonight."

"Sorry."

"Stop apologizing." I stood and offered him my hand. "Come on. You're tired, and you've been rubbing at that neck since you got here. Let me get the knots out."

Bennett took my hand, and I led him into my bedroom. He slipped off his shoes and sat down on the edge of the mattress.

338

I walked into the bathroom and grabbed the half empty bottle of baby oil I kept under the sink for my dry skin. "Take off your shirt, so I don't get it oily."

When watching me pour oil onto my hands didn't invite any lewd comments, I knew whatever was bothering him was more than neck pain and being tired. I got up on my knees behind him and began to massage the baby oil into his skin. His chin dropped to his chest as I worked my fingers into the muscles.

"You weren't kidding. You're *so* tense. It's like one giant knot back here."

Bennett made a sound that was a cross between a groan of pleasure and pain as I dug my fingers deeper into his flesh.

"Feel good?"

He nodded.

After I'd loosened the muscles in his neck, I figured I'd loosen another muscle. So I reached around his chest and unbuckled his belt while kissing the back of his neck. Then I climbed off the bed and stood between his legs before dropping to my knees.

The sound of the zipper on Bennett's jeans echoed through the room. Reaching into his pants, I cupped his cock, and he let out a loud, shaky breath. I'd thought it was the sound of his self-control slipping, but when I looked up, I found his eyes shut and his face twisted in pain.

"Bennett?" I pulled back. "What's wrong?"

His eyes opened. "Nothing."

"Don't tell me it's nothing. You look so upset."

He stood and took a few steps away from me. "I'm sorry."

"Stop saying that. What's going on with you?"

I waited quietly for him to say something, but he just continued to take deep, steady breaths, in and out. It seemed like he was trying to pull himself together, rein in his control.

Bennett ran a hand through his hair. "*Fuuuuuck*!" He sounded angry, but I could tell whatever it was, he was angry with himself, not me.

"Talk to me."

He paced a few times and then sat back down on the edge of the bed, head in his hands and fingers pulling at his hair.

I knelt in front of him. "Bennett?"

I watched his Adam's apple bob up and down as he swallowed. And then his shoulders started to shake. At first, I thought he was laughing—some sort of maniacal laughter that needed to come out because it was either that or break down and cry.

But then he looked up.

And I saw his eyes filled with unshed tears.

My heart stopped.

He wasn't laughing; he was silently crying—doing everything in his power not to let it out.

"Oh God, Bennett. What's wrong? What happened?"

chapter 44

Annalise

I held him tight.

His shoulders shook for so long, I knew I needed to brace for the sound when it finally came. It was an ear-splitting, heart-breaking, soul-crushing noise when it did. I had no idea what could possibly cause so much pain. But I knew I wanted to take some of it away for him.

I rubbed his back, stroked his hair, assured him with tender words that everything was going to be okay. Whatever it was, this was pain that had built for a long time. It wasn't new, not the type that happens when you lose someone unexpectedly or suddenly find out the man you thought you knew wasn't the man you fell in love with. The pain that emanated from Bennett was the kind that had spent years bottled up—like a volcano that erupts after a hundred years of being dormant and suddenly its fire is shooting three-hundred feet into the air.

I started to cry with him, even though I had no idea what we were crying about. It was just too emotional to watch and not be moved to tears of my own. We held each other for such a long time.

"It's going to be okay," I whispered. "It's going to be okay."

Eventually Bennett's shudders started to slow. I wasn't sure if it was because I'd brought him comfort or he just had no more tears to cry. He took a few long, deep, shaky breaths in and out, and his grip on me loosened.

His face had been buried in my neck. I wanted to look at him, to see his face, but I was half afraid that once I pulled back and saw the pain in his eyes, I'd lose it all over again, even if he was okay.

When both our breathing had returned to normal and neither of us was crying anymore, I cleared my hoarse throat. "Do you want me to get you something to drink? A water or something?"

Bennett shook his head, keeping it down so I couldn't see him, but one of his hands lifted to my face.

He pressed his palm to my cheek and whispered, "Thank you."

"Anytime." I smiled sadly, taking his hand from my face and bringing it to my lips. "Anytime."

He lifted his head and leaned his forehead to mine. His eyes were swollen and red, but the half smile he managed was real. "Thanks for the offer. But I'm hoping that was the first and last time you'll be seeing that."

He sounded more like Bennett already.

"Do you want to talk about it?"

He looked up. "Not yet."

"Okay. Well, you know where to find me if you do."

He grinned sadly. "In Texas?"

I started to laugh. "Boy, that didn't take you long. And here I was thinking you'd be nice to me after how nice I was to you. I should've known better."

Bennett scooped me up and surprised me by swinging me up to the top of the bed near the headboard. He climbed on top of me. "Are you saying I owe you one?"

I nodded with a giant, ear-to-ear grin. "Maybe more than one."

He chuckled. "Well, I'd better get started on that right away."

His face moved to my neck once more, only this time he definitely wasn't crying. We wrapped ourselves around one another. Not ten minutes ago, we'd both been emotional wrecks, and now those feelings had transformed into want and need.

Bennett kissed me passionately, with so much tenderness and worship. Our desire for one another had never been an issue, but this moment felt different for some reason. When he broke the kiss to slip off my clothes, he looked down at me as if no one else in the world existed. The smile he wore when he pushed inside of me touched me deeply. I knew in my heart that something had changed. Then he solidified that feeling by making love to me for the very first time.

———

"I told Lucas the truth about me tonight."

The room was pitch dark. I'd just started to doze off and couldn't be sure if I'd heard him right. "The truth?"

I felt him nod, even if I couldn't see it. My head was tucked into the crook of his shoulder, and he continued to stroke my hair gently as he spoke.

"Sophie was my best friend. People thought it was weird that we spent so much time together but weren't hooking up. She was like the little sister I never had, even though we were the same age. We were nineteen when she got pregnant with some loser's baby. Her mother kicked her out, and she came to stay with me in my dorm room for a while and then went back home. It went like that off and on for years. But after I graduated, she couldn't take it at home with Fanny anymore. We got an apartment together so we could share expenses and I could help out with Lucas while she went to cosmetology school at night."

He paused, and I waited in silence until he was ready to continue.

"One night she got out of class early. Lucas was already asleep in her room. I'd met a woman in our building, and we'd started hanging out once in a while. Sophie walked in on me and her having sex in my room." He blew out a deep breath. "I don't even remember the woman's name. Anyway, Sophie freaked out, saying Lucas could've walked in on us, and we had a big fight. The next night, she dropped Lucas off at her mother's instead of leaving him home with me when she went to school. Or at least I thought she went to school. A buddy of mine called later that night and said he was at a bar, and Sophie was there, and she was pretty loaded. So I drove to pick her up. It was a shitty night, pouring out, and I found her making out with some dirtbag biker. There was a big scene—the biker wanted to kick my ass, but I got her the hell out of there before she did something stupid."

He took another deep breath.

"Our fight continued in the car, and Sophie kissed me."

344

"She kissed you?"

"I thought she was just drunk at first. I pushed her off me and told her to cut the shit. But she started to cry. Then everything came out. She told me she'd been in love with me for years. Apparently the night before hadn't been about finding me with another woman while Lucas was sound asleep; it was because she had feelings for me."

"Oh, wow. And you had no idea?"

"None. Like a fucking blockhead, I didn't see any of it. Until long afterward. And I didn't handle it very well. I told her that was ridiculous, and she was like my little sister."

"Ouch."

"Yeah. That didn't go over too well. She was pretty upset, so I thought I better take her home." He paused. "We never made it. I missed a stop sign because of some trees weighed down from the rain, and there was an eighteen-wheeler coming. We skidded, and the car flipped a few times."

I turned over onto my stomach. "Oh my God, Bennett."

He shook his head. "I shouldn't have been driving while I was upset and pissed off, not at night with bad visibility and wet roads."

I clutched my chest. The story itself was heartbreaking, but then I remembered what he'd said earlier. "*I told Lucas the truth tonight.*"

"Lucas didn't know any of this?"

He nodded. "Not until this afternoon. It's a long story, but Sophie kept these journals, and her mother recently read them. Lucas almost read them, too. The last entry in her journal was written the day before she died and said she was going to tell me about her feelings. Her mother knew we'd had a fight the night Sophie died, but when she read the journals, she realized what we must've been fighting about. Fanny never liked me to begin with, and rightly blames me for the accident."

He sighed. "She only lets me stay in Lucas's life because I help her out financially. Lucas and I both got a settlement because the tree should've been cut back and the trucker was speeding, but his is in a trust, and Fanny only gets a stipend for his living expenses each month. I've always known I needed to tell him I was driving. I just thought I could wait until he was a little older." He shook his head. "Reading those journals stirred up a lot of feelings. For both of us."

I shut my eyes. "Oh God, Bennett. I'm so sorry. You told him all that today? I'm guessing it didn't go well?"

"He could have told me never to contact him again. So I guess it could have been worse."

It didn't take a shrink to figure out why Bennett didn't do relationships. A woman he cared for deeply had told him she was in love with him the night she died in a car accident—an accident that happened while he was behind the wheel, an accident he obviously harbored a lot of guilt over.

In an instant, the rest of the missing pieces of Bennett Fox clicked into place. Such a complex man, with scars inside that ran a lot deeper than the one on the outside from the accident.

"He'll come around. He's a smart kid, and in the little time I spent with you two, it was clear how much you care about him. I'm sure he was just upset at the shock. It must've felt like a big secret kept from him."

"He thinks I've been spending all this time with him out of guilt for what I did. And honestly, I do have a lot of guilt. But that's never been the reason I stayed involved in Lucas's life."

We were quiet for a long time. I needed to wrap my head around everything he'd shared, and Bennett obviously needed space. But first…I needed to ask one more question.

"Bennett?"

"Hmm?"

"Have you ever talked to anyone about this? I mean, the *whole story*. What Sophie meant to you, what she shared the night she died, and the relationships you've had since then—or lack of relationships?"

He shook his head.

"Thank you for telling me. I know it's been a long day, but I want you to know I'd love to hear all about Sophie. When you're ready."

He looked into my eyes. "Why? Why would you want to hear about her?"

"Because she's obviously very special to you, she's the mother of the boy you love, and whether you realize it or not, she's helped make you into the man you are today."

Annalise

I reread the letter I'd typed to Jonas a second time. I wasn't ready to give it to him just yet. But typing it brought me one step closer. It felt right—like trying on a pair of jeans that hadn't fit for a really long time, and suddenly the zipper closed. It had been a long time since anything in my life really felt like it fit.

My desk phone rang, so I quickly folded the letter into an envelope and stashed it in my drawer. I figured it was Bennett calling from two offices down to yell at me to hurry my ass up since I said I'd be ready in ten minutes at least a half hour ago.

"Annalise O'Neil." My voice was almost sing-songy.

But when I looked up, with the phone cradled between my shoulder and ear, Bennett was standing in my doorway. I smiled.

Until the voice on the other end of the line came through the receiver.

"Anna? Hey. I figured you might still be at the office."

Andrew.

I don't know why, but I panicked. "Ummm... Yeah. I'm still here. Hang on one minute." I held the phone pressed against my chest and spoke to the man currently ogling me from the doorway. "It's my mom. I'll just be a few minutes."

Bennett nodded. "Take your time. Give me your keys. I'll pull your car around the front so we can load your presentation stuff in when you're done."

I fished inside my purse, hoping he didn't notice the flush creeping up my face. Luckily, he didn't seem to. He took the keys and kissed my forehead before leaving my office. I waited, listening to his footsteps fade until they were in the distance, and for the sound of the front door of our offices opening and closing.

I lifted the phone back to my ear.

"Hi. What's going on? Is everything okay?"

"Did I catch you at a bad time?"

I sat down. Was there ever a good time for an ex to call out of the blue? "I'm just getting ready to leave. What's up?"

"Still working too late, I see." He was teasing, but I wasn't in the mood for small talk.

"I'm actually heading out to get some dinner. So I need to make this fast, Andrew. What's going on?"

"Dinner as in a date?"

That pissed me off. I huffed. "I really need to go."

"Okay. Okay. I just wanted to let you know I'll be joining Lauren and Trent for your dinner tomorrow night."

"Why?"

"Because I want to see you."

"What for?"

Andrew sighed. "Please, Annalise."

"This is a *business* dinner. Last time I checked, you had no interest in your family's business."

"I'm still a shareholder. And I've been helping out over there the last few months—revamping copy for the catalog and stuff."

His parents had always wanted him involved in the family business, but Andrew had stuck his nose in the air when they'd suggested he take a role that involved writing in their empire. Anything but literature was beneath him.

"Fine. Whatever. I need to run."

"I'm looking forward to seeing you."

The feeling was *not* mutual. "Goodbye, Andrew."

⁓

"Have you heard from Lucas?"

Bennett rubbed my shoulder. We were in what had become our usual post-sex sleeping mode—his left arm wrapped around me, my head resting on his chest, his fingers tracing my shoulder while we talked.

"I texted him this afternoon to remind him I'd be by Friday before school to say goodbye. He's leaving for Minnetonka with Fanny directly after classes end. I hate that he'll be gone for three-and-a-half weeks while we're in this fucked-up place. I should've pushed Fanny harder to let me tell him after he was back."

"Maybe the time will be good for him—make him realize he misses you."

"I don't know about that."

350

"Did he text you back?"

"One word: fine."

I smiled. "That's better than nothing. He'll come around. He just needs some space."

Bennett kissed the top of my head. "You nervous about tomorrow night?"

Because I had a guilty conscience, I immediately thought he meant about seeing Andrew, even though I hadn't mentioned he was coming to my presentation with Lauren and Trent.

"No," I snapped.

He chuckled. "You're really a shit liar. I don't even need to see your red face to know you're full of shit."

Now would have been the perfect opportunity to mention that Andrew was joining us for my meeting. But I didn't. I knew it would upset him, and he'd had enough stress lately.

When Andrew had called earlier, my immediate reaction was defensiveness. I was still angry over how things ended, and I didn't want him trying to get back into my good graces—if that was what he even wanted. Anger was easier to deal with. But the more I thought about it, the more I thought maybe seeing Andrew was just what I needed.

While I'd tossed around the idea of quitting a few weeks ago, it had seemed sort of ludicrous to risk so much for a far-fetched chance with a man who had no interest in a relationship. But after last weekend—after Bennett had confided in me about what had happened with Lucas's mother—I wasn't so sure he had no interest in a relationship. He just didn't feel he *deserved* happiness. He harbored a lot of misplaced guilt.

I needed a sign that going with my heart was the right thing to do. Maybe seeing Andrew would make me certain what I felt for Bennett wasn't some sort of a rebound. I needed to be sure my emotions were real and not a fantasy.

Bennett yawned. "You'll do great."

I'd almost forgotten we were still talking about tomorrow night. "Thanks. You all ready for your presentation?"

"Just about."

"How soon after do you think we'll hear about the board's decision?"

Bennett's hand at my shoulder stilled. "Not sure. Pretty fast, I think."

Which meant I could have less than a week to figure out if Bennett and I would be separated by more than a thousand miles.

"Your ideas were really great."

I turned from staring out the big bay window in Lauren and Trent's living room to find Andrew walking toward me with a glass of wine in each hand. He extended one to me.

"No thanks. I'm driving."

He smiled. "More for me, then. My car is in the shop, so Trent picked me up on his way home from the office."

I nodded.

Andrew had been pretty quiet while I presented my ideas before dinner, and then he'd stayed in the background of our conversation while the four of us shared a meal.

I took a minute to look at him. He wore a button-up shirt, untucked, with a pair of dark denim jeans and loafers. He had a light beard, which really surprised me. In fact, his entire laid-back look surprised me.

"You look different," I said.

He sipped his wine. "Is that a bad or good thing?"

I looked him over again. "Good. You look relaxed. I don't think I've ever seen you in a beard except when you were on a multi-day writing binge."

He nodded. "You always said you liked me with facial hair."

That was true. I'd always liked him with some scruff. But he didn't...so he never had any.

I looked over my shoulder toward the kitchen. Lauren and Trent had insisted on cleaning up and not allowing me to help. But they'd been gone a while.

Andrew drank more of his wine, watching me over the rim of his glass. "I asked them to give us a little time to talk."

"Oh." I nodded. Feeling suddenly uncomfortable, I turned my attention back to the big window. It had been pouring all night. "It's really raining out there."

Andrew kept his eyes glued to me. "I hadn't noticed."

He walked to an end table and set his wine down. When he returned, he stood a little closer to me. "You look beautiful tonight."

I looked over at him, and our gazes caught. The warmth of his smile threw me back to a long time ago. We used to be happy. That smile used to make my insides feel warm—the way Bennett's did now. Only Bennett's smile did so much more to me. It made me feel warmth and excitement, and even though he gave me nothing to indicate he felt more than a mutual, physical attraction to me, it made me feel loved and taken care of.

Andrew reached out and pushed the hair from my face. His fingers brushed my skin. I felt it, warm and soft, but only a shadow of what it felt like when I was around Bennett. Bennett could pass me a pencil in a meeting, and the accidental brush of our fingers lit my body on fire. Andrew's touch was the comfort of a cozy blanket—a familiarity. I couldn't remember the last time Andrew and I had been on fire. Had we ever been? Or had I just grown comfortable in the security of what I'd known?

He leaned in a little closer. "I miss you, Anna."

I stared at him. His lips were so close and his familiar scent all around me. Yet...I had no desire to kiss him. *None.*

A smile sprouted at the corner of my lips. I was excited to feel nothing, and in that moment, I made up my mind. I was going to take a chance with Bennett.

Andrew misread what was going through my mind and leaned in for a kiss.

My hands jumped to his chest, stopping him just short of our lips meeting. "No. I can't."

Lauren and Trent picked that moment to emerge from the kitchen. I took a step back, putting distance between Andrew and me before they joined us in the living room.

"All done with the clean-up." Lauren smiled. "And Trent only broke one plate tonight."

Trent put his hand on his wife's back. "I keep thinking she'll stop making me do dishes if I bust another one. But she just keeps buying more and forcing me to help."

I was grateful for the interruption. I also suddenly wanted to get the hell out of here and surprise Bennett on my way home. We had something to celebrate tonight, even if he had no idea what was about to happen.

"Thank you so much for dinner. It was delicious."

"Thank *you*," Lauren said. She looked at her husband. "We both loved your ideas. I don't even think we need to hear the other presentation, to be honest."

"That's very sweet. But I definitely want you to have the campaign you like best, so maybe keep your mind open until after you see what Bennett presents when you meet with him on Monday."

Plus, if you go with my ideas, I might be asking you to follow me to a new firm. I need at least a few days to get my resume floated out there.

Trent nodded. "Sure. Of course."

"I hope you don't mind, but I'm going to get going. The rain is really getting heavy out there, and I don't want to be driving with flooded streets."

"Oh. Of course," Lauren said. Her eyes shifted to her brother and then back to me.

"Would you mind giving me a lift?" Andrew said. "That way Lauren and Trent don't have to go out in this weather."

"Ummm..." I couldn't very well say no. Andrew's house was right on my way home, and it was pretty nasty out there. "Sure. No problem."

Maybe this was good. We'd kept the door open an inch, and it was finally time to close it and say goodbye. I could tell him on the way that I'd met someone. It was the right thing to do after eight years. And I didn't need any hard feelings between Lauren and me, if we were going to be working together.

The four of us said goodbye. It felt strange to be leaving their house with Andrew—we'd had dinner so many times as couples. Together, Andrew and I made a run for the car. But the rain was coming down sideways, and we were both drenched by the time we slammed the doors behind us.

"Damn." Andrew shook off his arms. "It's really raining."

I swiped water from my face and started up the car. "Yeah, awful."

"You want me to drive?"

Driving in this was the last thing I wanted to do. But that didn't matter. "No, I'm good. Thanks." Looking in my rearview mirror, I took a deep breath and whispered, "Checking for oncoming cars," before putting the car into drive. "Pulling away from the curb."

"This is one of the things I missed the most."

I heard the smile in Andrew's voice, but I kept concentrating on the road. It was pouring like I'd never seen before, and the streets were already starting to flood.

"Not sure if that's a compliment or an insult that this is what you missed the most."

I white-knuckled the steering wheel and navigated my way to the highway. The windows were starting to fog up, and when I looked in the side view mirror to merge onto the highway, I could only see a blur of lights through the cloudy driver's side window. The rearview wasn't much better because of the fogged-up back window. So I pressed the button to roll down my window and get a better look. But just as I did, a car passed, sending a big splash of water through my open window and directly on my face.

My innate reaction was to hit the brakes. But that caused me to hydroplane on the merge. I gripped the steering wheel, and my car started to fishtail out of control.

The car pulled to the right, toward the traffic moving on the highway, and I jerked the steering wheel to the left.

Everything happened in slow motion after that.

We started to spin.

I lost all sense of what was forward and what was backward.

Lights flashed in my eyes.

And I realized it was because we were facing the wrong way.

On the merge of the highway.

A horn started blare.

The car coming toward us swerved to the right.

But there wasn't enough room for two of us.

I braced for impact.

We got hit.

It was loud and jarring.

My body jolted to the left and then to the right.

Andrew screamed my name.

Then everything became quiet again.

I started to think we might be okay.

And then...
We got hit a second time.

chapter 46

Bennett

I pulled up in front of Lucas and Fanny's house a few minutes early and checked my phone for the tenth time since last night.

Still nothing.

I'd texted Annalise to see how her presentation went and never heard back. Even if she'd gotten home early and went to bed, she'd definitely be up by now. Most days she was in the office by seven.

I'd had a fucked-up, anxious feeling all night after I didn't hear back. But that was probably more due to the shit going on with Lucas and having to say goodbye for three weeks after what went down last weekend.

I shoved my phone back into my pocket, looked up at Fanny and Lucas's house, and took a deep breath before getting out of the car.

Fanny opened the door with her usual sunny disposition.

"He could use some spending money for his vacation."

I shook my head. *Yeah? So give him some.* "Fine. Is he ready?"

She slammed the door in my face, and I heard her shriek, "Lucas! Get your butt moving!"

My heart started beating erratically when I heard his big feet clomping down the stairs. I had no idea what I'd do if this kid didn't come around. The palms of my hands started to sweat.

The door swung open, and Lucas stepped out, putting on his backpack.

I treaded lightly, keeping my hands in my pockets. "Hey."

He lifted his chin to me. "Hey."

It's a start.

"You ready?"

He nodded, and we got into my car. I turned on the ignition and tried to make small talk. "You excited for your trip to Minnetonka?"

Lucas wrinkled his face like he'd smelled something sour. "Would you be?"

He had a point. "Go in the glove compartment. Take out the tan envelope. I printed you out some information on local lakes last night. There're a few within walking distance of where you're going that sound like they have good fishing. There's some cash in there, too, so you can get bait and lures and stuff."

He took the envelope and stuffed it into his backpack. "Thanks."

We made some more small talk on the short drive to his school, but it was stilted conversation and basically consisted of me talking and him saying *yeah, no,* or *thanks.*

It could have been a lot worse, I supposed.

When we reached the front of his school, we were still a few minutes early, so I pulled to the curb and put the car in park.

"Listen, buddy…" I cleared my throat. "…about what I told you last week."

He looked down, but didn't make an attempt to get out of the car at least.

So I continued. "I'm sorry. I'm sorry the accident happened. I'm sorry I didn't tell you until now. But that was never why I spent time with you." I dragged my fingers through my hair. "I'm not going anywhere. Take some time if you need it. Be mad at me for the accident. Be mad at me for taking too long to talk to you. Hell, I'm mad at myself for everything. But I'll be here every other week after you get back just like I've always been because I love you—and while I feel guilty about a lot of things, that guilt has nothing to do with the time we spend together."

Lucas glanced over at me, and our eyes met for a brief second. Then he reached down and lifted his backpack. He opened the car door and started to climb out, but paused to grumble, "Same."

I waited until he walked into school to pull away. I'd been dreading telling him for so many years, but we were going to get through it. It would be slow going to win back his trust, but we were going to do it together.

And it was the first time I believed maybe, just maybe, I might get through it, too.

Where the fuck is she?

I walked straight to Annalise's office to tell her about Lucas, but her door was closed. Her light was off, too. I dialed her number again on my way to ask Marina if she'd heard from her today.

She hadn't, and my call went to voicemail again.

By eleven o'clock, I was worried. It was one thing for her to blow me off, but to not show up or call the office? Something wasn't right. I went by Jonas's office, but he was in a meeting, so I asked his assistant to have him give me a call as soon as he got out. I must've hit redial fifty more times between then and when Jonas finally got out of the conference room.

He walked into my office without knocking and tossed an envelope on my desk. "You just couldn't help yourself, could you?" He was *pissed*.

"What are you talking about?"

"I confided in you that the board was going to keep you here. And you just couldn't wait to rub it in Annalise's face, could you?"

I held up both my hands. "I have no idea what you're talking about. I didn't tell Annalise anything."

"Then what is that letter about?" His eyes pointed down to the envelope.

I opened it and read.

Dear Jonas,

Please accept this as my letter of resignation and two weeks' notice that I will be leaving the position of Creative Director for Foster, Burnett and Wren. While

I have enjoyed my time working for you and appreciate the opportunity you afforded me, I have decided to remain in the San Francisco area and pursue other opportunities.

Thank you.

Annalise O'Neil

I held the paper out to him. "What the hell is this?"

"Seems to me like a resignation."

"When did she give this to you? Why would she resign?"

Jonas put his hands on his hips. "I assume she resigned because she wants to remain in the San Francisco area—like she wrote in her letter. But no one except the two of us knew she was the one who'd be relocated. She had to have found out that information somehow."

"Well, it wasn't from me. She gave this to you this morning?"

"I found it in her drawer when I went in to look for the files I needed to cover the meeting she didn't show up for today."

Something wasn't right. Annalise wouldn't just quit. Even if she were pissed, she wouldn't not show up for a scheduled client meeting. She took pride in the way she handled herself, always fair and professional. And why wouldn't she talk to me about something like this?

I re-read the letter one more time and then dropped it on my desk and grabbed my jacket off the back of my chair. "I gotta go."

I was at the door to my office before Jonas could object. "Where are you going?" he yelled after me.

"To figure out what the hell is going on."

"Annalise?" I banged on her door again, even though I was pretty sure she wasn't home. I'd rung every bell until someone buzzed me in the front door and then bolted to her apartment before I got kicked out. Her car wasn't parked on the block, and no sound came from inside. Yet I banged louder.

Eventually, the neighbor across the hall opened his door. He cradled a cat in his arms the way most people would cradle a baby. "I don't think she came home last night."

"Oh?"

He scratched at the cat's belly, and the thing purred loudly. "She was supposed to feed Frick and Frack for me last night. I left the cans on the table, but they're still there." He looked down at the cat and spoke to it, rather than me. "Mr. Frick here has forgiven me, but Mr. Frack won't even come out of his room. I'm lucky my flight this morning wasn't delayed or my babies would have starved."

Starved? I shook my head. *Whatever.* "When was the last time you spoke to her?"

"Yesterday morning when I gave her my key."

I turned and started back toward the stairs without saying another word. The cat freak yelled after me.

"When you see her, tell her she owes Frick and Frack an apology."

Yeah. That'll be the first thing we discuss.

I sat in my car outside of her apartment building double-parked, trying to figure out what the hell had happened. She hadn't come home last night and had quit without ever even discussing it with me?

Actually, she *had* mentioned work the other night. Well, sort of. She'd asked if I thought we'd be together next year if one of us weren't forced to relocate to Texas. And I'd said no. I knew I'd hurt her, but was she so upset with me that she'd up and quit without even letting me know?

I hadn't thought so.

Although…

She had been quiet the other night. I'd even asked her a few times if everything was okay. She'd said she was just nervous about her Pet Supplies presentation. My gut thought something more was bothering her. Now that I thought about it, she'd been quiet ever since that call from her mother. I hadn't pushed.

Was it a coincidence that she'd had dinner with her ex's sister last night? Maybe it reminded her that all men were assholes.

Even so, she would have at least come home last night.

Unless…

I shook my head. No, she wouldn't go there. She sees what a douche that guy is now.

Doesn't she?

But where the fuck *did* she sleep last night?

I started my car and dug my phone out of my pocket. No missed calls. No missed texts. Frustrated, I hit redial again before heading back to the office. Maybe she'd shown up at work while I was gone. We'd probably passed each other on the highway. She'd crashed at Lauren and

Trent's house last night and her cell phone had died. It had been raining pretty hard, and she didn't like to drive to begin with. It made sense.

Yeah, that's what happened.

Deciding that had to be it, I tossed my phone on the passenger seat and put my car in drive, forgetting I'd already hit re-dial. Which was why I was confused when a man's voice came through the speakers of my car.

"Hello?"

I furrowed my brow, waiting for the rest of the commercial on the radio.

"Hello?" the voice said again.

The illuminated cell phone on the seat next to me caught my attention. *Shit.* My cell had connected through my Bluetooth and was coming through my car. But who the hell did I accidentally call?

"Who is this?" I asked.

"Andrew. Who is this?"

I froze. *What the fuck?* Lifting the cell phone to look at it, I confirmed Annalise's name on the screen, and the call timer underneath was ticking away the seconds.

"Where's Annalise?"

"She's in bed. Sleeping. Can I help you with something?"

The blood in my veins started to boil. "Yeah. Put Annalise on the goddamn phone!"

"Excuse me?"

"You heard me. Put Annalise on the phone."

Click.

"Hello?"

Silence.

I screamed louder. "Hello?"

The asshole had hung up on me.

Fuck.

Fuck.

"*Fuuuuuck*."

I hit redial. The phone didn't even ring this time, just went right to voicemail. So I hit redial again.

Then again.

Then again.

I called over and over. But it kept going straight to voicemail. The fucker was either hitting reject call, or he'd turned her phone off. Either way, he was keeping me from talking to Annalise.

chapter 47

Bennett

I sat at my desk for hours, going through all the emotions.

Pissed.

How could she fucking do that to me...to us? Didn't she know how I felt about her?

No. She doesn't.

Why? Because I was too much of a pussy to tell her.

Denial.

There was probably a perfectly logical explanation for this. Maybe she'd met with Andrew for a business meeting—something related to Pet Supplies & More. Maybe Lauren had pulled her brother into the loop and wanted Annalise to show her presentation to him this morning.

Yeah. That was probably it.

Except she'd been in bed when he answered her fucking phone.

In *his* fucking bed.

Not mine, where she should've been.

Why? Because I was too much of a pussy to admit I was *afraid* to give things between us a real shot. She'd been brave enough to ask me the goddamn question. Yet I'd taken the cowardly way out.

I kept replaying the conversation we'd had the other night

"If things were different between us, would we be here a year from now?"

And my bullshit response. *"No. Because I like being single. I like my freedom and not having to answer to anyone or have any responsibilities."*

Well, you got what you asked for, dickhead.

Bargaining.

If I could just talk to her, I could fix it. I knew she had feelings for me; I could see it in her eyes—the way it hurt her when I told her we wouldn't be together a year from now, even if things were different at work.

I'd been trying to convince myself I liked my freedom, when all along I never wanted to let go of her.

Because I was afraid.

Fucking pussy.

I needed to talk to her—go over to that douchebag's apartment and kick his ass, if that's what it took to see her. She'd give me a chance. What we had was real.

Wasn't it?

How the fuck would I know? I'd never had anything real in my life except the way she made me feel.

We could separate by a thousand miles—one of us in Texas and the other here—but it wouldn't matter. Because physical distance wouldn't change what was in my heart.

In my heart.

Fuck.

My head fell back against my chair, and I looked up at the ceiling of my office, blowing out a deep breath.

I'm in love with her.

In.

Fucking.

Love.

How the hell did this happen?

I haven't loved a woman since...

Sophie.

And look what happened the last time I got close to a woman. Sophie didn't get a chance to feel what it was like to be loved back. Why should I get to?

I didn't deserve to be loved by a woman like Annalise.

I didn't deserve Sophie's love.

I didn't deserve to have Lucas's love either.

Yet somehow he gave it to me. And I was selfish enough to take it.

My mind kept jumping all over the place.

Annalise had feelings for me; I knew that somewhere deep in my black heart.

But I hadn't done a damn thing to show her how I felt.

I needed to tell her, but more than that, I needed to show her.

Her damn ex had said one thing and done another for years. If I had any chance of fighting for her, she needed to see I had more than words.

I just hoped it wasn't too late.

Jonas had been getting ready to leave for the night when I knocked on his door. But he put down his briefcase since I planted my ass in a chair across from him anyway.

He sat, took off his glasses, and rubbed his eyes. "What's going on, Bennett?"

I shook my head. "I fucked up with Annalise."

Jonas blew out a deep breath. "What did you do?"

"Don't worry. It's nothing you might be thinking. I didn't sabotage her presentation or cheat in anyway. And I didn't tell her about the decision with our positions."

He nodded. "Okay. So what happened?"

"You know that no-fraternization policy we have?"

Jonas closed his eyes and frowned. I didn't need to say more.

"So you won the job, but lost the girl."

"I got it backward."

"How are you going to fix it?"

I thought I'd be nervous, but I suddenly felt calm. Slipping the envelope from the inside of my suit jacket, I leaned forward and set it on Jonas's desk. He glanced down at it and then up at me, smiling sadly.

"I'm guessing this is your resignation?"

I nodded.

"Have you spoken to Annalise?"

"I haven't been able to reach her."

"And yet you're handing me this right now, anyway? What if you lose the job but still can't get the girl back?"

I stood. "That's not an option."

Jonas opened his drawer and took out the envelope containing Annalise's resignation. He extended it to me.

"Top left drawer of her desk. Sitting right on top. I never found this."

I exchanged my letter for hers. "Thanks, Jonas."

"Hope you get the girl."

"You and me both, boss. You and me both."

I'd filled her voicemail. Now every time I called, it just went straight to a message saying the phone number I'd reached could no longer accept messages. I blew out a ragged breath and leaned my forehead against the steering wheel. I'd been sitting in front of her house since four-thirty. It was almost eight now, and there was still no sign of her. I grew more and more anxious by the minute. But eventually she'd have to come home.

I waited what seemed like forever. Every time a flash of light started down the road, I'd grow impatient to see if it was her car. But each one passed right on by. Until finally a set of headlights in the rearview mirror slowed and pulled into the empty spot behind me. But I was disappointed again, finding a Toyota logo on an SUV. *Not her.*

My shoulders slumped. A minute later, the headlights turned off, and I heard the sound of a door opening and closing. A man had gotten out of the SUV and was heading toward the door of Annalise's building. At first I thought nothing of it. But then a dog barked, and the guy turned his head, giving me a glimpse of his profile. My heart started to pound. He looked a hell of a lot like Annalise's stepfather, Matteo.

Rolling down the passenger window, I leaned over and called his name. "Matteo?"

The man turned. It took a few seconds for him to register who I was, but then he started toward me as I stepped out of the car. "Bennett?"

I nodded. "Do you know where Annalise is?"

"The hospital. Her mother, she stay with her. I just come to get some of her things."

"Hospital?" I felt sick. "What happened?"

Matteo frowned. "You don't know? She had a very bad car accident."

chapter 48

Annalise

My eyes fluttered open at the commotion. They felt so heavy. Just like my arms and legs.

An alarm I'd been hearing off in the distance started to beep louder. A woman in blue walked up next to me and did something, and the annoying sound silenced. I heard her speak, but it sounded muffled, as if I was underwater and she wasn't.

"She needs her rest. If you two are going to upset her, I'm going to have security show you both to the door."

I heard a man's voice mumble something, or maybe it was more than one man's voice, I couldn't be sure. *If I could just kick my feet a little bit, I could probably reach the surface and hear better.* I tried to kick, but couldn't get enough momentum going. The woman in blue put her hands on my legs, stopping the little movement I'd managed to muster.

"Shhh. You rest, Miss Annalise. Don't let these boys upset you. God gave this nurse a mouth and a lot of back to toss visitors out when necessary."

A nurse. She was a nurse.

I tried to speak, but my mouth was covered. I lifted my arm to grab whatever was blocking it, but couldn't get it higher than an inch or two off the bed. The nurse moved closer and brought her face close to mine.

She had curly black hair, dark chocolate eyes, and lipstick on her front tooth when she smiled. "You're in the hospital." She stroked my hair. "There's a mask over your mouth so you can breathe easier, and drugs are making you feel sleepy. Do you understand?"

I nodded a little.

She flashed her teeth again, and I stared at the lipstick. *Someone should really tell her.*

"You have two visitors, Miss Annalise. Your parents, and your friends are here, too. They're out in the waiting room. Do you want me to tell these boys to let you rest?"

I slanted my eyes to the other side of the bed, and two faces leaned over.

Bennett?

Andrew?

I looked back at the woman and shook my head.

"How about we have them visit with you one at a time?"

I nodded my head.

She spoke to the men and then to me again.

"Do you want Andrew to visit right now?"

I moved my eyes to see his face, then looked back at the nurse and shook my head.

She smiled. "Good. Because the other one looked like he might rip my head off if I made him leave."

375

A minute later, Bennett was at my side, his face right where the woman's had been. He took my hand in his; it was so warm and held my fingers so tight.

"Hey." He leaned down and kissed my forehead. My eyes locked onto his. "There's my beautiful girl. Are you in pain?"

Pain? I didn't think so. I couldn't even feel my toes. I shook my head.

"I spoke to your mom. She said you're going to be fine. Do you remember the accident?"

I shook my head.

"You had a car accident. There was a storm and a lot of rain, and the merge to the highway made you hydroplane."

Memories started to come back in flashes. Raining so hard. Hitting the brakes. The bright lights. Headlights. The loud bang. Being jolted from side to side. *Andrew*.

I tried to lift my hand to take the mask off my face.

Bennett realized what I was attempting to do. "You have to leave it on for now."

I frowned.

He bent to our joined hands and kissed the top of mine. "I know. Keeping your mouth shut is a challenge for you." He smirked. "But I have a shitload to say, and I have no idea how long I'm going to get to sit here alone with you, so this kind of works for me." His face turned serious, and he looked away for a minute before taking a deep breath.

"I lied."

His gaze returned to mine. No words were necessary for him to know my question.

He squeezed my hand and moved closer. "When you asked me if we'd be together a year from now if one of us wasn't relocated, I said we wouldn't. I said I liked being single and having my freedom. But the truth is, I was terrified. I was terrified that I'd fuck things up if we stayed together. You don't deserve to be hurt again and..."

Bennett paused, and I watched as he attempted to swallow his emotions. When he looked up again, his eyes were welled with tears.

"You don't deserve to be hurt again, and I don't deserve to have love."

It crushed me to hear him say those words. He deserved so much good in his life.

Bennett closed his eyes and steadied himself to continue. "But I'm done caring about what I deserve or you deserve—because I'm selfish enough to not give a fuck that I don't deserve you, and I'll work hard every day to become the man you *do* deserve." He smiled and brushed his hand down my cheek. "I love you." His voice broke. "I freaking love you, Annalise."

We were interrupted by the nurse wearing blue scrubs. She leaned over my face from the other side of the bed, opposite of Bennett. "Just going to add some medicines into your IV. They might make you a little groggy."

Oh good. Someone told her about the lipstick on her teeth. I watched her push some medicine into my IV line. I turned back to Bennett, but my eyes became even heavier. *So, so heavy.*

Bennett was slumped over in the chair next to me, sound asleep.

I looked around. It was a different room than I'd been in earlier. *Wasn't it?* Or did I dream the other room—the big, windowless one with a dozen beds and only a curtain separating me from the patients on either side. Now I was alone in a big room with a door, except for the man sleeping next to me. And a window behind him told me it was nighttime.

My neck felt stiff, so I tried to move my head from side to side. The slight brush of the sheets woke the sleeping giant.

He smiled and leaned forward. "Hey. You're awake again."

I lifted my arm to grab my mask, but Bennett stopped me. "Don't take that off yet. Let me call the nurse. They lowered your sedation dosage, but they wanted to check your breathing and vitals before trying without the mask. Okay?"

I nodded. He disappeared and came back a minute later with a nurse.

I didn't recognize this one. She listened to my chest, took my blood pressure, and watched the monitor for a minute.

"You're doing great. How do you feel?"

My ribs were killing me, but I nodded to say I felt okay anyway while pointing to the mask.

"You want to take it off?"

I nodded again.

"Okay. Let me go get you some ice chips. When we take it off, you're going to be really dry from all the forced air for three days."

Three days? I'd been in here for that long?

When the nurse returned, she set a Styrofoam cup with a spoon down on the tray next to my bed and then reached around my head and loosened the strap that had been holding my mask in place. Slipping it off, she waited nearby, her eyes moving between the monitor and me.

"Take a few deep breaths."

First I opened wide to stretch out my cramped jaw, and then I did as she instructed. My face was so sore, especially my nose.

She listened to my chest again, then slung her stethoscope around her neck. "You sound good. How do you feel?"

My hand raised to hold my throat. My voice croaked out a low, "*Dry.*"

"Okay. Well, we need to go slow. But I'll keep an eye on your stats from the nurse's station and give you two a little time." She turned to Bennett. "One or two ice chips at a time. That should help moisten her throat."

The door hadn't even closed when Bennett had the ice chips in his hand and spoon at my mouth. I would have laughed at his eagerness if my side didn't hurt so much.

He spooned some chips into my mouth and then leaned down and brushed his lips to mine. "That was a long nap you took. I finally started to talk to you about my feelings, and your response was to conk out for twelve hours."

I'd almost forgotten about everything he'd said earlier. But once he reminded me, every word came back, crystal clear. Although I wanted to hear him say it again. So I put on my best confused face. "Feelings?"

Bennett's eyes widened. "You don't remember me pouring my heart out to you yesterday?"

I shook my head, but I couldn't stop my smile. He noticed.

"You're screwing with me, aren't you?"

My smile widened. "I want to hear it again."

Bennett stood and ever-so-carefully climbed onto the bed next to me. "Oh yeah? What part do you want to hear?"

"All of it."

A smile spread across his handsome face, smoothing out some of the worry lines. He snuggled his mouth to my ear. "I love you."

I grinned. "Again."

He laughed. "I love you, Annalise O'Neil. I fucking love you."

After I made him say it a dozen or more times, Bennett filled me in on my injuries. The soreness in my chest was due to a broken rib. I hadn't even noticed the cast on my left wrist from a fractured ulna, and apparently I had bumps and bruising all over. The worst of it had been a partial collapse of one of my lungs, which they had treated with a needle to suck out the air from around the outside of the lung, and it had re-inflated on its own. Basically, I was damn lucky.

More things started to come back to me the longer I stayed awake. I remembered that Mom, Matteo, and Madison had all been here. And Andrew, too. He had two black eyes and a bandage on his nose, but he'd said he was fine.

"Did everyone go home?"

Bennett nodded. "I promised your mom and Matteo I'd call if anything changed. They'll be back first thing in the morning. Madison threatened my life if I didn't text her updates every few hours." He fed me more ice chips. They felt so good on my sore throat. "She's pretty damn scary."

"What about Andrew? Were you arguing with him earlier in my room?"

The smile on Bennett's face fell. "I'd been calling your phone all night. When I finally got through, he answered. And the douchebag told me you were in bed. Didn't mention in the hospital or anything. Then he hung up on me."

Oh boy. "You must've thought..."

The clench of his jaw answered.

"You thought I went back to him?"

"I didn't know what to think."

"How did you find out what happened?"

"I camped out in front of your apartment. Eventually Matteo showed up."

Wait... "So when did you speak to Andrew then?"

Bennett shrugged. "I don't know. Early in the afternoon. Maybe about one?"

"But you waited in front of my building even though you thought I'd gone back to Andrew?"

He cupped my cheek. "I wasn't losing you without a fight."

That made my heart swell. "You would have taken me back even if I'd—"

Bennett put his finger to my mouth and stopped me from continuing. "Don't even say it. I don't even want to

381

know why you were in the car with him. Just tell me we're good and it won't be happening again."

"Nothing happened with Andrew. I was giving him a ride home because he said his car was in the shop. He was at Lauren's house for dinner."

Bennett's head dropped. "Thank freaking Christ. Because I quit my job. You're stuck with me here in San Francisco."

My eyes went wide. "What? Why would you do that?"

"Because I'm not letting you move to Texas."

"Uh...I think you're getting a little ahead of yourself. *You're* the one who would be moving to Texas when *I* win."

Bennett rolled his eyes as he smoothed hair away from my face. "Yeah, you're probably right. But either way, we're both staying put now."

Bennett

"You're supposed to be resting." I tossed my keys on the kitchen counter and set down a bag of groceries. I'd gone to the office for a few hours while Annalise's mom took her to a post-release check-up.

"I'm fine. I got this. The doctor said I'm doing great." Annalise bent to dig a pot out of the bottom of the cabinet. The view of her ass was spectacular, but I didn't want her to hurt herself. I wrapped my arms around her waist and lifted her out of my way.

"Let me."

She sighed when I emptied the contents of the cabinet onto the counter so she could pick what she needed. "You know, I'm going to have to function on my own anyway. You need to start looking for a new job, and I should probably be going back to my apartment. I've been here almost two weeks, and you're going to get sick of me soon."

I pushed a piece of hair from her face. "The doctor said you need to go slow because your lung is still recuperating. You're not ready for three flights of stairs in your walk-up. You need an elevator."

I'd made Annalise come home with me after she was released from the hospital. She'd agreed because I hadn't given her much choice. But she was getting stronger every day, and soon enough she'd be fine to go home, even if that day wasn't today. I just wanted her here.

"I could stay with my mom for a while. She has a spare bedroom on the first floor."

I slipped a finger under her chin and lifted so our eyes met. "Are you sick of me?"

She cupped my cheeks. "God, no. How can I be sick of you when you wait on me hand and foot and wash my hair in the bathtub so I don't get my cast wet?"

"Then why do you want to leave?"

"I don't. But I also don't want to overstay my welcome, Bennett. I feel up to doing things now, and except for the stairs, there's no reason I need to be here anymore."

I shook my head. "No reason? How about you *want* to be here?"

She softened. "Of course I do. But you know what I mean."

I lifted her up and set her on the kitchen counter so we were eye to eye. "I don't, actually. So let's talk. Do you like my place?"

She turned to look at the living room and the view out the windows. "Uh, it makes my place look like a shithole. It's depressing walking into my apartment after leaving yours."

"So you like the apartment. How about the roommate?"

She leaned forward and pressed her lips to mine. "He's spoiling me. Plus, the view when he comes out of the shower in just a towel blows the view of the Golden Gate Bridge from the living room out of the water."

I wound her ponytail around my hand and kept her mouth to mine when she attempted to pull back. She opened when I slid my tongue between those luscious lips. I kissed her long and hard, and my heart felt full again.

The last few weeks, I'd been happier than I'd been my whole life. I knew I didn't want this to end. The kiss was all the assurance I needed.

"Good." I gave her pony a light tug. "Then it's settled. You'll move in. I'll arrange for a moving company to go over to your place this weekend and pack up your stuff."

Annalise's eyes widened. "What?"

"You like the apartment better than yours. You're hot for your roommate." I shrugged. "Why leave?"

"Are you...are you asking me to move in with you permanently?"

I looked back and forth between her eyes. "I'm saying I want you here when I get up in the morning, and I want you here when I go to bed at night. I want your four different newspapers spread all over our bed, and your ridiculous amount of shoes filling our closet. I want you wearing my T-shirts to cook us breakfast when you're feeling up to it again, and I sure as shit want you underneath me, on top of me, on your knees on our bedroom floor, and tied to the headboard while I eat you for dessert." I paused. "Is that any clearer?"

She chewed her bottom lip. "There's something I need to tell you first."

385

I stiffened. "What?"

She rubbed her nose with mine and wrapped her arms around my neck. "I love you, Bennett Fox."

I dropped my head and let out a big rush of air. "Are you trying to give me a heart attack? Saying there's something you need to tell me? I thought... I don't even know what I thought. But it didn't sound fucking good."

Annalise laughed. "Sorry."

I squinted. "I'll give you sorry. What the hell took you so long to tell me that, anyway? You left me hanging out there for weeks."

She grabbed my T-shirt into two fistfuls and tugged me to her. "I wanted to be off the painkillers and meds that made me groggy so you'd have no doubt I meant it."

I pulled my neck back. "You stopped the meds? The doctor said it was okay?"

She looked down and scraped her fingernail along my arm. Then she looked up under her lashes with the sexiest fuck-me eyes. "He also said it was okay to resume *all activities*. I just need to go easy."

I'd been sporting the start of an erection since I walked in the door and saw her bent over. I needed confirmation before I got my hopes up. It had been a long-ass three weeks since her accident. "*All* activities?"

She wiggled her eyebrows. "All."

The kitchen counter was the perfect height, and I wouldn't crush her in this position. Plus, no wasting time walking to the bedroom. Reaching around to her ass, I pulled her to the very edge of the counter and pressed my growing hard-on between her legs. I felt the heat of her pussy through my pants and groaned.

Did I mention it had been *three* weeks?

"The right thing to do would probably be to make love to you right now. But I'm going to have to owe you slow and sweet, because I need you hard and fast before I'm calm enough to go slow."

She ran her tongue along my bottom lip and then bit down unexpectedly. "Hard works for me."

Her clothes were off in two seconds flat. I sucked her gorgeous tits, biting down until she let out a sound that was a cross between a moan and a yelp. God, I fucking missed her. Missed being inside her. Missed burying myself so deep that my cum couldn't find its way back out. It was surreal how much I wanted this woman. *Needed* this woman. Craved this woman—even when I hadn't wanted to.

Taking her mouth, I mumbled against her lips. "I fucking love you."

I felt the smile even if I couldn't see it on her face. "I fucking love you, too."

I kissed along every exposed piece of her skin I could reach while unzipping my pants. When my boxers joined them on the floor, my erection bobbed against my abdomen.

It took every ounce of willpower in me to slow things down. I stood and looked her in the eyes. "You okay? Your breathing's okay?"

She responded by gazing down between us, running her thumb over the glistening head of my cock and then bringing her finger up to her lips to lick. "*Mmmm...* All good. How about you?"

I groaned and fisted my cock, bringing it between her legs to test the waters and finding her gloriously wet. Feeling ready to explode before we'd even started, I pushed inside in one long, hard stroke and kissed the living shit out of her until I started to get concerned about her heavy breathing.

She smiled up at me, panting, but looked perfectly fine. I returned the sentiment as I began to move—slow and steady—never breaking our gaze as I pumped in and out of her.

God, this woman. I'd spent half of my life building a million obstacles to put in the way of love. Yet when I met Annalise, all the hurdles did was show me how much she was worth jumping over every one of them.

I tried to hold back, squeezing my eyes shut tight to avoid seeing how beautiful she looked. But when she whispered my name like a prayer, how could I *not* watch.

"Bennett. *Oh God.* Please."

There was no sweeter sound than the woman you loved moaning your name. It was also sexy as fuck. That was it. I broke.

My thrusts sped up, and I began to fuck her harder and harder. Every muscle in my body tightened while she clenched around me, her nails digging into my back as her orgasm hit. Watching my cock go in and out of her was the most stunning sight. But knowing she loved me made it that much sweeter. God knows why the hell she'd given me her heart, but I had no intention of ever giving it back.

When her body began to go slack, it only took a few pumps for me to find my own release. I kissed her lips and wrapped her in my arms, careful not to put too much pressure on her chest.

Leaning my cheek against the top of her head, I felt almost content. *Almost*. Just one little thing bothered me.

"So I didn't hear a definitive yes as your answer."

"What was the question?"

"Move in with me?"

Annalise pulled her head back. "But what would I do with that nice cowboy hat you gave me the second day we met if I stayed here in California?"

"I've been fantasizing about you wearing that thing and riding me for months. You'll be wearing it plenty."

She giggled, but she'd be finding out soon enough that I wasn't joking. I couldn't wait to watch her play cowgirl.

"So is that a yes?"

"Yes. I'll move in with you." She stopped the spread of my smile when she held up her pointer. "But under one condition."

I raised a brow. "A condition?"

She nodded. "I'm paying half the costs. Considering I'm the only one who's going to be employed pretty soon, I want to pay half...or more if I can afford it, while you look for a new job."

No way I was letting her pay anything—not in the traditional sense anyway.

"Actually, I'm not going to be looking for a job."

She furrowed her brow. "Why not?"

"Because I have something better in mind."

"Okay..."

"And I was hoping maybe you'd be interested in a new position as well."

She tilted her head. "A new position? Let me guess... on my back or all fours?"

I smirked and tapped her nose with my finger. "That wasn't what I was thinking—but I like where your mind is, my dirty girl."

"You're being very sketchy, Fox. Spit it out. What's going on?"

"I'm going to start my own agency. I want you to come work with me."

Annalise

Two years ago on this day, I'd been devastated.

I lit the last two candles and dimmed the lights in the living room. *Perfect.*

The fireplace was going, the table was set with the china my mom had given me when I moved out, two dozen candles set the mood for romance, and I had Bennett's favorite meal in the oven. I looked around and smiled. *Finally* this man would have a date with a girlfriend on Valentine's Day.

Last year I'd planned a special February fourteenth, but like most things since I met Bennett Fox, our night didn't go as expected. We got a call that morning from Lucas. He was at the hospital with his grandmother. He'd woken up to find her unresponsive and called 911. Turned out she'd had a stroke.

A week later, she passed in her sleep while still in ICU. And our lives took an unexpected turn once again.

Two years ago, my boyfriend of eight years had dumped me on Valentine's Day. Today I'm raising a teenager with a man who makes me want to simultaneously strangle and straddle him. Yet I've never been happier.

The day after Fanny died, Bennett petitioned the court for temporary custody. We filed for permanent custody a few months later. I pushed for Lucas to talk to a counselor, concerned he might be struggling with the loss of the second woman in his life to have raised him. As his guardian, Bennett went with him for a few sessions, and he wound up also seeing the counselor on his own a few times to work through his lingering guilt over the loss of Sophie. It did them both a lot of good.

I picked up the framed photo on the bookshelf in the living room and ran my finger over Sophie's smiling face. "Don't worry. They're happy. I'm taking good care of your boys."

Over the last year I'd found some solace in talking to her at different times—when Lucas was acting out, or when Bennett frustrated me with his incessant overprotectiveness. I felt eternally indebted to her for the beautiful life I had today, and I told her so often.

I heard the key in the door and leaned over the kitchen counter, exposing an eyeful of cleavage as I waited for my crazy man to come in. He opened the door, and his eyes immediately zoned in on what I displayed. Tossing his keys on the counter, he set down two bags. His eyes flickered up to mine and back down to my cleavage twice before he even noticed the apartment was filled with candles.

"Where's Lucas?"

"Sleeping at his friend Adam's," I said with a coy tilt of my head.

A wicked grin crossed Bennett's face. He walked toward me with such an intent look that goosebumps broke out over my arms. I had to work to stand still and not squirm with anticipation.

He slipped one arm around my waist and tugged me flush against him, while the other gripped the back of my neck. "I'm going to make you scream so loud, the neighbors might call the police."

His kiss knocked the breath out of me. I had no doubt he intended to make good on his threat.

We'd had to take our sex life at home down a notch since we became full-time parents to a teen. While before we'd had sex all over the apartment—up against the wall, on the living room floor, kitchen counters, in the shower—after the arrival of Lucas, our activity needed to be somewhat confined, as did its volume.

Although that didn't stop Bennett—he just became more creative. He'd send the entire staff home early so we could have uninhibited sex in the office. That tended to happen after the two of us had argued over how a certain account should be handled. We might be on the same team now, but a heated disagreement still made my man frisky. Sometimes I rattled him on purpose for just that reason.

"How did the meeting with Star go today?" I asked. "Did you tell Tobias I said hello?"

Bennett's eyes flashed.

See? Just like that. One of the easiest ways to get him riled up was to poke the jealous lion. It had always been a sore spot that Star had changed their mind at the last minute and gone with my campaign. Tobias had convinced the others it was the way to go, and that had only fanned the flame of envy Bennett carried. Oh, and by the way, Pet Supplies & More went with my campaign, too. Which meant I'd won two of out three, and it would've been Bennett wearing the cowboy boots. But it all worked out in the end. I'd taken both my new accounts and a whole bunch of others with me when I left Foster, Burnett and Wren and went to work for The Fox Agency.

"You're just asking to walk funny tomorrow, aren't you, Texas?"

The nickname had stuck.

I smiled. "Happy Valentine's Day, sweetheart. We broke your streak."

Bennett's brows drew together.

"You never had a date with a girlfriend on Valentine's Day, remember?"

"Ah. It's Valentine's Day." He smiled mischievously. "I totally forgot about that. Hate to spoil your plans." He looked around the room. "Seems like you went to a lot of trouble. Such a shame."

I frowned. He forgot Valentine's Day? Other plans?

"*Really?* We have the entire house to ourselves for a night and you made plans on Valentine's Day?"

"Sorry, babe."

Talk about disappointment. The lid on the pot full of water on the stove to cook the pasta started to make noise. Apparently there were two things boiling now.

I stepped around Bennett and went to the kitchen. Grabbing a pot holder from the drawer, I turned down the heat and lifted the top to let out the steam. But as the seconds passed, I became more and more annoyed that Bennett had spoiled the evening I'd planned. I'd even gotten him a few gifts I didn't feel like giving him anymore.

Never one to hold back when it came to fighting with him, I clanked the lid down on the counter and decided to share how upset I really was.

Only when I turned, he wasn't standing there anymore.

He was down on one knee.

I gasped in shock.

Bennett held a black velvet box in his hand and smirked. "You were going to rip into me, weren't you?"

My heart was beating out of my chest. I covered it with my hands. "Of course I was. Why did you screw with me like that?"

He reached out and took my hand. "You did all this because I never had a date with a girlfriend on Valentine's Day. I'm hoping that streak continues and I'll be having a date with my fiancée."

My eyes started to tear.

He squeezed my hand, and I noticed the box in his other one shaking. My confident nemesis-turned-love-of-my-life was nervous to propose. Underneath all the tough exterior was a man with a giant, soft heart—it's why he suffered so much for so long and put up a wall to protect it from breaking again.

Bennett swallowed, and the humor in his face was replaced by sincerity. "When I met you, I was broken, and I didn't want to be fixed. You vandalized my car, tried to take my job, and called me an asshole, all within a few hours of strutting into the office. I did everything I could to hate you, because somewhere down deep inside, I knew you were a threat to my need to be miserable.

"When I insulted you, you invited me to a meeting even though you were my competition and you could have gone alone. When I made an ass of myself telling you your mom was hitting on me, you encouraged me to stay for dinner. When Lucas's grandmother died, it was you who immediately said we needed to take him. You should've run the other way, but that's not who you are. You're a beautiful woman, but the true beauty that shines from you comes from the inside."

He shook his head. "I don't deserve such selfless love. I can't imagine how I deserve you. But if you'll let me, I want to spend the rest of my life trying to live up to half of what you somehow see in me."

Warm tears started to stream down my face.

"Annalise O'Neil, I want to argue with you every day at the office and make up with you every night in our bed. I want to fill your belly with crazy-haired little blond babies who look just like you and overflow our home with happiness. I want to grow old with you. So, will you not be my girlfriend and do me the honor of being my fiancée this Valentine's Day instead?"

I dropped to the floor, almost knocking him over as I wrapped my arms around his neck. "Yes. Yes." I kissed his face again and again. "Yes. Yes, I'll marry you."

Bennett steadied us and pressed his lips to mine. His thumbs wiped the tears from my eyes. "Thank you for loving me even when I hated myself."

My heart let out a big sigh. That's the thing about love. We don't fall in love with the perfect person; we fall in love despite a person's imperfections.

"I love you," I said.

He lifted my hand and slipped a beautiful emerald-cut diamond on my finger. "I didn't see you coming, Texas. Didn't see you coming."

"That's okay." I smiled. "Because you'll never see me going now, either."

acknowledgements

To you—the *readers*. Thank you taking this journey with me and allowing Bennett and Annalise into your minds and hearts. With so many books to chose from, I'm honored that many of you have been with me for so long. Thank you for your loyalty and support.

To Penelope – I couldn't imagine doing this without you by my side. Thank you for putting up with my neurotic ass on a daily basis. I can't wait to see what our next adventure is!

To Cheri – Thank you for being the best assistant at signings a girl could ask for! And for always being there to support me at every turn. Books brought us together, but friendship made us forever.

To Julie – Thank you for your friendship, inspiration and strength.

To Luna – You're usually the first person I chat with each morning, and I can always count on you to start my day off with a smile. Thank you your friendship and support.

To my amazing Facebook reader group, Vi's Violets – Thank you for the enthusiasm and excitement that you bring every single day. Your encouragement is my daily motivation!

To Sommer – Thank you for wrapping my words inside beautiful covers. Your designs bring my books to life!

To my agent and friend, Kimberly Brower – Thank you for all that you do and always doing more than is required. There is no agent that is as creative and open minded to new opportunities as you.

To Jessica, Elaine and Eda – Thank you for being the dream team of editing! You make my stories and *me* better.

To Mindy –Thank you for keeping me organized and pulling everything together!

To all of the bloggers – I've said it for years, but it still holds true today—you're the glue of the book world—keeping authors and readers connected and working tirelessly to share your passion for books. Thank you taking your precious time to read my stories, write thoughtful reviews, and share graphics that bring my books to life.

Much love

Vi

About the Author

Vi Keeland is a #1 *New York Times*, #1 *Wall Street Journal*, and *USA Today* Bestselling author. With millions of books sold, her titles have appeared in over a hundred Bestseller lists and are currently translated in twenty-five languages. She resides in New York with her husband and their three children where she is living out her own happily ever after with the boy she met at age six.

Other Books by Vi Keeland

Standalone novels
The Naked Truth
Sex, Not Love
Beautiful Mistake
EgoManiac
Bossman
The Baller
British Bedmate (Co-written with Penelope Ward)
Mister Moneybags (Co-written with Penelope Ward)
Playboy Pilot (Co-written with Penelope Ward)
Stuck-Up Suit (Co-written with Penelope Ward)
Cocky Bastard (Co-written with Penelope Ward)
Left Behind (A Young Adult Novel)
First Thing I See

The Rush Series
Rebel Heir (Co-written with Penelope Ward)
Rebel Heart (Co-written with Penelope Ward)

Life on Stage series (2 standalone books)
Beat
Throb

MMA Fighter series (3 standalone books)
Worth the Fight
Worth the Chance
Worth Forgiving

The Cole Series (2 book serial)
Belong to You
Made for You

Made in the USA
San Bernardino, CA
04 July 2019